DREAM EYES

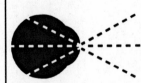

This Large Print Book carries the
Seal of Approval of N.A.V.H.

DREAM EYES

JAYNE ANN KRENTZ

LARGE PRINT PRESS
A part of Gale, Cengage Learning

GALE
CENGAGE Learning·

Detroit • New York • San Francisco • New Haven, Conn • Waterville, Maine • London

LIBRARY OF CONGRESS CATALOGING-IN-PUBLICATION DATA

Krentz, Jayne Ann.
   Dream eyes / by Jayne Ann Krentz.
     pages ; cm. — (Thorndike Press large print basic)
   ISBN-13: 978-1-4104-5440-9 (hardcover)
   ISBN-10: 1-4104-5440-1 (hardcover)
   1. Psychics—Fiction. 2. Large type books. I. Title.
PS3561.R44D74 2013
813'.54—dc23   2012045025

ISBN 13: 978-1-59413-671-9 (pbk. : alk. paper)
ISBN 10: 1-59413-671-8 (pbk. : alk. paper)

Published in 2014 by arrangement with G. P. Putnam's Sons, a member of Penguin Group (USA) LLC, a Penguin Random House Company.

Printed in the United States of America
1 2 3 4 5   17 16 15 14 13

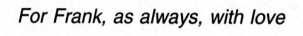

For Frank, as always, with love

ACKNOWLEDGMENTS

A very special thanks to Stephen Castle, a course director for the National Association of Underwater Instructors (NAUI), an instructor trainer for the Public Safety Diving Association (PSDA) and an instructor trainer for TDI. He owns AAI Neptune Divers, Las Vegas, and he is cavern/cave-certified. I am grateful for his technical assistance and advice. Also, I'm proud to say, he is my brother. Really, it is just so useful having an expert in the family. Any errors in the text are mine, all mine.

ONE

The dead diver was wedged like a bone in the stone throat of the underwater cave they called the Monster. The body — still clad in a tank and regulator, fins, buoyancy compensator and mask — shifted gently in the subtle current. One gloved hand rose and fell in spectral warning.

Turn back.

But for Judson Coppersmith there was no going back.

The locals on the island claimed that the flooded cave beast swallowed divers whole. The adrenaline junkies who were foolish enough to ignore the signs outside at the entrance never got far inside the uncharted labyrinth of underwater passages. The smart ones turned back in time. But the explosion in the dry section of the cavern had sealed the aboveground exit and canceled that option. His only hope was to try to swim out to the sea through the Monster.

There was no darkness as dense and relentless as that of the interior of an underwater cave. But the clarity of the water was surreal. The beam of the flashlight sliced through the deep night like a laser, pinning the body.

He swam closer and took stock of the dead man's equipment. Relief swept through him when he saw that the killers had not bothered to drain the victim's air tank. He stripped it off the bloated body, tucked it under one arm and helped himself to the diver's flashlight as well. Throughout the process, the dead eyes stared at him reproachfully through the mask.

Sorry, pal, but your gear is of no use to you now. Not sure it will do me any good, either, but it will buy me a little time.

He eased past the body and focused the sharp light on the twisted rock passage. The urge to swim forward as quickly as possible was almost overwhelming. But impulsive decisions would kill him as surely as running out of air. He forced himself to drift for a few seconds.

There it was, the faint but steady pull of the current. It would either be his lifeline or the false lure that drew him to his death. He slipped into the stream of the ultra-clear water and allowed it to guide him deeper into the maze.

The islanders claimed that there was an exit to the sea. That had been proven years ago by a simple dye test. A coloring agent poured into the cavern pool had emerged a short distance offshore. But the island was riddled with caves, and no one had been able to find the underwater exit point. Divers had died trying.

It was getting hard to breathe off the first tank of air, the one he had grabbed when he had been forced into the water. It was almost empty. He took it off and set it down on a rocky ledge with great care. The last thing he needed now was to stir up the sediment on the floor of the cave. If that happened, he would be forced to waste precious time waiting for the current to clear out the storm of debris. Time meant air usage. He had none to spare. There was, in fact, a staggeringly high probability that he would not have enough air regardless of how carefully he managed the one commodity that meant life or death.

He slipped on the dead man's tank and waited a beat, drifting upward a little. Sometimes in a flooded cave the current was stronger toward the roof of the tunnel.

Once again he sensed it, the faint, invisible tug that urged him deeper into the flooded labyrinth.

Sometime later — he refused to look at his watch because there was no point — the flashlight began to go dark. He used it as long as possible, but the beam faded rapidly. The endless night closed in around him. Until now he had never had a problem with darkness. His paranormal night vision allowed him to navigate without the aid of normal light. In other circumstances, the natural para-radiation in the rocks would have been sufficient to illuminate his surroundings. But the strange aurora that had appeared in the cavern and the explosion that had followed had seared his senses, rendering him psychically blind. There was no way to know if the effects would be permanent and not much point in worrying about it now. The loss of his talent would not matter if he did not make it out of the flooded catacombs alive.

He fumbled with the flashlight that he had taken off the body, nearly dropping it in the process of switching it on. The chill of the water was making him clumsy. The thin 3mm suit he wore provided only limited protection. Although the island was in the Caribbean, he was in freshwater here in the cave, and the temperature at this depth was unpleasantly cold.

Ten minutes later, he rounded a bend and saw that the rocky corridor through which he was swimming narrowed drastically. He was forced to take off his tank and push it into and beyond the choke point. He barely managed to squeeze through after it. The nightmare scenario of getting stuck — unable to go forward or back — sent his heart rate climbing. He was suddenly using air at an even faster rate.

And then he was on the other side. The passage widened once more. Gradually, he got his breathing back under control. But the damage had been done. He had used up a lot of air.

He got the first clue that the current was guiding him in the right direction when he noticed that the once crystal-clear water was starting to become somewhat murky. It was an indication that he had reached the point where the freshwater of the underground river was converging with seawater. That still left a lot of room for things to go wrong. It was entirely possible that he would discover the exit only to find out that he could not fit through it. If that happened, he would spend his last minutes as a condemned man gazing upward through the stone bars of his cell at the summer sunlight filtering through the tropical sea.

The second flashlight slowly died, plunging him into absolute darkness. Instinctively he tried to heighten his talent. Nothing happened. He was still psi-blind.

All he could do now was try to follow the current. He swam slowly, his hands outstretched in an attempt to ward off a close encounter with the rocky walls of the cave.

At one point, to keep his spirits up more than anything else, he took the regulator out of his mouth long enough to taste the water. It was unmistakably salty. He was now in a sea cave.

When he perceived the first, faint glow infusing the endless realm of night, he considered the possibility that he was hallucinating. It was a reasonable assumption, given the sensory disorientation created by the absolute darkness and the fact that he knew he was sucking up the last of his air. Maybe this was the mysterious bright light that those who had survived near-death experiences described. In his case, it would be followed by for-real death.

One thing was certain. If he survived, he would never again take the light of a summer day for granted.

The pale glow brightened steadily. He swam faster. Nothing to lose.

Two

"You're too late," the ghost in the mirror said. "I'm already dead."

There was no accusation in the words, just a calm statement of fact. Dr. Evelyn Ballinger had always been logical and even-tempered in life, reserving her deepest passions for her work. There was no reason why death would give her a personality transplant. But knowing that did nothing to temper the terrible sense of dread and guilt that chilled Gwen Frazier's blood. If only she had opened the e-mail last night instead of this morning.

If only. The two most despairing words in the English language.

She crossed the cluttered, heavily draped room that Evelyn had converted into an office. All of the rooms in the house were dark. Evelyn had never liked sunlight. She claimed it interfered with her work.

Gwen's movement through the room

stirred the still air. The crystal wind chimes suspended from the ceiling shivered, producing an eerie music that seemed to come from beyond the grave. The sound raised the hair on the back of Gwen's neck.

In the doorway behind her, Max, Evelyn's burly gray cat, meowed plaintively as if demanding that Gwen fix the situation. But there was no fixing death.

The body was crumpled on the floor beside the desk. Evelyn had been in her early seventies, a large, generously proportioned woman who had been caught in a fashion time warp like so many others who resided in the small town of Wilby, Oregon. With her long gray hair, voluminous tie-dyed skirts, and crystal jewelry, she had been a model of the proudly eccentric look that Gwen privately labeled *Hippie Couture.*

Evelyn's blue eyes stared lifelessly at the ceiling. Her reading glasses lay on the floor. A photo had fallen beside one hand. The pinhole at the top of the picture indicated it had come from the corkboard over the desk. There was no blood or obvious bruising on the body.

"No sign of an injury, you'll notice," the mirror ghost said. "What does that tell us?"

"Always the instructor," Gwen said. "You can't help yourself, can you?"

"No point changing now, is there, dear? I repeat my question. What does the lack of an obvious injury indicate?"

"Could be natural causes. You were seventy-two years old, a type two diabetic who insisted on eating all the wrong foods, and you were absentminded when it came to taking your meds. You refused to lose weight, and the only exercise you got was an occasional stroll down by the river."

"Ah, yes, the river," the ghost said softly. "You won't forget the river or the falls, will you, dear?"

"No," Gwen said. "Never."

She knew there was no hope, but she made herself check for a pulse. There was only the terrible chill and the utter stillness of death. She got slowly to her feet.

"This scene looks dreadfully familiar, doesn't it?" the ghost said. "Brings to mind what happened two years ago."

"Yes," Gwen said. "It does."

"Another person connected to the study is dead by what appears to be natural causes. Bit of a coincidence, don't you think?"

Gwen looked at the vision in the mirror. The ghosts were always wispy, smoky images — never sharp and clear like photographs. For the most part, the specters she encountered were strangers, but she had known a few of them all too well. Evelyn Ballinger had now joined that short list. Evelyn had been both mentor and friend.

"I'm sorry," Gwen said to the ghost. "I didn't see your e-mail until this morning. I called you right away. When you didn't answer your phone, I knew something was wrong."

"Of course you did, dear." The ghost chuckled. "You're psychic."

"I got into the car and drove down here to see you. But it's a four-hour trip from Seattle."

"You mustn't blame yourself, dear," the ghost said. "There is nothing you could have done. It happened last night, as you can see. I was working here in my office. You remember that I was always a night owl."

"Yes," Gwen said. "I remember. Your e-mail to me came in around two o'clock this morning."

"Ah, yes, of course. You would have been asleep."

But she hadn't been asleep, Gwen thought. She had been walking the floors of her small condo, trying to work off the disturbing images from the dream. It had been two years since Zander Taylor's death, but each summer in late August the night-

18

mares struck. Her talent for lucid dreaming allowed her to control the dreams to some extent, but she had not been able to dispel them. Each time she dreamed the terrifying scenes from that summer of death, she came awake with the same unnerving sense that it had not ended with Taylor going over the falls.

"I was up," Gwen said. "But I wasn't checking e-mail."

She stepped back from the body and dug her phone out of her tote. Max meowed again and lashed his tail.

"I'm sorry, Max. There's nothing I can do. It's too late."

Max did not look satisfied with that response. He watched her intently with his green-gold eyes.

She concentrated on punching in the emergency number and tried not to look at the mirror. Talking to ghosts was not a good thing. It made other people — potential lovers as well as friends — extremely nervous. After all, there were no ghosts. She was really talking to herself, trying to make sense of the messages that her odd form of intuition picked up at the scenes of violent death.

She usually went out of her way to avoid such conversations because she found them incredibly frustrating. There was, after all, very little she could do for the dead. That was the job of the police.

Years ago she had come to realize that if she was seeing ghosts in mirrors, windows, pools of water and other reflective surfaces, it meant that she had stumbled into one of the dark places in the world, a place tainted with the heavy energy that was laid down at the time of violent death. As the old saying went, murder left a stain. But she was not a cop or a trained investigator. She was just a psychic counselor who interpreted dreams for her clients and earned a little money on the side writing scripts for a low-budget cable television series. There was nothing she could do to find justice for the dead.

"When Wesley Lancaster finds out about my death, he'll probably want you to turn it into a script for his show," the ghost in the mirror said. "I can see it now. *Was this reclusive paranormal investigator murdered by paranormal means? Is there a link to the mysterious deaths that occurred in this same small town two years ago?*"

"You're distracting me," Gwen said. "I'm trying to call 911."

"Why bother? We both know where this is going. The authorities will assume that I died of natural causes."

"Which is entirely possible."

"But your intuition is telling you that I was murdered like the others."

"My intuition has sent me in the wrong direction before," Gwen said.

"You're thinking about what happened two years ago, aren't you?"

"Of course I am. I've been thinking about it all night and during the drive from Seattle."

Gwen turned her back on the ghost in the mirror and focused on the crisp voice of the 911 operator.

"What is the nature of your emergency?" the woman asked.

"I just found the body of an old friend," Gwen said. "Dr. Evelyn Ballinger."

"Ballinger? The crazy old lady who lives out on Miller Road?"

"I'm sure your professionalism would be an inspiration to 911 operators everywhere," Gwen said.

She rattled off the stark facts and verified the address.

"I've got cars on the way," the operator said. "Your name, ma'am?"

"Gwendolyn Frazier."

"Please stay at the scene, ma'am."

"I'm not going anywhere."

Gwen ended the call and wondered if

Harold Oxley, the Wilby chief of police, would be among the first responders. Probably. It was a small town, after all.

When she turned back to the mirror, the psychic vision made a tut-tutting sound.

"No one except you and the killer will know that I was murdered, let alone that I was killed by paranormal means. The perp will never be brought to justice, not unless you do something about this."

Just like last time, Gwen thought.

"There's nothing I can do," she said. "I'm not a cop and I'm not a private investigator."

"No, but you owe me, don't you? When you were locked up at the Summerlight Academy, I taught you how to handle your talent. And I'm the one who got you the job writing those scripts for *Dead of Night.* We were friends. And this time it's different, isn't it? Two years ago, you didn't know any psychic investigators. But now you are aware of a certain security consulting firm that specializes in the paranormal, aren't you?"

The annoying thing about talking to ghosts was that it was a lot like talking to yourself, Gwen thought, which was pretty much exactly what was going on.

She closed the phone and dropped it back into her tote. For the first time, she noticed that there was an empty space on top of the desk. A film of dust traced the outline of the place where a laptop had once sat.

"He took your computer," she said. She thought about that glaring fact. "Maybe this was a home-invasion robbery."

"In that case, I probably would have been killed in a more traditional fashion, don't you think?" the ghost asked. "Perhaps with a gun or knife or a blow to the head."

"Something violent happened here, I can sense that much, but there's no sign of a struggle, and you would have fought back."

"Not if I was caught unawares," the ghost pointed out.

"There was violence done here, but it's possible that your death was due to a heart attack or a stroke brought on by the shock of the robbery."

The ghost smiled. "But the only thing missing is my laptop. You know as well as I do that it was not a particularly valuable, high-end machine. There's my old backpack sitting on the chair. Why don't you see if the thief took my money and credit cards?"

Gwen crossed to the chair and picked up the small, well-worn backpack. The crystal wind chimes shivered again, unleashing another string of spectral notes. Max crouched in the doorway, flattened his ears and meowed again.

There was fifty dollars and two credit cards inside Evelyn's wallet. Gwen set the pack back down. So much for the home-invasion theory.

"As for other motives, you know me," the ghost continued. "I wasn't dealing drugs out the kitchen door. I didn't cultivate a marijuana plantation in the woods behind the house. I was very fond of my crystal jewelry, but none of it was expensive."

"You also had a cell phone." Gwen turned on her heel to survey the room. "But I don't see it."

"Gone, like my computer."

"Phones are small. It could be anywhere. Maybe it's in the kitchen or your bedroom."

Sirens howled in the distance. It sounded as if the 911 operator had sent the community's entire fleet of emergency vehicles. Gwen realized she did not have a lot of time to search for the missing cell phone.

She whipped through the study, opening and closing drawers as quickly as possible. There was no sign of the phone.

The sirens were closer now. Gwen slammed the last drawer shut and raced past Max, out into the hall. The cat hurried after her.

She paused at the entrance to the kitchen

and did a quick survey. The old-fashioned tiled countertops were bare except for a row of pottery canisters and an ancient coffee-maker.

Turning, she dashed upstairs, Max at her heels, and did a swift foray through the two small bedrooms. She was on her way down-stairs when the first patrol car roared into the drive.

She rushed back into the office. The chimes clattered restlessly, as though impatient with her lack of progress.

"My death is going to be the biggest news in town by noon," the ghost observed. "There hasn't been this much excitement around here since Mary, Ben and Zander died two years ago."

"There can't possibly be any connection between your death and what happened two years ago," Gwen said.

"Are you certain of that?"

"It's been *two years.*"

"But you're still dreaming about what happened, especially at this time of year, aren't you? You've known all along that some piece of the puzzle was missing."

Gwen pulled one of the curtains aside. Her heart sank when she saw Harold Oxley extricate his big, heavily padded frame out from behind the wheel of one of the patrol cars. Dark glasses shielded his eyes, but she could see that two years had taken a toll on the man. The mild exertion of heaving himself out of the vehicle was enough to turn his broad, jowly face an unhealthy shade of red. His uniform shirt was stretched tight across his rounded belly. He moved stiffly, like a man who was plagued with multiple joint issues. But the gun on his hip was as large as ever, and there was nothing to indicate that he would be any more open to the possibility that there were paranormal aspects involved in a death than he had been two years ago.

Gwen let the curtain drop back into place and turned around. She stopped at the sight of the photograph on the floor. *It had not simply fallen off the corkboard,* she thought. *It looked as if Evelyn had ripped it off in her dying moments and clutched it as she went down.*

"It's important, dear," the ghost said. "Why else would it be there right next to my hand?"

Gwen picked up the photo and looked at the seven people in the group shot. She was the third person from the end in the bottom row. The picture had been taken two years ago, shortly before the murders had begun. Mary Henderson and Ben Schwartz were in the picture. So was Zander Taylor. They were all smiling for the camera.

"You kept this photo tacked to your bulletin board," she said. "Why is it on the floor?"

"An intriguing question," the ghost said.

A heavy fist rapped authoritatively on the front door. Gwen dropped the photo into her tote and went down the hall. Max padded after her.

She opened the door.

"Chief Oxley," she said politely.

Harold Oxley yanked off his sunglasses and looked at her with an expression that made it clear he was no more thrilled by their reunion than she was.

"Cindy said the 911 call came in from a Gwendolyn Frazier," Oxley said. There was grim resignation in his growly voice. "I hoped it was just a coincidence."

"Evelyn was a friend of mine," Gwen said. She was careful to keep her own voice cool, calm and as innocent-sounding as possible. "We stayed in touch."

"Two years ago, you and I met over three dead bodies. You leave town and there are no unexplained deaths for the whole time you're gone. You come back to town and we have ourselves another dead body. What am I supposed to do with that?"

27

"Two years ago, you concluded that all three of those people died of natural causes," she said. She struggled to keep her temper under control, but she knew she probably sounded as if she was speaking through set teeth. So much for the innocent act.

"Not Taylor." Oxley narrowed suspicious brown eyes. "He went over the falls and drowned."

"You called his death a suicide."

"Uh-huh. I'll want a statement from you today."

"Of course."

A young officer and two medics arrived at the door behind Oxley. The medics carried emergency equipment and a stretcher.

Oxley peered into the hallway. "Where is she?"

"In her office." Gwen moved out of the way and opened the door wider. "It's to the right."

Oxley, the young officer and the medics tromped past her and Max and disappeared around the corner.

Gwen stood in the doorway and watched the light summer rain fall steadily in the trees that surrounded the house. She listened to the commotion and the muffled voices that emanated from the far end of the hall.

Max pressed his heavy frame against her leg. She reached down to scratch him behind the ears.

"I know you're going to miss her," she said gently. "I will, too."

After a while, she remembered the photograph she had found on the floor. She opened her tote and took out the picture. Once again she examined each face in the image. It was impossible not to do the math. Three of the people she was looking at had died two years ago, and now the photographer, Evelyn, was also dead.

Gwen turned the photo over and saw two words scrawled on the reverse side. *Mirror, mirror.*

THREE

"What makes Gwen think that Ballinger was murdered by paranormal means?" Judson Coppersmith asked.

He was on the porch of the small cottage, tilted back in a wooden chair that was propped on its two rear legs. The heels of his running shoes were stacked on the railing. He held the phone tightly to his ear so that he could hear his brother over the dull roar of the breakers crashing on the long strip of beach.

There was a storm coming in on the Oregon coast, and the little town of Eclipse Bay was going to take a direct hit. He was looking forward to it. With luck the energy of the gale would prove distracting, at least for a while. He needed a distraction. Lately the days seemed endless and the nights were even longer.

The layers of gray that surrounded him — from the leaden sky to the weathered boards of the cottage — went well with the gray mood that had descended on him after he'd made it out of the flooded caves. He wasn't sleeping well, which was a good thing because when he did sleep, the dream was intense. And it was getting worse.

"Gwen is a talent," Sam said patiently. "Like us, remember?"

Oh, yeah, I remember you, Dream Eyes, Judson thought. He'd encountered her on only one occasion — a month ago when he'd driven to Seattle to meet Sam's fiancée, Abby Radwell — but he wasn't likely to forget Gwen Frazier.

The four of them had gone out to dinner together at a restaurant in the trendy South Lake Union neighborhood of the city. He'd taken one look into Gwen's witchy green-and-gold eyes and immediately started contemplating a long hot night spent amid sheets made damp with sweat. He had convinced himself that the attraction was mutual. There was no way he could have been wrong about the energy that had sparked in the atmosphere between them that night. *No way.* There had certainly been no doubt in his mind that Gwen was exactly the distraction he had needed to get his mind off the damn dream.

But the vision of a night of sexual relief

had gone down in flames when Gwen had looked at him and said those four little words. *I fix bad dreams.*

It was at that point that he realized he had completely misinterpreted the look in her mysterious eyes. She hadn't seen him as a potential lover. She had viewed him as a potential client — vulnerable and in need of her professional expertise.

He now had a new four-word rule. *Never date psychic counselors.*

"Gwen sees auras, doesn't she?" he said into the phone. "Dead bodies don't have auras, so I don't understand how she could pick up much at a crime scene."

"Abby says that Gwen's talent is a lot more complex than she lets on," Sam said. "Don't forget those two have known each other since they were locked up in high school together."

"Locked up?"

"After their psychic talents started to manifest, Abby and Gwen both wound up in a boarding school for troubled youth, the Summerlight Academy," Sam explained. "In Abby's case, her family figured she was psychologically disturbed. Gwen ended up there after the aunt who had raised her died. It's a long story and not a happy one. Abby says there were bars on the windows."

Judson exhaled slowly. "That had to be rough."

"Knowing Abby and Gwen has brought home to me the fact that you and I and Emma don't always appreciate just how damn lucky we were to grow up with parents who managed to deal with the paranormal side of our natures."

Meeting Abby Radwell had changed a lot of things for his brother, Judson thought. Sam had fallen for Abby like the proverbial ton of bricks after Abby had hired him to investigate a case that had involved murder, revenge and a rare psi-encoded book.

The couple had announced their intention to marry immediately. Willow Coppersmith had flown into a mild panic. Claiming some rights as the mother of the groom, she had beseeched Sam and Abby to wait until she could plan a more formal wedding.

A compromise had been reached. The wedding was scheduled for the end of August, less than three weeks from now. Judson was pretty sure that the negotiation had been Abby's doing, not Sam's. Abby had struggled all of her life to find a real family. Now that she was about to join the Coppersmith clan, she wanted to start off on the right foot with her new mother-in-law.

The gala celebration was going to take place at the family compound, Copper Beach, on Legacy Island. The normally secluded enclave in the San Juans was now abuzz with activity as Willow and the wedding planner she had hired exercised their remarkable talents for organization to pull together a large-scale event in a short span of time.

Judson suspected that there were probably no more than five men on the face of the planet who would have enjoyed the commotion associated with the planning of a big wedding. Sam was not among those five, but he was the groom, so he was stuck coping with the hubbub created by the constant comings and goings of caterers, photographers and florists.

Judson felt a little sorry for him, but he figured Sam could handle the situation. In any event, he knew that in his present mood he would not be good company. Also, in his present state, it was best to avoid Willow. She had a mother's intuition. If she found out about the recurring dream and the sleepless nights, she would freak. That was the last thing anyone — especially Sam and Abby — needed.

"Look, I understand that you want to take a break before we decide what we're going to do with Coppersmith Consulting," Sam said. "But this is a family situation. Abby says that Gwen is really upset about Ballinger's death. Gwen wants an investigation, and she's not going to get that from the local cops. All we're asking you to do is make a quick trip to Wilby and figure out what happened to Ballinger."

"What if it turns out that Ballinger was murdered by paranormal means? What the hell will Gwen expect me to do about it? It's not like this is one of our old agency jobs where I can go in, analyze the scene and turn the problem over to Spalding so that he can make the problem go away. Regular cops and prosecutors don't think much of the woo-woo stuff. They need hard proof to build a case, and that's not always available."

"I'm aware of that," Sam said.

"It's why we don't do much private work, remember?"

"I know, but this falls into the friends-and-family category," Sam said.

"I get that, but that still begs the question. What will Gwen Frazier expect me to do if I determine that her friend was murdered but can't find any usable evidence?"

"You'll think of something," Sam said. "You always do. This is very important to Abby. She says Gwen needs closure."

"Closure for what?"

Sam cleared his throat. "Evidently Gwen has a history there in Wilby."

"This thing is starting to sound more complicated by the minute."

"Two years ago, Gwen was one of seven subjects in a research study conducted by the dead woman. The study was designed to try to find a way to prove the existence of paranormal talents."

"Safe to say that the study was a failure," Judson said. "No way to prove what can't be scientifically measured. The Coppersmith R-and-D lab has been working on that problem for years."

"Sure. But that's not the big story about what happened in Wilby two years ago."

"There's more?"

"Turns out one of the research subjects in the Ballinger study, a guy named Zander Taylor, was a serial killer who specialized in stalking and killing people who claimed to be psychic. Until he arrived in Wilby, most of his targets were probably frauds — a mix of storefront fortune-tellers, tarot card readers, mediums and assorted scam artists."

A flicker of awareness arced across Judson's senses. Something that might have been curiosity stirred inside him. It was the first time he had felt anything other than the weight of the gray since he had returned from the island. He took his feet down off the railing and stood.

"Let me take a flying leap here," he said. "This Zander Taylor wanted a challenge. He volunteered for the research study in order to find himself some real psychics to murder."

"You do know how the bad guys think," Sam said. "You nailed it. He succeeded in killing two members of the research study before he tried to murder Gwen. Obviously, he failed but it was a near thing, and Abby says Gwen was badly traumatized by the attack. Now Ballinger's death has brought back all the bad memories and vibes."

Another tendril of curiosity flickered through Judson. He looked down at the amber-colored crystal in his ring. The stone was glowing with a little energy in response to his slightly jacked talent.

"How come we've never heard of Taylor?" he asked. "That kind of story should have been all over the news. I can see the headlines now. *Serial Killer Stalks Psychics.*"

"Taylor never made the news because no one ever realized that he was killing people,"

Sam said. "In the case of the Wilby murders, the first two deaths were attributed to natural causes. Taylor's death was ruled a suicide."

Judson contemplated the restless, gray ocean. "What did the local cops say about the deaths?"

"I'm told that the Wilby chief of police — guy named Oxley — had his suspicions but he couldn't prove anything. That was fortunate for Gwen."

"Why is that?"

"Because Gwen was the one who reported all three deaths," Sam said. "You know how that would have looked to any halfway competent cop. The person who finds and reports the body usually goes to the top of the suspect list."

"And this morning she finds another body." Judson whistled softly. "What are the odds, huh?"

"You can see it from Oxley's point of view."

Judson wrapped one hand around a wooden post and watched the summer storm sweep in over the ocean. "Okay, got to admit there's an interesting pattern here."

"Evidently, when Oxley arrived at the scene this morning, he did not hide the fact that he doesn't like coincidences."

"He really believes that Gwen may be responsible for all of the murders?"

"He never could prove that there were any murders, but, yes, he has his suspicions. Gwen is in no immediate danger of arrest, but for her own peace of mind, she needs to find out what is going on. She knows Abby so she knows that you and I are in the psychic investigation business."

"We were in the business before I pretty much put us out of business," Judson said.

"We'll find another client. Got to be more where that one came from."

"Very funny."

"I'm serious," Sam said. "Losing our number one client is no big deal, given what we now know about said client."

"Except that, aside from the security work we do for Coppersmith, Inc., it was pretty much our only client. And we didn't lose the client. I destroyed the whole damn agency."

"Not a problem," Sam said. "We'll find a replacement. At last official count, there were close to a thousand different government agencies, departments and offices involved in the U.S. intelligence community — and a couple thousand more private contractors. I'm sure we can find one that is interested in the services of a consulting firm that specializes in paranormal investigations. But for now, we need to do something about Gwen Frazier's case."

The wind sharpened. So did Judson's senses. This time it would be different, he thought. This time Gwen needed him. She would not be able to treat him like one of her psychic counseling clients.

"All right, I'll drive to Wilby and take a look," he said.

There was a short pause on the other end of the call.

"One more thing you should know about Gwen Frazier," Sam said finally.

"Yeah?"

"She sees ghosts," Sam said.

"What the hell?"

But it was too late. Sam had already ended the connection.

Judson stood quietly, letting the energy of the oncoming storm and the prospect of seeing Gwen again stir his senses.

After a while, he turned and went back inside the cottage to pack for the long drive to Wilby.

Ghosts were no big deal. He saw a few every night in his dreams.

FOUR

Gwen sat at a small table in the tearoom of the Riverview Inn and watched the dark-haired man with the eyes of a raptor enter the lobby. An eerie storm of amber lightning flashed and sparked in the atmosphere around Judson Coppersmith. The disturbing heat in his aura had not diminished since the disastrous evening in Seattle. His dreams were growing more powerful.

The effect that Judson had on all of her senses had not lessened, either. A near-violent rush of awareness, an effervescent excitement mingled with dread and an uncanny sensation of *knowing,* shivered through her. The same intuitive certainty that had both compelled and alarmed her that night in Seattle came crashing back. *This is the one.*

The paranormal fire that surrounded Judson roared in the cozy lobby of the old Victorian inn. But Gwen knew that she was the only one who could see the flames. The handful of guests seated in the wingback reading chairs did not look up from their books and magazines. Riley Duncan, the front desk clerk, did not take his eyes off his computer screen.

Trisha Montgomery, the proprietor of the Riverview Inn, was seated across the table from Gwen in the tearoom. She, too, was oblivious.

"Between you and me, you should try to stay out of Nicole Hudson's way while you're in town," Trisha said. She lowered her voice to a conspiratorial whisper. "That woman isn't right in the head. You know as well as I do that she wasn't what anyone would call stable two years ago. I can tell you for a fact that her mental health hasn't improved in the past two years."

"Don't worry," Gwen said. She suppressed a small shudder. "I have no intention of crossing paths with Nicole if I can avoid it."

"That won't be possible, not if you hang around for more than a day or two," Trisha said dryly. "Wilby is one very small town."

Trisha was in her late thirties, an attractive woman with short, curly brown hair that framed a fine-boned, heart-shaped face. Gwen had met her two years earlier at the start of Evelyn's research study. At the time, Trisha had been a newcomer to Wilby, a newly minted multi-millionaire who had made her fortune in the high-tech world. She had retired at an early age to do what she had always dreamed of doing — run a quaint B&B in the Oregon woods. To the surprise of just about everyone in town, she had made the old inn a year-round success.

Gwen tried to pay attention to Trisha, but her eyes kept returning to the lobby where Judson was approaching the front desk. She knew that the storm of amber light that blazed around him was a vision conjured by her psychic senses. Normally, she kept her talent tamped down when she was around other people. But today she was tense and very much on edge and therefore not in full control. Her other sight had flared a moment ago when Judson had opened the door. Even though she had been anticipating his arrival, seeing him for the first time after a month of thinking about him far more often than was good for her had rattled her senses and raised her talent.

What on earth was going on in Judson's dreams that caused her to perceive him like this — a hard, relentlessly determined man walking through a storm of hot amber light?

She had a talent for analyzing dreams, but

she needed context to comprehend what her intuition was trying to tell her. Judson was still very much an enigma, and given his reaction to her offer of dream therapy that night in Seattle, she had a feeling that he intended to remain a mystery.

He must have sensed that he was being watched because he stopped before he reached the front desk and raked the small lobby with a single glance, sizing up the handful of guests the way a predator considers potential prey.

She knew that he had jacked up his talent a little because at that point some of the guests belatedly became of aware of something dangerous in their midst. A few of them raised their eyes from their magazines or broke off conversations long enough to glance around, instinctively searching for whatever it was that had raised the hair on the back of their necks.

But as was so often the case, they chose to ignore the primal message that their senses were sending. After all, this was a warm, safe place, and the newcomer looked well dressed, calm and controlled. He made no overtly threatening moves.

The guests went back to their magazines and conversation. Perhaps their intuition had told them what had been clear to Gwen when he walked through the door. They were safe. None of them was Judson's intended prey today. He was here for her.

With an effort of will, she forced her vision back down into the normal zone. The surreal ultra-light fire winked out, but the sense of recognition was as strong as ever. This was the man she had been waiting for — not just since she had made the phone call to Abby — all of her life. Her pulse beat faster. Her fingers tightened on the teacup.

Pull yourself together, woman. She had always been a dreamer, but she had learned long ago not to get carried away by her own dreams.

At that instant, Judson looked at her through the open French doors of the tearoom. Another unsettling jolt of awareness thrilled her senses. She was pretty sure that she saw a flash of heat in his topaz eyes.

She inclined her head in what she hoped was a cool, polite acknowledgment of his presence. He returned the small gesture — equally cool and polite — and continued on to the front desk to check in.

Gwen turned her attention back to Trisha.

"Is Nicole still running the florist shop?" Gwen asked.

"Oh, yes," Trisha said. "She's really good at the business, even if she is a bit nutty.

45

Handles all the weddings, funerals and high school proms in the area. She does the weekly arrangements here at the inn." Trisha angled her delicate chin toward the floral display that sat on the round table in the lobby. "But last month I stopped by her shop to discuss some changes I wanted to make in the flowers that go into the rooms. The door of her office was open. I'm telling you, the inside looked like some kind of weird shrine to that man she was seeing two years ago, the one who went over the falls."

Unease twisted through Gwen.

"She's still carrying the torch for Zander Taylor?" she asked, just to be certain.

"I'm afraid so." Trisha made a face. "And she still blames you for his death. As far as I can tell, Zander Taylor was the only serious relationship she has ever had. She's great with flowers and animals, but not with people. I thought you should know. You might want to be careful around her."

"I appreciate the warning," Gwen said.

"I see you booked a week with us for yourself and this Judson Coppersmith," Trisha said, probing gently.

"I need time to arrange Evelyn's funeral and take care of her legal and business affairs," Gwen said. "Judson is going to help me."

Trisha frowned. "No offense, but why you? Didn't Evelyn have any family?"

"No. She left everything to me."

"I see. I hadn't realized that." Trisha gave her a commiserating smile. "You probably won't have any trouble selling the house she lived in here in town, but what on earth will you do with the old lodge out at the falls, the place she called her research lab?"

"I have no idea," Gwen said truthfully. "I suppose I'll hire someone to clean out the equipment and the instruments she installed and then try to sell the place. I'm hoping I can get things wrapped up in a week, but there's a lot to handle."

"This Judson Coppersmith you're expecting is a friend?"

"Not exactly, more of a financial adviser," Gwen said. She was proud of the smooth way that came out. She had been working on Judson's cover story all morning. "He's had some experience with this sort of thing, settling estates and such."

Trisha's expression cleared. "Good, because I think you're going to need some help. I doubt that Evelyn paid much attention to her business affairs. All she cared about was her research."

"I know."

"She was a real eccentric in a town full of

that particular breed, but I'm going to miss her."

"So will I," Gwen said.

Trisha cleared her throat. "Sara, one of my housekeepers, says there's a large cat in your room."

"Evelyn's cat, actually. Max. I couldn't leave him there at the house. There's no one around to feed him. I didn't know what to do with him, so I brought him here with me. I hope that's not a problem. I brought his litter box with me. I'll pick up some cat food later."

"It's okay." Trish smiled. "I allow pets."

Judson had finished at the front desk. He walked through the doors of the tearoom, a leather bag in one hand. His profile suited his hawk-like eyes, Gwen thought, all sharp planes and angles. There was a prowling, muscular grace in his stride. He wore khakis, a gray crew-neck pullover and low boots. The unusual amber-colored crystal in the black metal ring on his right hand caught the summer light streaming through the window. For a heartbeat, she could have sworn that it glowed, as if infused with some energy. *Just like his eyes,* she thought.

Judson stopped at the table and pinned her with his bird-of-prey eyes.

"Hello, Gwen," he said.

"Judson. Nice to see you again." She managed a bright, welcoming smile. "You made good time. This is Trisha Montgomery. She owns the inn."

"Welcome to the Riverside Inn," Trisha said, smiling warmly.

"Thanks," Judson said.

"I understand you'll be staying with us for a few days while you help Gwen settle Evelyn Ballinger's affairs," Trish continued.

Gwen knew a rush of panic. She had not had time to brief Judson on the cover story she had concocted.

Judson looked at Gwen, utterly unfazed, his brows elevated ever so slightly. "That's right."

Gwen breathed a sigh of relief and flashed him an approving smile. He had handled the situation very smoothly. As well he should, she thought. He was a security consultant, after all.

Trisha got to her feet and took her computer bag off the back of the chair. She hitched the strap of the bag over one shoulder. "If you two will excuse me, I need to have a chat with my cook. Please let me know if I or anyone else on the staff can help in any way."

"We'll do that," Judson said.

Trisha went briskly toward the kitchen.

Judson lowered himself into the chair across from Gwen. He set the leather bag on the floor near his feet.

"So, we're here to settle Ballinger's affairs?" he said, speaking in very neutral tones. "That's our story?"

"Well, it's not like I can announce that we're conducting a possible murder investigation, now, is it?" Gwen said. She spoke crisply, authoritatively. It did not require psychic intuition to know that with a man like this a woman had to take charge right at the outset and stay in charge. Guys like Judson Coppersmith were far too accustomed to giving the orders.

"Probably best not to bring up the word *murder* yet," Judson agreed. "You'd be amazed how that subject tends to upset people."

"I realize we can't discuss it in public. The room I booked for you is next to mine on the third floor. There's a connecting door so we can talk privately without being seen coming and going from each other's rooms."

"Wow," he said, his voice still perfectly neutral. "Connecting doors."

She was starting to get flustered. "The inn is a little more expensive than either of the two motels in town, but it's actually a good bargain when you consider that we get breakfast and afternoon tea."

"Afternoon tea?" Judson repeated thoughtfully. "Will there be scones and clotted cream?"

She narrowed her eyes. "I'll be picking up your expenses, of course."

Something that looked suspiciously like amusement came and went in his eyes. "I'll keep track and make sure you get a detailed accounting when I send you my bill."

No doubt about it, he was laughing at her.

"I realize that you consider this case very low-rent compared to the jobs you're accustomed to handling for some no-name government intelligence agency. But Abby assured me that due to some unfortunate circumstances on your last mission, you are currently without a client and that you would give this investigation your full attention."

Judson's smile was slow and dangerous. "Rest assured you have my full attention, Gwen Frazier."

A middle-aged woman in a white pinafore apron appeared at the table. Her nametag read *Paula*. She handed Judson a menu and beetled her brows in a severe manner.

"It's almost four o'clock," she warned. "Tearoom closes at four. We're out of sandwiches and cakes. I think I've got a couple of scones left, but that's it."

"Just coffee, please," Judson said.

"Huh." Paula was obviously disappointed that Judson was not going to argue about the closing time, but she recovered quickly. "Cream and sugar?"

"Black," Judson said.

Naturally, Gwen thought. How else would a man like Judson Coppersmith take his coffee?

Paula eyed Gwen. "More green tea?"

"Please," Gwen said.

"Heard you've got Evelyn Ballinger's cat upstairs in your room," Paula said.

"That's right," Gwen said.

"Gonna take it to the pound?"

"No, I'll probably haul Max back to Seattle with me." Gwen paused. "Unless you know someone who might like a nice cat?"

"Nope. Got too many cats around here already. Folks from Portland are always driving up here to dump their unwanted cats and dogs on the side of the road. Besides, according to Sara, the housekeeper, Evelyn's cat isn't a nice cat. Sara says it hissed at her from under the bed when she cleaned your room today."

Paula stalked off toward the kitchen.

Judson waited until she was out of earshot.

"Looks like you've got yourself a cat."

"For now, apparently." Gwen said. She lowered her voice again and leaned forward a little. "How long do you think it will take you to conduct the investigation?"

"Depends how far you want me to go with it." Judson kept his own voice at a normal, conversational level.

She frowned. "What does that mean?"

"It will take me about five seconds at the scene to determine whether or not your friend was murdered."

"Really? Your brother made it clear that you're a professional investigator and that you have a talent for this sort of thing, but five seconds at the scene of the crime doesn't sound like enough time to conduct a thorough investigation."

Judson swept her misgivings aside with a slight motion of one powerful hand. "Murder is murder. It leaves a calling card, even when it's done by paranormal means. But you already know that, don't you? You must have sensed something when you found your friend's body — something that made you suspect foul play."

She drummed her fingers on the table. "Okay, obviously, I have my suspicions, but my talent is kind of dicey when it comes to this sort of thing."

"Dicey?"

"I read dreams and view auras. I don't investigate murders. Look, the bottom line here is that I need to be absolutely certain about what happened to Evelyn. That means that I need an investigator who is willing to spend more than five seconds at the scene."

"Is that right?" Judson lounged back in his chair and shoved his booted feet straight out under the table. He hooked his thumbs in his wide leather belt. "What, exactly, do you want from me?"

"Well, I expect you to determine cause of death, for starters."

"You mean, you want to know if Ballinger was killed by paranormal means."

"Yes. I admit that given her health history it's not beyond the realm of possibility that she had a heart attack or a stroke. I want to be sure."

"What else?" Judson asked.

"If you conclude that she was murdered, I want you to find the killer, of course."

"See, that's where things can get — what was the word you used? Oh, yeah, dicey."

She narrowed her eyes. "Complicated?"

"Very complicated."

"Because you aren't particularly good when it comes to identifying the killers?" she asked in her sweetest tones.

"Nope. I'm good at that, too."

He broke off when Paula returned to the table with his coffee and the check for Gwen to sign. Paula hovered while Gwen scrawled her name and a tip on the little slip of paper.

Paula took the signed paper and departed in the direction of the kitchen.

"She didn't look impressed with the tip that you left," Judson observed.

"Well, she should have been impressed. It was a good tip. I've worked as a waitress. Everyone knows that ex-waiters and -waitresses always overtip, even when the service is lousy."

"I'm just saying she didn't look impressed."

"And she doesn't like cats, either. Forget Paula. Let's get back to the subject at hand. You said you're good at identifying the bad guys. So what is the hard part of a murder investigation for you?"

Judson picked up his coffee. "The complication in situations like this is finding the type of evidence that we can take to the local cops, the kind they need to make an arrest and build a case."

"But isn't that what you and your brother do?"

"Not exactly," Judson said. "Mostly we work off the record."

"Off the record?"

"Didn't Abby explain what it is that Coppersmith Consulting does?"

Gwen hesitated. "She said you conducted security investigations for a government agency that recently shut down due to severe funding cuts."

Judson looked pained, but he did not correct her.

"That's true," he said. "But the great thing about working for our former client was that the guy in charge wasn't overly particular about the sort of legal technicalities that regular law enforcement has to deal with. Sam and I were hired to gather intelligence and make security recommendations. We were not in the business of making arrests."

"I see."

"Is there a problem here?" Judson asked.

"I'm not sure yet. Did your brother warn you that if we do manage to prove that Evelyn Ballinger was murdered, the local chief of police will probably consider me to be the lead suspect?"

Judson drank some coffee and lowered the cup. "I believe Sam did mention that possibility, yes."

"Let's get something straight here, Judson. I'm employing you to find the person who murdered Evelyn Ballinger, assuming she was murdered. I expect you to do so in a way that keeps me out of jail."

"I usually charge extra for that kind of work."

She stared at him, speechless for a few seconds. Judson used the time to down more of the coffee.

"Are you serious?" she finally managed.

"No." His smile was cold steel and his eyes burned. "Don't worry, you're getting the friends-and-family rate. That means you won't pay extra for little add-on services like making sure you don't get arrested for murder. I'll throw those in for free."

"Gosh, thanks." Her temper threatened to flare, but she wrestled it to the ground. It wasn't like she had a lot of options when it came to investigators, she reminded herself. "What, exactly, do you propose to do first?"

"According to *Psychic Detecting for Dummies,* the first step is to visit the scene of the crime." He glanced at his watch. "I'll do that later tonight when I can get inside without being seen."

"There's no reason to sneak around. As it happens, I have the keys."

"Well, hey, that sure makes life simpler. Can I ask why you happen to have the keys to the victim's house?"

Gwen braced herself. "Evelyn didn't have

a lot. She spent her life studying the paranormal."

"Not a profitable career path unless you're
a scam artist."

"No," Gwen agreed. "But what Evelyn did
possess, she left to me."

Judson's brows rose slightly. "This case is
getting more interesting by the minute. You
do realize that in some circles the fact that
you are Ballinger's sole heir might be viewed
as a motive for murder?"

"Trust me, the thought has crossed my
mind more than once today."

FIVE

Judson let himself into his room on the third floor and tossed the black duffel onto the bench at the foot of the big four-poster bed. One thing was now blazingly clear. Nothing had changed when it came to his reaction to Gwen. When he had seen her there in the tearoom, he had experienced the same rush of sensual hunger — the same bone-deep thrill — that had slammed through him a month earlier when he'd met her for the first time in Seattle.

She'd hit his senses like an intoxicating drug that night. He'd gotten the same exhilarating shock today.

If anything, his reaction was even stronger this time, probably because he'd been thinking about her nonstop for the past month.

She was tall for a woman, just the right height for him, Judson thought. Attractive, but not in the generic cover-girl style. What she had was a hell of an edge.

She wore her dark hair snugged back in a sleek knot that emphasized her regal nose, high forehead and deep, watchful, witchy eyes. Her curves were subtle but one hundred percent feminine. There was a sleek, feline quality about her that appealed to all of his senses.

Which immediately brought up the obvious question. Where was the man in her life? According to Sam and Abby, there was no significant other in Gwen's world. But that seemed unlikely. *Who do I have to kill to get to you, Gwendolyn Frazier?*

The old floorboards creaked beneath his boots when he crossed the room. The inn dated from the late eighteen hundreds. According to the black-and-white photographs on the walls, it had started out as a private mansion. The lumber baron who had built it had used it as a summerhouse to entertain guests and business colleagues.

He stopped at the window to study the view. The river was visible through a thick stand of trees. From where he stood, he could not see the falls. He thought about what he had managed to discover concerning the events of two years ago. The first two deaths had occurred less than three weeks apart. Gwen had found both bodies. A few days later, Zander Taylor had gone over the falls, an apparent suicide. Gwen had been the one who had called 911 on that occasion, too.

It was all very murky, but the one fact that stood out was that the series of mysterious deaths had ceased following Taylor's death. The surviving members of Ballinger's research project were all still alive according to Sam. At least they had been until this morning.

But now the director of the project was dead. And once again it was Gwen Frazier who had found the body.

He contemplated the heavily forested landscape for a while. There was a lot of wilderness left in the mountains of Oregon. Every year, people went out hiking in this part of the Pacific Northwest and disappeared forever. The rough terrain provided ample hiding places for all kinds of predators, including the human kind. A killer could commit murder and vanish into the woods for as long as it suited him.

He turned away from the window and yanked off the crewneck pullover. Opening his leather bag, he took out a fresh edition of the shirt in a slightly different shade of gray, grabbed his overnight kit and went into the grand, Victorian-style bathroom to freshen up. He wasn't used to working for private pay clients, but he suspected that neatness counted; at least he was pretty sure it counted with a client like Gwen. Downstairs in the tearoom she had made it clear that she had some doubts about both his talent and his commitment to the job. He'd better get his act together before she fired his ass.

He had to consider the reputation of Coppersmith Consulting, he told himself. It wasn't like he could afford to lose another client.

It took him half a second to recognize the guy in the mirror. His eyes didn't appear quite as bleak and soulless as they had for the past few weeks. He'd been right about one thing: Gwen Frazier was the distraction he'd been needing.

He tucked the clean shirt into the waistband of his khakis and left the giant bathroom.

A muffled meow stopped him. He turned toward the connecting door. It was closed and locked on his side, but he could see the shadows of four paws under the lower edge. The cat meowed again, sounding curious this time, and began to pace back and forth on the other side of the door.

Judson unlocked the door on his side, but when he tried the handle, he discovered that it was still secured on Gwen's side.

"Sorry, cat," he said. "You're stuck in there for now."

There was another muffled meow from the other room. This time the cat sounded irritated.

"Take it up with the boss lady," Judson said.

He went back across the room and paused to brace his right boot against the bench at the foot of the bed. He pulled up his pant leg and checked the pistol in the leather sheath strapped to his ankle.

Satisfied that he was appropriately dressed for business — probably overdressed for this job — he let himself out into the hall and went back downstairs. A disturbing whisper of energy arced across his senses when he realized that Gwen was not waiting for him in the lobby.

The desk clerk looked up from whatever he was working on and squinted through his black-framed glasses. He was in his early thirties, with a stocky build and sandy brown hair that had evidently been thinning for a while. The comb-over style was not working for him. His nametag read *Riley Duncan.*

"If you're looking for Ms. Frazier, she went outside to talk to a guy," Riley said.

Judson nodded. "Thanks."

He looked out the window and saw Gwen in the parking lot. She was not alone. A tall man with a shoulder-length mane of blond hair was with her. Something about the way the two stood together made it clear that they were not strangers. Gwen's tightly crossed arms and angled chin told him that she was not happy with the way the conversation was going.

He pushed open the front door and went outside. It was late afternoon, and the Pacific Northwest was still basking in the long days of summer. But here in the mountains, twilight fell early, even at this time of year. The shadows were already creeping over Wilby.

Anticipation heated Judson's blood as he walked toward Gwen and her companion. Maybe this was the guy he was going to have to kill to get to Gwen.

Gwen was facing the entrance of the inn. She was still wearing the trousers and dark, long-sleeved pullover that she'd had on earlier but she had added a lightweight black jacket. She saw him immediately. Relief followed by an urgent warning flashed through her eyes. Her smile was too bright and too welcoming. It was the smile a woman gave to a man with whom she was intimately involved. *What's wrong with this picture?* Judson wondered.

"Oh, there you are, Judson," she said quickly. "I was just explaining to Wesley that you and I have plans for this evening. This is Wesley Lancaster. Wesley, this is Judson Coppersmith."

It didn't take any psychic talent to know that he had just been promoted from the role of financial adviser to that of lover, Judson thought. No problem. He could work with that. He moved to stand very close to Gwen, his shoulder just brushing hers.

"Lancaster," he said. Taking his cue from Gwen, he was careful to keep his tone civil, at least until he figured out what the hell was going on.

"Coppersmith." Wesley acknowledged the introduction with a short, brusque inclination of his head that went well with his short, brusque greeting. It was clear that he was not thrilled to learn that Gwen was not alone.

At close range, it was clear that somewhere along the line a few Vikings had contributed to Wesley's gene pool. He was tall, narrow-hipped and strategically muscled in the manner of a man who spent a fair amount of time at his gym. A strong jaw, high cheekbones, light-colored eyes and the elegantly styled sweep of blond hair added to the image. All he needed was an axe, shield and helmet to complete the look, Judson thought.

Instead of the battle armor, Wesley wore a pair of hand-tailored black trousers and a dark blue silk shirt. The collar of the shirt was open partway down his chest. A slouchy linen jacket, a pair of Italian loafers and some designer shades finished the look. But Judson was sure that no self-respecting Viking warrior would have been caught dead at his own funeral pyre looking like he was dressed to make a pitch at a Hollywood film studio.

"Wesley is the ghost hunter on *Dead of Night,* the television show that investigates reports of old hauntings and paranormal occurrences," Gwen said.

That explained a lot, Judson thought.

"Is that right?" he said. He made himself stop there. No sense pushing the envelope by adding that he considered all ghost hunters to be frauds and that he had never heard of the show.

"Gwen tells me that the two of you are in town to handle Evelyn Ballinger's funeral and her affairs," Wesley said.

"That's right." Judson went for casual, still

trying to get a feel for the vibe between Wesley and Gwen. They clearly shared a past, but beyond that things got murky fast. "What brings you to Wilby?"

Wesley blew out a long sigh and looked troubled. "I came here to see Evelyn. I've been trying to contact her for several days now. She stopped replying to my e-mails, and she wouldn't respond to the messages I left on her voice mail. I decided to grab a plane to Portland and drive up here to Wilby to find out what was going on. It came as a hell of a shock to discover that Evelyn died sometime last night."

"Why were you so concerned about her when you couldn't get in touch?" Judson asked. "Close friends?"

"Business associates," Wesley said grimly.

Gwen unfolded her arms and shoved her hands deep into the pockets of her jacket. "Evelyn did some contract work for Wesley. She was his primary researcher. She checked out stories of hauntings and paranormal activity. It was her job to identify locations that were suitable for episodes of *Dead of Night.* After Wesley made his choice, I wrote up the script."

Judson looked at her. "*You* did the scripts?"

"Yes," she said. She glared, silently daring

67

him to challenge that.

"For a series that investigates haunted houses?" he said carefully.

"Yes," she said. Ice dripped from the word.

Wesley scowled. "You got a problem with that, Coppersmith?"

"No," Judson said. "I knew Gwen was a psychic counselor, but I didn't realize that she had been writing fiction, that's all."

Gwen raised her eyes toward the evening sky and looked mildly annoyed.

"*Dead of Night* is not fiction," Wesley snapped. "We deal with real hauntings. Gwen's scripts are based on the actual details and rumors that surround old murders and mysterious disappearances and deaths."

"I see," Judson said. "How many people work for you?"

Wesley eyed him with impatience. "Several, why?"

"Just wondered if you're in the habit of hopping a plane and driving a couple of hours to see one of your staff whenever you can't get in touch by phone or e-mail."

Out of the corner of his eye, he saw Gwen's expression sharpen. He felt energy stir and knew that she had heightened her talent. She was studying Wesley's aura. *What do you see, Dream Eyes?*

Wesley was getting angry. "Evelyn was late with the results of her last research project. She'd missed two deadlines. Every time I asked her if she had finished researching the next location, she told me that she just needed another few days to finish. Finally she stopped taking my calls. *Dead of Night* operates on a very tight schedule. I can't afford to sit around and wait on a researcher. So, yes, when I couldn't get hold of her, I came here to see her in person. I had no clue that she'd died during the night."

"What time did you arrive?" Judson asked.

"You know, I really don't owe you any explanations, Coppersmith." Wesley turned back to Gwen. "Think about what I said. If you're interested in taking over the research as well as the scriptwriting, I'll make it worth your while. I'm in a real crunch here. I need your help."

"I'll think about it," Gwen promised.

"Do that," Wesley advised. "But do it fast. I'll give you the same salary that I gave Evelyn. We both know that between the research and the scriptwriting, you'll make a hell of a lot more than you will in the psychic counseling business."

"I know," Gwen said. She studied him with an assessing expression. "How long do you plan to be in town?"

"I've got to get back to Portland tonight to catch a plane to California first thing in the morning. We're filming all day tomorrow. But you can reach me on my cell. Call anytime, day or night. I'll need an answer soon, Gwen."

"I understand."

Wesley hesitated. "Do you have any idea what she was working on there at the end?"

"No. She never sent me any notes. Usually the two of us batted around ideas for a show before we settled on a couple that we thought would work for you. But I hadn't heard from her in nearly two weeks."

"If you find anything connected to *Dead* when you go through her files, let me know."

"All right," Gwen said.

"It's weird," Wesley said. "The last time I spoke to her — about a week ago before she stopped taking my calls — I got the impression that she was working on something really big. You're sure she didn't drop any hints?"

"None."

"Well, that's it, then. Shit." Wesley's jaw hardened. "I'm dead serious about my offer, Gwen. Evelyn would have wanted you to take over her job. Think of it as carrying on her legacy of research into the paranormal. And I can guarantee you that the money is good."

"I promise I'll think about it." Gwen took one hand out of her jacket pocket and glanced at her watch. "It's getting late. You'll have to excuse us, Wesley. Judson and I have some business to attend to."

"Yeah, right. Business." Wesley shot Judson a narrow-eyed look and then jerked open the door of a nearby car. He got behind the wheel and looked up at Gwen.

"Don't forget," he said. "If you turn up that last research file she was working on, call me."

"Okay," Gwen said. "But I can tell you right now that it was probably on her computer and her computer is missing."

"Shit." Wesley slammed the door and fired up the car.

Judson watched the vehicle roar out of the parking lot.

"Guess we can't add him to our suspect list," Judson said. "Sounds like he depended on Ballinger to keep his show on the air."

"She was certainly important to him," Gwen said. "So it doesn't seem like he would have had a motive. Also, if I'm right, Evelyn was killed by paranormal means. That means it's practically impossible that Wesley killed her."

"Why do you say that?"

"I've known Wesley since the days of the Ballinger study. I'm almost positive that he doesn't have any strong psychic talent. Heck, he doesn't even believe in the paranormal. He just thinks it makes good television."

"Okay, that explains a few things." Judson took her arm and steered her toward his black SUV. "First things first. Let's go have a look at the scene and find out whether or not we're dealing with murder and, if so, whether it was murder by paranormal means. We'll figure out what to do from there."

"Well, actually, first things first means a stop at the Wilby General Store before it closes. I've got a cat to feed."

"Fine. Cat food first. Then the murder investigation."

He discovered he liked holding her arm. He liked it a lot. When he opened the passenger-side door of the vehicle, Gwen paused, glancing at his hand.

"Your ring," she said.

"What about it?"

"It's infused with a little energy. It's a paranormal crystal like the one your brother, Sam, wears, isn't it?"

Judson glanced at his ring. The amber crystal was faintly luminous. The stone was responding to his slightly jacked senses,

"Yes, it's hot," he said. "My father gave it to me when I was in my late teens. Sam and Emma got crystals as well. They're each unique."

He used his grip on Gwen's elbow to give her a boost up into the passenger seat, closed the door and walked around the front of the SUV to the driver's side. He took another look at the ring. The crystal had been infused with energy that night in Seattle when he'd contemplated the possibility of getting Gwen into bed. It was hot again tonight. Probably for the same reason. He got a little rush just thinking about her. Being physically near her was a real ride.

Over the years, he had learned that the crystal resonated with the energy of his talent. When he was really in the zone, the stone glowed like molten amber. The ultralight it gave off, however, was from the paranormal end of the spectrum. Only someone who was sensitive to psi could perceive the heat in the crystal.

He'd noticed energy stirring on several occasions in the crystal. But until he had met Gwen, it had never heated with this unique color. It was the glow of sunlight, he thought, the same light that had guided him out of the flooded caves.

He opened the door, got behind the wheel, cranked the big engine and drove out of the small parking lot.

"Want to tell me what made you decide to give Thor the impression that you and I are sleeping together?" he asked.

There was a short, startled pause from the other side of the vehicle.

"Thor?" Gwen repeated, as if she wasn't sure she had heard him correctly.

"Sorry." He shifted gears. "I think it's the hair."

She smiled. "Wesley does have a certain sense of style." She stopped smiling. "But I certainly never meant to imply that you and I were romantically involved. Are you sure that's how it came across?"

He tightened his grip on the wheel. "Oh, yeah."

"Are you positive?"

"Call it male intuition," he said.

"I wasn't trying to project that sort of impression, believe me. I just wanted him to know that I had —"

"Backup?"

"Yes, backup." She was clearly pleased. "That's the right word."

"Why?"

"Wesley can be a trifle obsessive when it comes to his show. I don't want him interfering with our investigation."

"Do you think that he would?"

"Ha. In a heartbeat if he thought it might be fodder for an episode of *Dead of Night*. What could be more made-to-order than an investigation into the mysterious death of a woman who conducted research into the paranormal?"

"Is his series really popular?"

"It has attracted an audience on cable, but between you and me, I think it's struggling," Gwen said. "You can only do so many ghost stories, you know. After a while, they all tend to be alike. Evelyn and I did our best, but it's hard to keep coming up with new angles."

"Especially since there are no such things as ghosts."

"That fact was the least of our problems," Gwen said. "Between us, Evelyn and I did a good job of coming up with interesting locations and good scripts because we focused on genuine murders. We stuck with the really old ones, of course — historical mysteries."

"The kind where everyone involved is long dead."

"Right. The last thing we wanted to do was get sued by irate relatives of the deceased. Anyhow, once we had the mystery and the location, I just invented a ghost for the story. No problem."

"Or have to wonder if you should go to the cops with whatever evidence you found?"

She glanced at him swiftly and then looked straight ahead through the windshield. "There would be no point going to the police in most cases. They wouldn't pay any attention to a psychic counselor."

"No, probably not. But you're okay with the real cold cases?"

"Yes." Gwen brightened. "I view them as fascinating puzzles. To tell you the truth, I think that Evelyn and I solved a lot of very old murders for *Dead of Night,* but of course there's no way to prove it."

"Because everyone involved is dead."

"Yep."

"Were you telling Wesley the truth when you said that you didn't have any idea what Evelyn was working on recently?"

"That was the absolute truth," Gwen said. "I've been busy with my clients and finishing an earlier script for *Dead.* I hadn't heard from Evelyn in a while, but that wasn't unusual. I just assumed she was consumed with her research. When she got caught up in a project, she became very, very focused."

"Are you talking about her research for

Dead of Night?"

"No," Gwen said. "She just took that job to pay the bills. Her real passion was serious research into the paranormal. She set up an entire lab out at the old lodge near the falls. That's where she spent most of her time."

"When was the last time you heard from her?"

"I got a very cryptic e-mail message from her late last night telling me that she had stumbled onto something very important. She wanted to talk about it in person, not over the phone." Gwen looked out the side window at the river. "But I didn't read my e-mail until this morning. I tried to call her immediately, but by then it was too late."

He caught the faint tremor in her voice.

"There was nothing you could have done," he said quietly.

"I know." Gwen trapped her hands between her knees and continued to stare out the window at the river. "I know."

Brooding on what ifs never went well, he thought. He should know. The solution, he had learned, was to stay focused on the present.

"Let's stick with what we have," he said. "You're thinking that if Ballinger was murdered, there may be a connection to whatever she was working on just before her death."

"Yes." Gwen turned back to look at him. "You heard me tell Wesley that her computer was missing. Her cell phone was gone, too."

"I agree that under the circumstances that needs some explaining. You don't trust Thor — Lancaster — do you?"

Gwen winced. "I wouldn't say that, not exactly. It's just that when you're dealing with Wesley, you have to keep in mind that he always has an agenda and that he'll do or say whatever it is he needs to do or say to get what he wants. The trick to dealing with him is to remember that the most important thing in his world is the future of *Dead of Night.* If you filter everything through that lens, you can work with him. He's no worse than any other career-obsessed person, male or female. In fact, I've met worse."

"Got any specific reasons for not trusting him?"

Gwen was silent for a few seconds.

"I guess I'll have to go with the obvious answer," she said. "Female intuition."

"I respect intuition," he said. "But I like hard facts, too. Correct me if I'm wrong, but earlier I got the impression that you and Lancaster have some history that involves more than a business association."

"Two years ago, when we met here in Wilby, he tried to get me into bed."

Judson's gut tightened. "Do you distrust every man who wants to sleep with you?"

"Only when the man in question neglects to mention that he's married. That tends to piss me off."

Judson exhaled slowly and loosened his death grip on the wheel.

"Okay," he said. "I get that. So, did you find out about the wife before or after?"

She gave him a cold glance. "It's not really any of your business, is it?"

"No. But I am a trained psychic investigator. I tend to be curious by nature." *Especially when it comes to you,* he added silently. "Sorry. You're right. Not my business. Moving right along —"

"Before."

"What?"

"I found out that Wesley was married before our relationship progressed to the physical stage," she said stiffly.

"Is he still married?"

"No. Evelyn mentioned several months ago that Wesley and his wife were divorced."

"Was Lancaster here in Wilby two years ago when the deaths occurred?"

"Yes," Gwen said. "He was here."

"Now there's been another death and Lancaster is here again."

"I noticed that amazing coincidence, myself," Gwen said. "Here we are. That's the Wilby General Store. You can park in front. We're in time. Luckily Buddy doesn't close much before five-thirty."

Six

Buddy Poole, proprietor of the Wilby General Store, leaned on the counter and peered at Gwen over the rims of gold-framed reading glasses.

"So, you took Evelyn's cat, eh?" he said. "That's mighty noble of you, but I'd better warn you up front Max is used to the expensive stuff. The high-end cat food, canned wild salmon and the good tuna fish. Evelyn always bought him the best — same brands that people eat. Gotta tell ya, my dogs don't eat nearly as high on the hog as that cat."

"He's going to have to modify his gourmet tastes if he hangs around me," Gwen said. "Buddy, I'd like you to meet Judson Coppersmith. He's a friend of mine."

"Nice to meet you," Buddy said. He stuck out a big hand. "Welcome to Wilby. Sorry it's such sad circumstances that bring you here."

Judson shook hands across the counter. "Call me Judson."

"You bet. Heard Gwen had a friend with her. You're stayin' over at the inn?"

"That's right," Gwen said. "Trisha has very kindly allowed me to keep Max in my room, but I need some cat litter and food for him. I don't suppose you know anyone who might like a nice cat?"

"Nope. I'm a dog man, myself. Got a couple of Rottweilers that would probably view Max as a chew toy."

The Wilby General Store had changed little in the two years that she had been away. The grocery aisles and the small fresh produce section occupied the left-hand side of the premises. Shelves and tables displaying the wares of the local artisans were arranged on the right.

Buddy Poole hadn't changed, either, she thought. He was a sturdy, stocky man with a bushy gray beard and a receding hairline. He wore a plaid shirt and a pair of pants held up by red suspenders.

"Real shame about poor Evelyn," Buddy said. He exhaled heavily and shook his head. "We're all gonna miss her. She was a fixture here in Wilby." He looked at Gwen. "Heard you were the one who found her body."

"Word gets around fast," Gwen said.

"In this town it does. Sorry it had to be you. I know the two of you were friends."

"Thank you," Gwen said. "About the cat food, I'll go with the expensive stuff for now. I think Max has been traumatized enough. You know how cats are when you take them out of their territory."

"Heard they don't settle well into new surroundings," Buddy said. "With dogs, it's different. Long as they're with their pack, they're happy campers." He bustled around the end of the counter. "You'll be wanting the wild salmon, then. And fresh eggs. Evelyn always fed him eggs. Got a refrigerator in your room? If not, I'm sure Trisha would let you store a carton of eggs in her kitchen."

"I've got one of those minibar refrigerators," Gwen said. "There's enough space for a half-size carton of eggs."

"We'll need a can opener, too," Judson said, "and the cat litter."

"Aisle three." Buddy started back toward the counter with a couple of cans of salmon and the eggs.

Two people, clearly summer visitors, not locals, ambled into the store. The subtle draft created by the opening and closing of the front door sent a faint shiver of all-too-familiar music through the atmosphere. The melancholy sound iced the back of Gwen's neck. She knew that from now on whenever she heard wind chimes, the image of Evelyn's body lying on the carpet would drift like a ghost through her thoughts.

She saw that Judson was studying the small display of crystal wind chimes suspended from the ceiling.

"Sell a lot of those?" he asked Buddy.

"Sure do," Buddy said. He set the cans of salmon on the counter. "Local lady named Louise Fuller makes 'em. Very popular with the tourists. Just about everyone around here has one of her little musical sculptures hanging on the front porch or somewhere inside the house. Couple of other craftspeople in Wilby make chimes, but no one makes 'em the way Louise does. The sound is unique. I sell a lot of 'em at the crafts fairs, too."

"You're still doing the crafts fair circuit?" Gwen asked.

"Oh, sure." Buddy punched in numbers on the antique cash register. "I try to hit five or six a year. Lot of the craftspeople and artists here depend on the cash I bring back from those fairs. Nicole, the florist, looks after my dogs when I'm gone. You remember Nicole Hudson, Gwen?"

"I remember her," Gwen said.

Buddy winced. "Sorry. Forgot that you

and Nicole had some words after what happened out at the falls a couple of years ago." He cleared his throat and looked up from the cash register. "Will that be all?"

"Yes," Judson said. He fished out his wallet and put some cash on the counter.

"Wait," Gwen said. "I was going to pay for those things."

"We'll settle up later," Judson promised.

Buddy slipped the money into the till and handed back some change. He looked at Gwen above the rims of his glasses. "Don't want to get personal, but people are saying that Oxley gave you a hard time because of what happened to Evelyn."

"I think it's safe to say that Chief Oxley would prefer that I leave town as soon as possible," Gwen said. "And he's not the only one. But it's going to take a while to decide what to do with Evelyn's house and her old lab."

Buddy's bushy brows bounced up and down a couple of times. "Also heard that the television guy Evelyn used to do some work for is back. Any idea why he's hanging around?"

"He's looking for more ideas for his show," Gwen said, deliberately vague. "He left town a short time ago." She collected the sack of cat litter, food and eggs.

"Thanks, Buddy."

"You bet." Buddy exhaled. "Just so damn sad about Evelyn. Really gonna miss her."

"So will I," Gwen said.

SEVEN

Evelyn's small house was huddled in the trees at the end of the road. The windows were dark, just as they had been that morning when Gwen arrived. She felt the hair lift again on the nape of her neck. A shiver went through her.

Judson eased the SUV to a stop in the drive. He sat quietly for a moment, studying the house. Energy shifted in the atmosphere. The stone in his ring heated a little.

"You feel it, too, don't you?" she said.

He did not ask her for an explanation.

"Like a shadow over the house," he said. "You just know something bad happened inside."

"I knew this morning when I got here, before I even opened the door," Gwen said.

"Yeah, it usually hits me that way, too." He paused. "But only if serious violence was involved."

"Same with me." She did not take her eyes

off the house. "But at least in your business you get to do something constructive. You find justice for the victims."

"I hate to disillusion you, but most of my consulting work is — was — done for an intelligence agency. Justice wasn't the objective."

"What was the objective?"

"Information. I'm good at gathering that."

She turned her head and gave him a disturbingly insightful look. "But you don't find it very satisfying, do you?"

He hesitated. "Sometimes I think Mom was right. I should have joined the FBI."

"So that you could hunt bad guys? But you don't like to take orders or work as a member of a team. You and the FBI would not have been a good fit."

"No." He paused, frowning. "Did Sam tell you about my preference for working alone?"

"No."

Judson's irritation was palpable. "You can read that kind of personality trait in an aura?"

"I didn't get that information from your aura." She unbuckled her seat belt and opened the door. "Five minutes in your company was more than enough to reveal that aspect of your character, believe me."

She jumped down and slammed the car door a little harder than was necessary.

Judson cracked open the driver's-side door and got out. Together they went up the steps, crossed the porch and stopped at the door.

He watched her take the key out of her tote. When she got the door open, he moved into the front hall ahead of her. Energy whispered in the atmosphere, cold and intense. She knew that he had heightened his talent.

"The electricity is still on," she said. She stepped into the hall behind him and flipped a switch, illuminating the small space. "No need to work in the dark."

"Which way?"

"Down the hall to your right."

Judson moved along the hallway. "What happened to the Ballinger study?"

"Evelyn stopped it after the second member of the study group was found dead. She realized that something awful was happening, and she sensed that it was connected to her research."

"I'm going to want to hear about the three people who died two years ago," he said. "Especially how you came to find the bodies."

She had known this was coming, she reminded herself. She was prepared.

"I assumed you would want the details," she said.

He looked back over his shoulder. "Show me where you found Ballinger's body."

"All right, but I think I should show you this picture first." She took a photo out of her tote and handed it to him. "I found this on the floor beside her this morning. I'm not sure what to make of it but I think it might be important."

Judson studied the photo. "I recognize you. Who are the others?"

"It's a group shot of the members of Evelyn's research study. She kept it thumbtacked to her bulletin board. The fact that it had been ripped off the board and dropped on the floor bothered me for some reason."

"Ballinger is not in the picture."

"She was the one who took the photo. Three of the people in that picture are dead. Mary Henderson, the blonde on the left, Ben Schwartz, the man standing next to her, and Zander Taylor. Taylor is the good-looking dark-haired man in the first row."

"You're standing next to a serial killer."

She shuddered. "Don't remind me. His goal was to take us down in the order in which we were posed in the picture. It was all a game to him. He was annoyed because he had to make me his third target. He said I had interfered with the proper sequence of play."

Judson's eyes heated. So did his ring. "He told you that?"

"Shortly before he went over the falls. Yes."

"All right, we'll finish this conversation later. Let's take a look at the scene."

Gwen kept her talent tamped down so that she would not see the ghost in the mirror. She reached around the corner of the door frame, found the wall switch and flipped it.

Shock lanced through her when she registered the chaos inside the office. Desk drawers and cupboard doors stood open. Books had been swept off the shelves. Files had been pulled out of the metal cabinet and dumped on the floor.

"Good grief," she whispered, stunned.

"I take it things didn't look like this when you got here this morning?" Judson said.

"No," she said. "Someone searched this room sometime after I left today."

She was already tense and on edge. Her startled response to the scene in the office kicked up her talent. It was an intuitive reaction. Before she could suppress it, she was looking into the mirror.

The ghost appeared in the glass.

91

"Well, you knew that this was going to get a lot more complicated, didn't you, dear?" the ghost said. "That's why you brought along your very own psychic investigator. I must say, he looks interesting. Definitely a high-end talent. I do hope he's competent."

"You and me, both," Gwen said under her breath.

"What did you say?" Judson asked.

"Nothing." She dragged her attention away from the mirror, lowered her senses and looked at him. "Talking to myself. I do that sometimes. Bad habit." She swept a hand out to indicate the overturned office. "What happened here?"

"I'll go out on a limb here and say that it sure looks like someone was searching for something he expected to find in Evelyn's office."

"No kidding." She paused, frowning. "Maybe the killer didn't find whatever he was after on her computer so he came back to take another look."

"I don't think so." Judson prowled deliberately through the office, stopping briefly to brush his fingertips across the top of the desk. "I think we're dealing with someone else. Doesn't mean there isn't a connection between the second person and the killer, though."

"What makes you think that there was a second person here?"

"There's a lot of desperation and growing rage in this space. Whoever conducted the search started out with a high level of urgency and left in a frustrated fury."

Gwen was fascinated. "You can sense all that?"

"Sure," Judson said, "providing the emotions were laid down with a lot of intense energy as they were in this case. It's what I do, Gwen."

"All right, let's think about this. If there was a second intruder, maybe he was searching for whatever was on the computer or the cell phone, in which case he didn't find it because the killer got to the information first."

"That's a reasonable assumption." Judson crouched on the floor and shuffled through the folders that had been dumped on the carpet. "Some of these files go back thirty years."

"I told you, Evelyn devoted her life to the study of the paranormal. But in the end, she was never able to prove anything to mainstream science."

Judson opened several folders and examined the contents. "Looks like most of her research was focused on dreams."

"Much of it was, yes. That's why she and I became so close. I met Evelyn when I was in high school at the Summerlight Academy. She was a counselor there, the only one who really understood my psychic side. My aura vision is linked to my lucid-dreaming ability."

"Yeah?"

She flushed, remembering how bad things had gone that night in Seattle when she had made the mistake of offering to fix his dark dreams.

"Never mind," she said quickly. "It's complicated, believe me."

"I believe you." Judson got to his feet with the languid grace of a tiger. "You and Ballinger stayed in touch after you left Summerlight?"

"Yes." She watched Judson move through the room. "Well? What do you think? Did Evelyn die of natural causes because of the shock of a random home invasion? Or was she murdered?"

Judson stopped in the vicinity of the space where Gwen had found Evelyn's body. Energy heated the atmosphere.

"She was murdered," he said quietly. "No question about it."

Gwen thought she was prepared for that answer. It was the same conclusion that she had arrived at that morning. Nevertheless, Judson's matter-of-fact certainty made her catch her breath.

"By paranormal means?" she asked.

"Yes."

"Damn, just like last time." Gwen made fists with her hands. "I was hoping I was wrong."

Judson did not respond to that. Instead, he did another short circuit of the room and stopped again near the desk.

"What?" she asked. "I can tell that something isn't coming together for you."

Judson met her eyes. "Ballinger died here, where I'm standing. But I'm almost positive that the killer was not physically close to her when she died. He was standing over there, near the door."

"Oh, crap, are you sure?"

He gave her a politely patient look. "Analyzing crime scenes is what I do, Gwen."

"Yes, I know. Sorry, it's just that — never mind. I think I see where you're going with this."

"In my experience, it takes a very strong talent to overwhelm another person's aura and stop the heart," Judson said. "I've met very, very few psychics who can generate that much firepower and even fewer who can focus their talent so that it can be used as a lethal weapon. In those rare situations, the killer almost always needs to have physical contact with the victim. But there are exceptions."

A chill feathered her senses. "Yes, I know. You think that whoever murdered Evelyn used a paranormal weapon of some kind, don't you?"

"That's the only explanation that works for this scenario. According to what Sam and his lab techs have discovered, psi-based weapons have to be used at fairly close range. They aren't very powerful or accurate beyond a range of about twenty feet."

Gwen took a long breath and let it out slowly, with control. "I've heard the Coppersmith R-and-D lab does research in that field."

"Paranormal weapons have other limitations, as well. They can only be activated by someone who possesses some talent. And if they are crystal-based technology, they have to be tuned to the wavelengths of the individual who intends to use it. There are other issues, as well. Naturally occurring crystals that can be weaponized are extremely rare. Sam has tried growing them under lab conditions, but he's had only limited success."

Gwen wrapped her arms around herself.

"Still, such weapons do exist."

Judson met her eyes across the room. "You sound like you've had some personal experience."

"Two years ago Zander Taylor used a paranormal weapon to murder Mary and Ben."

Judson frowned. "Are you certain of that?"

"Yes," she said. "Because he tried to use it on me, too. Now it looks like Evelyn has been killed in the same way. It's as if Zander Taylor has come back from the grave and brought his damned camera with him."

"What camera?"

"That's what his dreadful device looked like, a small camera. Just point and shoot."

Judson watched her for a long moment.

"How did you escape?"

"We were in the lab. There's a great deal of energy in that place. Something went very wrong when Zander tried to use his camera. The device sort of exploded, I think."

Judson gave her a politely skeptical look. "Sort of exploded?"

"It's hard to explain. All I know is that he suddenly started screaming. He ran for the falls and jumped."

"That's all there was to it?"

"Pretty much."

"You're a damn good liar," he said. He smiled. "I like that in a woman."

EIGHT

"When did you start talking to yourself?" Judson asked.

He'd held the question back until after the waiter had brought two glasses of wine to the table. The name of the restaurant was the Wilby Café. It featured a typical Pacific Northwest menu that ran the usual gamut from salmon and Dungeness crab cakes to steak. The establishment's most outstanding virtue in his opinion was its convenient location. The café was located within walking distance of the Riverview Inn.

He could tell his question caught Gwen off guard. That had been his intention. She was expecting to be interrogated on the subject of Zander Taylor and the camera weapon. He'd get around to that eventually but he preferred the indirect route. It was usually easier to get straight answers out of people if they didn't see the questions coming. He'd spent enough time in Gwen's company now to know that she had long ago learned to keep secrets.

When it came to keeping secrets, he thought, they had a lot in common.

Gwen paused, her wineglass halfway to her lips, and looked at him for a long, considering moment. He didn't care about the delay. He could sit here and look into her eyes forever. He realized that he was still a little jacked. Not like he could shut down completely around her, he thought. Something about Gwen kept him on edge and heated his blood as well as his senses.

For a while he wondered if she was going to answer the question. She had a right to her privacy, but, damn, he wanted to know more about her. And he knew that the talking-to-herself thing was not just an old habit.

She reflected a moment longer. In the end she took a sip of wine and set the glass down very precisely on the table.

"I wasn't talking to myself today," she said. "I was in a waking dream, talking to Evelyn's ghost in the mirror."

She watched him, waiting for his reaction.

"Huh." He ran through the possible scenarios. "The ghost is some sort of dream-state image manifested by your intuition?"

Gwen relaxed visibly. Her eyes cleared and

she smiled. "Yes. That's exactly what happens when I see the ghosts. But it's almost impossible to explain that to people because it sounds like I'm claiming to have visions."

"Which is exactly what is going on, when you get right down to it."

"Sort of, yes." She eyed him, once again wary. "You don't appear too freaked. Most people look at me funny when I tell them about the ghosts. My aunt said I mustn't ever tell anyone about the visions. She said I should learn to ignore them. But after she died, I went into the foster care system. Eventually I made the mistake of confiding in a counselor. Everyone concluded that I was seriously disturbed. The next thing I knew, I landed in the Summerlight Academy. By the time I graduated, I had learned to keep my secrets, believe me."

"When did the ghost visions start?"

"When I was about twelve. They got stronger as I went through my teens."

"That's about the age when Emma, Sam and I came into our talents," he said.

"I'd see the ghosts in unexpected places, almost always on some reflective surface," Gwen said. "The first time it was a mirror in an old antique shop. I was terrified. Somehow I knew that it was not a real ghost, but in a way, that just made the experience more unnerving."

"Because you wondered if you were crazy."

"For a time, yes," she said. "So did everyone else around me. But it was Evelyn who helped me to understand that the visions are actually lucid dreams that occur when I'm awake. I can go into a lucid dream on purpose. But the energy laid down at the scenes of violence seems to trigger the ghost dreams."

"A lucid dreamer is someone who knows when he or she is dreaming, right? The dreamer can take control of the dream."

"Yes." Gwen took another sip of wine. "It's not an uncommon experience. A lot of people occasionally have lucid dreams. But in my case, the talent is linked to my psychic intuition and my ability to see auras. I've come to the conclusion that seeing ghosts at old murder scenes is actually just a side effect of my type of paranormal sensitivity."

"How did you figure out that the ghosts were always at old murder scenes?"

"After the first few instances, I went online and researched the locations where I had seen the ghosts. It didn't take long to find out that in most cases there was a record of a murder or unexplained death in the vicinity. My intuition was picking up some of the psychic residue and interpreting it as a vision of a ghost."

"The energy laid down by violence is powerful stuff," he said. "A lot of people are sensitive to it, even those without any measurable talent. Almost everyone has had the experience of walking into a room or a location that gives off a bad vibe."

"I know. But in my case the reaction is a little over-the-top."

"How bad was the Summerlight Academy?" he asked.

"I was miserable at the time, but looking back, it was the best thing that could have happened to me. I was very lonely at first and I was scared, but I soon met Abby and another talent, Nick Sawyer, there. The three of us bonded. I'm not sure why. We just did. We stuck together until we graduated, and we're still very close. We're family. The other good thing about Summerlight was that I met Evelyn there. She was the one who helped me deal with my talent."

"But most of the time you use it to do your psychic counseling work."

"I prefer living clients." She smiled over the rim of the glass. "They pay better."

That surprised a laugh out of him. "I can see the upside."

She stopped smiling and wrinkled her nose. "But living clients are also incredibly frustrating. I can pick up a lot of impressions when I view their auras, but those impressions are not helpful if I can't get context. To obtain that, I need cooperation from my clients. That isn't always forthcoming."

He raised his brows. "Are we, by any chance, talking about me now?"

"We are."

"I'm not one of your clients," he said very softly, very deliberately.

"True," she agreed. "But that could change. I've got room on my schedule."

"Not a chance in hell."

"Fine. Be like that." She finished off the rest of her wine and set the glass down. "Your dreams, your problem."

"That's how I look at it."

"At least you're not one of those clients who pays for dream therapy and then fails to take my advice."

He smiled. "Does that happen a lot?"

"Oh, sure, all the time. Clients book a session, spend forty minutes telling me about their dreams to give me context, I do an analysis, put them in a trance and help them rework the dreamscape until we discover the unresolved issues involved. Then we talk about the issues and I offer advice. The clients go away and return a month later complaining about the same problems."

"Because they didn't follow your advice?"

"It's very frustrating." Gwen shook her head. "I suppose I should be grateful for the repeat business but —"

She broke off because he had started to laugh. She watched him, her eyes widening with a mix of curiosity and bemusement.

He was even more surprised by his laughter than she was. It had been a while since he'd been able to laugh like this. A couple of people at a nearby table turned to look at him.

He finally settled into an amused smile and reached for a chunk of bread.

Gwen narrowed her eyes. "What's so funny?"

"You, the psychic counselor, wondering why people pay you for advice and then ignore the advice," he said around a mouthful of the bread. "Talk about naive. But it's rather sweet when you think about it."

"Excuse me?"

"People ask for advice all the time. They go to their friends for it. They talk to virtual strangers at the gym. They pay doctors, shrinks, therapists and psychics for advice. But very few people actually take the advice unless that advice happens to be something they are already inclined to do."

"That's a very insightful comment." She wrinkled her nose. "Still, it's one thing to have a person reject my help flat-out like you did. It's something else altogether when people pay you for expensive dream therapy and then ignore it. Do you know how disheartening that is?"

"Sure, I'm a consultant, remember? The pay is good in my line, but almost no one ever follows a consultant's advice."

She furrowed her intelligent brow. "I hadn't realized that."

"Look on the bright side: at least we both get paid for the advice we give."

"There is that."

The waiter put the plates of broiled salmon down in front of them and departed.

Gwen examined the salmon for a few seconds and then looked up.

"Do you think we'll be able to find Evelyn's killer?" she asked.

"Sure."

"You sound very certain of that."

He shrugged. "The case looks simple enough. It will take a while to sort out, but it's just a matter of following up on the leads. Plenty of those."

"I wish you had been around two years ago when Zander Taylor was stalking the people in Evelyn's research study. Maybe he could have been stopped before he killed Ben and Mary."

"One thing I've learned in the consulting business. Don't look back. Not unless there is information in the past that can be used to figure out what is going on in the present."

"It's a good rule." Gwen picked up her fork. "But in my line, I've learned that the past always impacts the present."

"Yeah," he admitted. "I've run up against that problem a few times, myself."

They ate in silence for a while. He tried not to watch Gwen overtly but it was hard to take his eyes off her. It was good to be here with her, basking in her delicate feminine energy. This was what he had needed ever since he had returned from the island, he thought. Gwendolyn Frazier was the fix he craved.

"It's usually better if you don't ask," she said matter-of-factly. She speared a tomato slice and ate it.

He went very still, vaguely aware that his ring was suddenly infused with a little heat.

"Better if I don't ask what?" he said, feeling his way as cautiously as he had when he had escaped the underwater cave.

"You're wondering what I see when I view your aura." She munched the tomato and swallowed. "I was just warning you that it's better not to go there."

He had known he would have to deal with this sooner or later. She was not the type to let go.

"You do realize that you've left me no option," he said. "Now I have to ask."

"I was afraid of that. Promise you won't get spooked?"

"I'm a talent. I take the paranormal as normal." He forked up a mouthful of fish. "Why would I get spooked?"

"My aura readings sometimes have that effect on people, even those who accept the reality of the paranormal," she said.

"What do you see in my aura?"

She hesitated. He could see the uncertainty in her eyes.

"Okay," she said. "But remember that my visions involve all sorts of misleading symbols and metaphors. When I go into my talent, I essentially slip into a trance, a waking dream. Those kinds of dreams can be just as hard to interpret as regular dreams unless I have context."

She paused to give him an encouraging smile.

"No context," he said. "Let's see what you can do without any hints or clues."

She stopped smiling.

"I was afraid you were going to say that," she said. "You don't believe that I can actually see anything useful, do you?"

"I don't doubt that you can see auras, and I'm convinced you're sensitive to heavy energy like the kind laid down at crime scenes. But read my dreams? No. I don't think anyone can do that."

She sat quietly for a moment, her incredible eyes luminous with a little psi. Energy shivered in the atmosphere. Two men at the nearby table glanced around uneasily and then went back to their meal.

Gwen lowered her talent. Her mouth tightened at the corners. "Your aura looks the same as it did a month ago when I met you in Seattle. You're stable. But I can tell that the dreams are getting more powerful. They aren't nightmares — not exactly — but there is a rising sense of urgency linked to them. You're not sleeping well, either. But there's something else going on, too, something I can't figure out without more context."

He made himself put his fork down with no outward show of emotion. "Is that the best you can do? Because any storefront fortune-teller could pull that kind of analysis out of a crystal ball. Everyone has a few bad dreams from time to time."

"I know," she said.

Her voice had gone flat and cold. He felt like he had just stomped on a butterfly.

"I apologize," he said. "I shouldn't have implied that you were a storefront fortune-teller."

"I'm aware of what the general public thinks about psychic counselors. Most people assume that we are entertainers at best and scam artists at worst."

"I know that your talent is genuine, Gwen. I shouldn't have said what I did. I'm sorry."

She relaxed. "Apology accepted. Do you want me to finish telling you what I saw in your aura?"

"Sure."

"There's not a whole lot more to tell. It's all that hot radiation in your dream currents that I find difficult to interpret. I'm sure it's psi. But the ultra-light is the same color as the energy I see from time to time in your ring. Did something happen to you that involved that amber crystal? Were you caught in an explosion? A fire, maybe?"

He thought that he was prepared for whatever vague analysis she came up with — prepared for anything except the possibility that she might actually be able to see into his dreams. There was only one way she could strike that close to the truth.

"I told Sam something of what went down on that last case," he said. "He told Abby and Abby told you. So much for keeping some things private within the family."

"You mustn't blame Sam or Abby. Neither of them told me anything about your dreams. As for what happened on your last case, it's no secret that you nearly got killed and that you had to swim out of an underwater cave — which does explain some of the urgency in your dream, of course. But there's something else going on. You're revisiting the same dreamscape again and again. My reading tells me that you're searching for something."

A dark chill whispered through him. "And you can help me find it?"

She smiled, her eyes filling with a wistful regret, as if she had just acknowledged to herself the loss of something she had longed to possess.

"I fix bad dreams, remember?" she said gently.

"I'm not interested in therapy. I can handle my own damn dreams."

"Right." She took a breath and pulled her cloak of cool, polite reserve around herself. "Now you see why I lead a very limited social life."

"What are you talking about?"

"You're thinking that it's as if I had caught a glimpse of one of your dreams, aren't you? It felt like an invasion of privacy."

He started to deny it but decided there wasn't much point. "Thought crossed my mind, yeah."

"If it's any comfort, I can't actually see your dreams."

He was starting to get pissed — with himself, not with her. He was the one who had challenged her to do a fast reading on his aura. The fact that he didn't like the results was his own fault.

"Good to know," he said.

"There's no need to growl at me."

"I am not growling."

"I know growling when I hear it," she said. "The thing is, heavy dreams affect the aura, especially if they recur frequently and especially if the dreamer has a lot of psychic talent. What I pick up is the dreamlight energy in a person's aura. My intuition then interprets that energy. I don't always get it right, and it's impossible to do an accurate analysis when I don't have any context. But I can usually see enough to start asking the right questions. That's where I'm at with your case."

"I'm not your case, and I'm not here to get psychic dream counseling," he said. "I'm here to solve a murder. You're the client, not me."

Anger flashed, quicksilver bright, in her eyes. In the next instant the shadows were back, veiling her secrets.

"No," she said much too politely. "You are not my client."

He felt as if she had just slammed a door in his face. And it was his own damn fault.

NINE

She had nobody but herself to blame for the glacial chill in the atmosphere between them, Gwen thought. She should have known better than to tell Judson the truth. She had been aware that she was rolling the dice when she described what she saw in his dreamlight energy. She had hoped that his own psychic abilities, combined with his understanding of the paranormal, would allow him to accept her talent. But she had placed a losing bet. Then she'd made the stupid mistake of doubling down on a very bad wager by trying to convince him to let her help him.

It wasn't the first time she had miscalculated with a man, but this time it seemed to matter a lot more than it usually did. She told herself it was better to get the truth out in the open before the relationship progressed any farther.

Then again, the only relationship she had

with Judson Coppersmith was that of client and hired investigator. She needed to keep that in mind at all times.

Show no weakness, she thought. It was the motto that Nick Sawyer had taught to Abby and her early on in their time at the Summerlight Academy. Definitely words to live by, then and now.

She and Judson finished dinner in a brittle, tension-laced silence and walked outside. The night air was crisp. Stars and a half moon glittered in an obsidian dark sky, but they did little to illuminate Wilby.

"I really do not like this town," she said, breaking the edgy silence.

"I'm not surprised, given your history here," Judson said.

"What's our next move?"

"There are a lot of next moves," Judson said. "Tomorrow I want to see the old lodge where you found the bodies and where Zander Taylor attacked you and then went over the falls."

"All right."

They started across the mostly empty parking lot. The lights of the Riverview Inn glowed in the distance.

"As a matter of curiosity, what did you see in Zander Taylor's aura?" Judson asked.

She thought about the visions that still

came back to haunt her in the darkest hours of the night. "Nothing that told me that he was a killer, at least not until he attacked me. Afterward I could make sense of at least some of what I had seen, but by then it was too late. That's the problem with my visions. I keep telling you, without context —"

"Without context you can't interpret what you see. You've made that clear. Tell me what you saw in Taylor's aura."

"I saw the kind of energy that I've come to associate with drug addiction. But I didn't see any indications of an actual drug in his aura. I mentioned the bad energy to Evelyn, but she said as long as he wasn't using at the time, she wasn't going to kick him out of the study. She reminded me that a lot of people with psychic talents end up experimenting with drugs at some point in an attempt to self-medicate. Sensitives often think they're going crazy. Sometimes they go to a doctor who thinks they're disturbed and puts them on medication. Either way, drugs are often a factor when it comes to dream therapy."

"The bottom line being that the indications of addiction were not a serious red flag."

"No, especially since he showed no obvious signs that he was on drugs at the time.

It was only later that I realized it wasn't drugs that he was addicted to — it was the killing."

"The ultimate game for a full-blown psychopath," Judson said.

"Game is exactly the right way to describe how Taylor viewed his kills. Evelyn and I were convinced that there had been many victims before he got to Wilby."

A van that had been driving down the street abruptly veered into the parking lot. The headlights pierced the night. The vehicle was moving much too fast and it was coming straight at them.

Judson was already reacting. He seized Gwen's arm and swept her into a protected zone created by two parked cars.

The van slammed to a halt less than three feet away. There was just time enough to read the words *Hudson Floral Design* before the driver's-side door shot open. A woman dressed in jeans, boots and a faded cotton shirt leaped out. Her dark hair was pulled back into a ponytail. She ignored Judson and fixed her full attention on Gwen.

"I heard you were back," she said. Rage and long-smoldering pain seethed in the atmosphere around her. "I also heard that Evelyn Ballinger is dead and that Oxley found you in the house with the body.

Sounds like you've gone back to your old habits."

"Hello, Nicole," Gwen said.

She kept her voice low and soothing, intuitively trying to counteract some of the other woman's anger. But she knew there was little hope of success. She was aware that Judson had gone ominously still. He stood very close and a little in front of her, partially shielding her with his body. She wanted to tell him that there was no immediate physical threat, but she wasn't altogether certain that was true. It had been two years since she had last faced Nicole. On that occasion Nicole, sobbing hysterically, had vowed vengeance.

Nicole rounded on Judson. "Rumor has it you're the new boyfriend. Better be careful. People around her have a bad habit of dying."

"Take it easy," Judson said.

"She murdered the man I loved two years ago and a couple of other people as well. I'll bet she killed Evelyn Ballinger, too." Nicole's voice rose. "Stick around long enough and you'll be her next victim. And watch what you eat. She uses poison, you see, so it always looks like a heart attack or an accident."

"That's enough," Judson said. This time

he put an edge on his words.

His ring heated a little, and Gwen was aware of an unnerving, deeply ominous sensation.

Nicole gasped and stepped back, startled. She turned quickly, searching the parking lot with an anxious expression, as if looking for something that might be coming up behind her. When she saw nothing, she burst into tears and turned back to face Gwen.

"How dare you come back here as if nothing ever happened?" she got out between sobs. "How dare you, bitch?"

She swung her hand in a vicious slap aimed at Gwen's face. Judson moved slightly, just enough to get in the way of the blow. He absorbed the impact on one broad shoulder. The scary heat in the atmosphere escalated a couple of degrees.

Nicole whirled and fled back to the van. She got behind the wheel and slammed the door shut. The vehicle careened out of the parking lot and shot off down the street.

The disturbing energy dissipated.

Gwen watched the taillights of the van until they disappeared. Eventually, she allowed herself to take a breath. Judson clamped a powerful hand around her arm and drew her out from between the parked cars.

"Who was that?" he asked. He sounded very matter-of-fact, as if nothing out of the ordinary had just happened.

"Nicole Hudson. She owns a florist shop here in town."

"I saw the sign on the van. She was Taylor's lover?"

"Yes. She blames me for his death. She never believed that he was a suicide. She thinks I killed him."

"I got that impression," Judson said. "You have quite a reputation in this town, don't you?"

"You have no idea."

Ten

When Judson and Gwen walked into the lobby, Riley Duncan looked up from whatever he was doing at the front desk. He gave Gwen a stern frown.

"Had a complaint from a guest on your floor, Ms. Frazier," Riley said. "The lady in three-oh-five says your cat is bothering her."

Gwen frowned. "How could Max bother anyone?"

"She said he meows loudly whenever someone walks past in the hall. I went up there to check and she's right. I could hear him on the other side of the door. Three-oh-five says the noise creeps her out. She doesn't like cats. She's afraid the cat will get out of the room and trip her up on the stairs."

"I'll keep Max away from her," Gwen promised. "Once he knows I'm back tonight, I'm sure he'll stop meowing. I think he's having abandonment issues. Evelyn raised him from a kitten, and he doesn't understand that she's gone forever."

"Probably doesn't like being cooped up in a hotel room, either," Riley said. "Cats are territorial, you know. They don't adapt well to new environments."

"I'm aware of that," Gwen said. "But I couldn't leave him out there all alone at the house. There's no one around to feed him." She cleared her throat. "I don't suppose you'd be interested in adopting him?"

"I'm not a cat person," Riley said. "Take him to the pound."

He went back to his computer screen.

Gwen and Judson went up the stairs. The meowing started when they reached the third floor. It reverberated down the hall. Gwen winced, took out her key and hurried forward. When she opened the door Max was waiting. He dashed through the opening.

"Max, no," Gwen said. "Come back."

Judson leaned down and scooped up the cat. "You don't want to go running off like that, Max. She's the one with the food. Not that you need any. You are a little on the hefty side. Do you lift weights?"

"Evelyn said that he's part Maine coon cat," Gwen said. "Maybe a *lot* Maine coon cat." She switched on the lights.

Max twitched his ears, but he allowed himself to be carried back into the room. Judson set him down on the floor while Gwen closed and locked the door.

"What are you going to do with him?" Judson asked.

"Take him back to Seattle, I guess, unless I can convince someone local to take him in, which is probably unlikely. Max does not have what you'd call a warm and cuddly personality."

"He looks tough."

"He is tough. But Evelyn loved that cat. I'm not going to take him to the pound, and if I turn him loose back at the house, he'll go feral. Cats that go wild don't do well."

"In that case, it looks like you've got yourself a cat," Judson said.

"Probably." She looked at Max. "Of course, if you take it into that blocky head of yours that you were born to be free, I promise not to stand in your way."

Max ignored her. He went into the tiled bath and took up a position next to his empty bowl. He glared at her from the doorway.

"Okay, okay," she said. She opened the minibar and took out the eggs. She cracked two into Max's bowl. "But don't blame me if you get too chunky to escape."

Judson went to the minibar. "How about a nightcap while we talk?"

"Good idea. I could use a drink after that encounter with Nicole."

Eleven

"Start at the beginning," Judson said.

Gwen settled into the oversized wingback chair and contemplated the gas fire on the hearth. The dancing flames cast a warm glow over the small space, but she could not seem to shake a deep chill. Max was stretched out on the cushion beside her. The low rumble of his purr was a comforting sensation against her thigh.

She searched for a place to begin.

"There's no way to know how many people Zander Taylor killed before he found his way to Wilby," she said. "And no way to prove that he murdered anyone. Evelyn and I did some research after he died, but it wasn't easy trying to trace his comings and goings. Neither of us was a professional investigator. But we found hints of what looked like a pattern."

"How did you piece it together?"

"Zander was very friendly — quite chatty.

He talked a lot about how good it was to be hanging out with other people like himself, people who had real talent. He went on and on about how many phony psychics there were in the world. After he . . . died, Evelyn and I made up a partial list of all the places he had mentioned in his conversations. Then we went online to check the local business directories for those locations."

Judson nodded appreciatively. "You searched for people who advertised psychic services and then you tried to match the names with local obituaries?"

She glanced at him, surprised. "Yes, exactly. We couldn't think of any other way to go about it. I mean, it's not like you can go online and search for a genuine psychic private investigator. Zander was right about one thing — lot of frauds out there."

Amusement briefly lit Judson's eyes. "Maybe Sam and I should run some ads offering psychic investigations. We're the real deal."

She smiled. "The problem is that your ads for Coppersmith Consulting would look exactly like the ads run by the frauds and fakes."

"So it comes down to, how do you convince people that you're a real psychic investigator? You're right. That's tricky."

"It was a very time-consuming process, but in the end Evelyn and I found enough matches — deceased fortune-tellers, palm-readers and other storefront psychics who had all died unexpectedly of natural causes — to convince us that Taylor had murdered a lot of people. We stopped searching for victims because there didn't seem to be much point continuing."

"Did Taylor tell you about his kills there at the end when he tried to murder you?"

"Yes. He was thrilled with himself because here in Wilby he was at last hunting real psychics, not the phonies."

Judson drank some of his brandy. "Killing other people of talent made the game more of a challenge."

"He said he thought it would be harder to kill genuine psychics, but it turned out that real talents were no more difficult to murder than normal people."

"When did you get suspicious that there was a killer in your midst?" Judson asked.

"Immediately after the first murder." Gwen stilled her hand on Max's furry side. Memories of that first terrible day flooded back. "I found Mary's body out at the lodge. She was lying on the floor near one of the workbenches at the back. I somehow knew she hadn't had a heart attack or an aneurism. There was something about the way she was positioned that told me she had tried to run. At least, that's what the ghost was telling me."

"You saw her ghost at the scene?"

"Yes, in the walls of the mirror engine," Gwen said. She resumed stroking Max, who twitched an ear and purred louder.

"What's the mirror engine?" Judson asked.

"The most exotic piece of test equipment that Evelyn constructed. It was her pride and joy. She built it primarily for me. She thought she could use the engine to measure and record the energy patterns that I generate when I go into my talent. Mary died near one of the mirrors, and that's where I saw her ghost."

"Did you pick up anything else?"

"Nothing useful," Gwen admitted. "I'll give Oxley credit for conducting a fairly thorough investigation. After all, Mary was only in her mid-thirties and there was no indication that she had a chronic underlying illness. But in the end, Oxley couldn't find anything. The medical examiner ruled that she had died of a heart attack."

"You found the second victim in the same place three weeks later?"

"Yes. Ben died near the mirror engine, too. My intuition told me that, like Mary, he had been trying to flee when he went down. But again, the authorities called it death by natural causes. In his case it was a little more believable because Ben had severe asthma and some other health issues. I realized I was in trouble on that occasion. I could tell that Oxley's cop instincts were stirring."

"Two dead bodies within one month, both found in the same location by the same person, would have that effect on any cop," Judson said.

"I talked to Evelyn. By then we were both very certain that someone had targeted her study subjects. She immediately canceled the project and warned everyone in the group. Most of the subjects panicked and left town."

"But you didn't leave Wilby?"

"No, I kept thinking there was something I was missing in the lab. I went back to take another look. Zander showed up. As soon as he walked into the lodge, I saw his aura. He was really jacked and terribly excited. The dream energy was bad, unwholesome. Wrong. I just knew that he was the killer. And he knew that I knew."

"What happened?" Judson asked.

"We were alone in the lab. He started talking, playing his game with me. He told me that he had planned to take us down in the order in which we appeared in the group photo. He said I'd ruined the plan and spooked the herd. That's what he called us, the herd. He said that because I'd interfered in his hunt, he was going to have to get rid of me out of order even though he had scheduled me to be last."

Judson watched her with dangerously hot eyes. "Go on."

"Zander reached into his jacket and took out what looked like a small digital camera and aimed it at me. He told me he had used it to kill Mary and Ben and a lot of phony psychics. Now it was my turn. He aimed the camera at me and started stalking me. I felt an icy sensation. My heart started to beat harder. I couldn't catch my breath. I started to run. He laughed and told me that was what the others had done. He said that the chase was the best part. I figured I had nothing to lose, so I fled into the mirror engine. He followed me. And suddenly he was screaming."

"He saw something in the mirrors?"

She took a deep breath and buried her fingers in Max's fur. It was time to choose her words very, very carefully.

"I told you, there was a lot of energy in the atmosphere that day. I was in my talent and so was Taylor. There was the additional energy of the camera, too. The mirrors are designed to enhance the effects of psi. I'm not sure exactly what happened, but I think Taylor saw things in the mirrors — maybe the images of some of the people he murdered."

Judson's expression sharpened. "He saw ghosts in the mirrors?"

"Yes, I think so. He shouted at them. *You're dead, damn you. Why don't you stay dead?* He started firing that strange weapon at the mirrors. There was a flash of brilliant light. It looked like a real camera flash or a strobe light except that it was hot psi. I could sense it. The energy bounced off the mirrors — straight back at Zander. He started screaming. He turned and ran out the front door of the lab. He kept running and he kept screaming, and when he got to the falls, he threw himself into the water. I ran out behind him. I was in time to see him go over. I will never forget the look in his eyes."

She stopped talking. For a time Max's rumbling purr was the only sound in the room.

Judson contemplated the fire. "Do you think that it was the reflected energy from his own weapon that killed Taylor?"

"That's the only explanation that makes any sense. All I can tell you is that in those last moments he went stark staring mad." She paused. "I sometimes have a few bad dreams of my own, especially at this time of year."

Judson's brows rose. "You can't fix your own bad dreams?"

"I haven't been able to fix these," she said. "As a strong lucid dreamer, I can usually structure a dream to some extent. The trick to handling a bad dreamscape is to find a way out. But I haven't been able to find an escape route through my Zander Taylor dream. So it keeps repeating. August seems to be the worst month."

"Because that's when the deaths occurred."

"Yes."

She stopped talking, waiting for the other shoe to drop — waiting to find out if Judson was going to buy her heavily edited version of events. She had told him the truth, she reminded herself. Just not quite all of it.

To her surprise, he reached across the small space between them. His strong, warm hand closed over hers.

"I don't have any helpful advice to give you," he said. "You don't ever forget watching someone die. Doesn't matter if the bastard deserved it. Violent death exacts a psychic toll from anyone unfortunate enough to be in the vicinity. I see that in my work and I've experienced it firsthand. No one is ever the same afterward. If the events of two years ago didn't give you a few bad nights, it would probably mean that you were missing something vitally important in the part of you that is supposed to make you a decent person. It's only the monsters that can kill without paying a psychic price. That's what makes them monsters."

She looked at him. "I'm the one who is supposed to be the psychic counselor here."

"Yeah, well, that's all the counseling you're going to get from me because I don't have anything else to offer. I'll warn you up front that what I just said isn't going to be any help in the middle of a bad night. All you can do is remind yourself that it was the outcome that matters. You saved not only yourself but all of the people Taylor likely would have murdered in the future. You take that information and you move forward."

"I get the feeling you've given yourself the same lecture recently."

"Yeah."

"Is it working for you?"

He looked at her and said nothing.

"Right," she said. She drank some more of her brandy. "You need closure, too."

He ignored that. "There's no doubt that it was Taylor's body they found?"

"None. Evelyn and I both knew him and so did Nicole. All three of us identified him."

"Did anyone come forth to claim the body?" Judson asked.

"No. It was Nicole who arranged to have Taylor cremated."

"What about the weapon?"

"The camera?" She shook her head. "I don't know what happened to it. I think about it a lot. I try to see it in my dreams. Evelyn and I went back to the lab the following day to look for it, but we couldn't find it. We assumed that it went into the river with Zander, but I've never been entirely sure of that."

"What makes you think it didn't get lost in the water?" Judson asked.

"I've replayed that scene over and over again in my dreams, using my talent to take a closer look. I could swear that Zander did not have anything in his hands when he ran outside the lab and went toward the falls. I think he dropped the camera somewhere inside the lab. I thought I heard it hit the concrete floor, but I might be wrong. But like I said, Evelyn and I searched that whole place the next day and we didn't find it."

"And now Evelyn Ballinger has died in a way that is very similar to the deaths of the two people who were killed by the camera weapon."

"Yes."

"You said you didn't go back to the lab until the next day," Judson continued. "That leaves an entire night during which someone could have searched the lab."

"But that would mean that someone else knew about the weapon and what it could do. It means that person knew where to search for it after Zander's body turned up in the river." Gwen caught her breath. "It means someone was aware that Taylor was murdering people with a crystal-based weapon and that he intended to murder me that day."

Judson's ring flashed with dark energy, but his expression did not change. "Yes," he said. "We're talking about an accomplice who may have decided to continue playing the game."

"But no one else in the study group has died in the past two years. Evelyn and I kept track."

Judson's did not take his eyes off the fire. "You said that Mary Henderson and Ben Schwartz were both victims of Taylor's kill-the-psychic game and that Taylor liked to see his prey run. He intended for you to die running, too."

"Yes. The chase excited him."

"What I sensed today at the scene told me that Ballinger's killer did not see her as a player in a fantasy game. He definitely got a rush out of the kill, but he was under control at the time, not excited the way I think he would have been if he had considered that murder a game."

"You could perceive that much?"

"It's the nature of my talent," Judson said. "I can sense the emotions the killer experienced when he made the kill."

She shivered. "It's as if you get a snapshot of the killer's mind."

He looked at her. "Yes."

"Tough talent. Must make for a lot of bad dreams."

He looked at her for a long moment, his eyes shadowed. Eventually he turned back to the fire.

"My talent doesn't make for good dreams or stable, long-term relationships," he said.

She recognized it for the warning it was and smiled.

"Welcome to the club," she said.

He smiled. "There's a club for people like me?"

"People like us. I've got dream disorder issues, too, and they make stable, long-term relationships very difficult. Impossible, in my case."

"Yeah?" Judson looked intrigued.

"You'd be amazed how fast a guy can run when you tell him that you see ghosts. In fact, men I have known have fled, screaming, into the night."

Judson's teeth flashed briefly in a wicked smile. "Sounds interesting."

"You think I'm joking, don't you?"

"Sure, but I get your point. You've had a few problems with long-term relationships. Good to know I'm not the only one."

There was no reason to tell him that she had not been joking, she decided.

"I think we can both blame our relationship problems on our talent," she said instead.

Judson nodded. "With the exception of Sam, no one else in my family understands. My mother and my sister are convinced that I've got major commitment issues. Their theory is that I'm obsessed with hunting bad guys, that I'm somehow addicted to using my talent. They're afraid, long-term, that will damage me psychically if not physically."

"Well, you're going to have to find a way

to deal with it because you need to hunt," Gwen said without stopping to think. "Your talent drives you to it, just as mine makes me see ghosts. It's not like either of us can just stop perceiving what we perceive."

"No," he said. "It's not like we have a choice."

"I'm not sure we'd want the choice. As hard as it is sometimes, I can't imagine that either of us would want to come upon a crime scene and not know that something bad had happened there. It would be like walking through a graveyard or across an old battleground and not sensing the dead and the dying under our feet. It would be . . . disrespectful, don't you think?"

He was surprised. Then his eyes tightened at the corners in a thoughtful expression. "Yes, that's exactly how it is for me."

"What about your father? Does he understand?"

"Dad tells himself and everyone else who will listen that my problem is that I just haven't found the right woman. But deep down he's worried that I won't get lucky the way he did with Mom and that it's his fault."

"Why?"

"He feels guilty because he's pretty sure the problem is my talent," Judson said. "He blames himself."

"Because he thinks you acquired your talent from his side of the family?"

"Because he *knows* I got it from his side." Judson's mouth kicked up at the corner. "Hell, it's the truth. He's probably responsible for Sam's and Emma's psychic abilities, too. But it's not his fault he got hit with a heavy dose of paranormal radiation forty years ago."

"Is that what happened?" she asked.

"It's a long story, but the bottom line is that Dad was caught in an explosion in an old mine back in his prospecting days. We have reason to believe that there was a lot of paranormal energy released in the blast. Sam and Emma and I are convinced that the ultra-light altered his DNA in a way that affected all three of his future offspring."

"That's an interesting theory," she said. "I have no idea where my talent came from. I never knew my parents. They were killed shortly after I was born. The aunt who raised me swore it didn't come from her side of the family. That would have been my father's side. But, then, Aunt Beth had a few issues of her own."

There was a long silence. Max rumbled on.

"How have you handled your relationship

issues?" Judson asked after a while.

"Mostly I just avoid them."

"The issues?"

"No, the relationships. It's easier that way." She stretched and settled deeper into the chair. "Well, now that we've established that neither of us is good long-term commitment material, maybe we should get back to our investigation. You said you didn't think that Evelyn was a victim of some terrible fantasy game. What does that tell us?"

"That she was killed for a very pragmatic reason." Judson got to his feet and went to the window. He stood looking out into the night. "You knew her better than anyone. Do you have any idea where we can start looking for her secrets?"

"Maybe," Gwen said.

She rose from the chair and crossed the room to take the photo out of her tote. She brought the picture back to show him what Evelyn had written on the back.

"Mirror, mirror," he read.

"I think I may know where she hid at least one very important secret," Gwen said.

TWELVE

The next morning, the old lodge was shrouded in a heavy mist. Judson shut down the SUV engine and studied the scene. The rustic, badly weathered structure was two stories in height. The architecture looked like it dated from the early nineteen hundreds. All of the windows on both floors were covered with metal shutters.

"What's with the blackout windows?" he asked.

"Evelyn was convinced that natural daylight and light in general from the visible end of the spectrum interfered with psi, making it harder to detect and measure," Gwen said.

"She was right. Sam and his lab techs have come to the same conclusion. So you are now the proud owner of this old firetrap as well as her house?"

"Yep, property taxes, utilities and all." Gwen fished a piece of paper out of her tote.

"I didn't want the lab and I have absolutely no use for the equipment inside, but I couldn't bring myself to tell Evelyn. Just about everything in there — all of the instruments and machines that she designed to study the paranormal — is a one-of a-kind device, designed and built by her."

"What did she expect you to do with the stuff?"

"She hoped that I would find a good home for her precious instruments and test equipment. There aren't a lot of people doing serious research into the paranormal, but there are a few."

He smiled faintly. "Like Coppersmith, Inc."

Gwen brightened. "Do you think that Sam and his R-and-D techs would be interested in some of her devices?"

"I think I can safely predict that Sam and his people would jump at the opportunity to examine whatever is inside that lodge. Can't guarantee they'll take every piece of equipment, though."

"I understand. But I know Evelyn would have been thrilled to have some genuine paranormal researchers give her inventions serious attention. Unfortunately, she never even knew that the Coppersmith lab existed."

"And Coppersmith was never aware of her work." He unfastened his seat belt. "Damn shame. You know, this isn't the first time that it has occurred to me that those of us with real talent need to come up with a way to find each other and communicate. It's like we're all working in the dark."

"Evelyn used to say that a lot, too."

"Did she spend a lot of her time here at the lab?"

"Are you kidding?" Gwen smiled. "This place was her life. She invested just about every dime she ever got into it. The security system is state-of-the-art because she wanted to protect the things she designed and built."

"Not like you can buy good quality paranormal instruments and monitors online. Believe me, Sam and his lab techs have tried." Judson opened the door and got out. "Let's take a look."

Gwen jumped out and walked around the front of the SUV to join him. He saw the gritty determination in her eyes and knew that going back into Ballinger's lab would not be easy for her. She had found the bodies of two friends there and nearly been murdered herself.

"When was the last time you were in there?" he asked.

"The day after Taylor attacked me."

"When you and Ballinger came here to search for the weapon."

"Yes."

She went up the steps to the heavy metal door. He followed her and stopped beside her. The numbers on the lock's keypad were illuminated in red. He recognized the manufacturer's logo on the small, square panel.

"I'm impressed," he said. "Ballinger really did spring for good security. Must have cost her a fortune to install this system."

"I told you, the stuff inside this place was important to her," Gwen said.

She keyed in the code. The red lights on the panel turned green.

"Does anyone else besides you have access to this place?" Judson asked.

"No, Evelyn changed the code after the murders. As far as I know, I'm the only one who has it now that she's gone."

He glanced at the paper in her hand. "She might have jotted it down someplace, just like you did, or stored it on her computer."

"Yes, that's quite possible. Evelyn was very focused when it came to her research, but she could be absent minded about other things. The code is not an easy one to remember. That's why I wrote it down."

Gwen frowned. "Are you thinking that the killer was after the code to this lab the night he murdered Evelyn?"

"Maybe, but murder seems a little over-the-top if that's all he wanted. It would be easier to break the code on this door or take a crowbar to one of the windows. Those metal shutters are designed to keep out light and the average burglar, but they're not armor plate."

"True."

Gwen opened the door. Judson looked into a cavernous, echoing space filled with deep shadows and the kind of heat that was the hallmark of paranormal energy.

Heavy currents of psi swirled and seethed inside the lodge, much of it similar to the kind that circulated in Sam's crystal vault and in the company's R&D facility. The atmosphere got downright electric when a lot of paranormal artifacts, crystals or other psi-infused objects were housed in a con-fined space.

But beneath the hot energy, he sensed something else — the unmistakable miasma of death and violence.

"You were right," he said, "The people who died here didn't die of natural causes."

"I can still feel it, too," Gwen said.

She pressed a glowing switch on a wall

145

panel. A strip of low-level floor lights winked on, illuminating a small area around their feet. The rest of the lab remained drenched in deep gloom.

Judson closed the door, shutting off the weak daylight. "No fluorescent overheads?"

"No," Gwen said. "There are task lamps at the various workstations, but most of the lab is lit with this kind of strip lighting. It's all on automatic sensors. Once we pass through a section, the lights will go off behind us."

"Ballinger really had a problem with visible light, didn't she?" he said.

"Evelyn found almost all light a distraction. Something to do with her talent, I think. She was very sensitive to ultra-light energy."

Gwen moved along the concrete floor. Another strip of lights winked on, revealing a few more feet of flooring.

"The mirror engine is at the back," she said, leading the way. "It takes up the entire rear wall."

He raised his other vision, increasingly intrigued as he followed Gwen through a maze of workbenches, cabinets and display cases. In addition to a vast array of odd tools and machines, there was a large collection of crystals and stones that he knew would fascinate Sam.

He eased his talent higher, opening himself to the energy-infused atmosphere. There was a lot of ambient psi around, but it was the dark currents of violence that riveted his senses.

He had recovered from the nightmare in the cave, but Gwen was right — as long as he had his talent, he would be compelled to hunt. She was the only woman he had ever met who got that part of him — got it and was not repelled or unnaturally attracted to it. She simply understood and accepted his nature.

And she had made it clear last night that she was not looking for a forever commitment any more than he was. By all logic and reason, that made her the perfect woman for him, the woman of his dreams.

Now, if he could just get her to stop insisting that he needed therapy.

Gwen came to a halt. "That's the entrance to the mirror engine."

But he had already sensed a heightening in the energy level as they neared the back of the lab. Hot psi cracked and snapped in the atmosphere, raising the fine hair on his neck and arms. His palms prickled.

"Whatever it is, it's powerful," he said. "I'm impressed."

"The engine was Evelyn's greatest creation." Gwen skirted a workbench. "She told me that originally she had envisioned it as just another small experiment. The first version was about the size of a walk-in shower. But the results were so extraordinary that she kept expanding the surface area dedicated to the mirrors. Eventually the engine grew to the size you see now."

The dark mirrored walls that formed the outside of the engine extended halfway to the vaulted ceiling. Judson estimated they were fifteen feet high. There was energy infused into every inch of the thick glass. Flashes of ultra-light appeared and disappeared in the depths of the reflective surfaces. He looked through the entrance and saw a hall of mirrors.

"Evelyn designed the interior in the form of a simple maze," Gwen said. "The idea was to maximize the mirrored surfaces inside. The result is that there are lots of twists and turns and short hallways and corridors that end in interesting passages."

"I've never seen anything like this, and I doubt that Sam has, either," Judson said. "He's going to be a like a kid in a sandbox. Where did Evelyn get the idea for building this engine? From her own research?"

"She told me that years ago she found

some notes describing the possibility of constructing a mirror engine in an old diary that she discovered in a library. Evidently a Victorian-era paranormal researcher named Welch tried to build a similar device back in the late eighteen hundreds, but there was a major flaw in the design."

Gingerly, Judson reached out to touch the nearest mirrored panel. A shock of psi zapped across his senses. Hastily, he yanked back his finger.

"What was the flaw in Welch's design?" he asked, shaking his fingers a little.

"Welch was a wack-job. He concluded that the most efficient way to trap strong energy in mirrors was to murder people. He planned to kill his victims in a chamber of mirrors that he had constructed in his mansion, hoping to infuse the energy given off at death into the glass."

"What the hell?" Judson looked at her. "Are you serious?"

"Oh, yes," Gwen said. "Evelyn showed me Welch's notes. She said he had been onto something but that he was wrong in his conclusions about how to fuel a true mirror engine."

"Good to know," Judson said. He studied the mirrored hallway with a growing sense of unease. "What happened to the first engine?"

"Evelyn wasn't sure, but from what she could find out, the mansion in which it had been constructed was destroyed in a huge explosion and fire. Her theory was that the engine got overheated and blew."

"How many other people besides you and Ballinger knew about the history of the mirror engine and Welch's theories of how to fuel it?"

"As far as I know, Evelyn didn't tell anyone else except me," Gwen said. "We discussed making the story of the first engine into an episode for *Dead of Night*. But Evelyn said she didn't want to turn that snippet from paranormal history into a TV show, for fear that some modern-day crazy might take it seriously."

"She was right. There's always a nutcase out there in the audience. But Zander Taylor murdered two people here in this lab and tried to kill you. Are you certain he wasn't aware of Welch's work?"

"As certain as I can be," Gwen said. "He did a lot of talking that day, boasting about all the psychics he had killed. But he never mentioned the mirror chamber or Welch's work. As far as Evelyn or I could tell, he was not interested in the science or the history of the paranormal. He just liked to commit murder by paranormal means."

"And he somehow came across an untraceable weapon that allowed him to fulfill his fantasy. Did he tell you when or how he found the camera?"

"No. All I can tell you is that Evelyn was certain it didn't come from her lab. But maybe she did find out recently." Gwen's expression sharpened. "Maybe that's the secret she hid inside the engine."

"What about lights inside the maze?"

"There's some more strip lighting in there," Gwen said. "But in a weird way you don't need lights inside. The mirrors give off so much energy that I think most people with a little talent could perceive the illumination. There is a lot of power in there, though. It can be disorienting."

She moved through the entrance. He followed. He thought he was prepared, but the hot energy of the mirrors crashed and churned like storm-tossed waves on a beach, igniting his senses.

"Damn," he said. "This is a real adrenaline rush, isn't it?"

Gwen glanced back over her shoulder. "Are you sure you're okay with being in here?"

"Oh, yeah."

Understanding brightened her eyes. "It is kind of a thrill ride, isn't it?"

"That's one way to describe it."

"The interesting thing is that it doesn't affect everyone the same way," she said. "The other members of Evelyn's study found it very disturbing. They said it gave them the same creepy feeling you get when you go into a dark alley or down a mine shaft."

She turned a corner and disappeared deeper into the chamber. He caught up with her. The energy in the mirror panels seemed to be getting stronger as they moved toward the heart of the engine.

Judson looked into the depths of a nearby mirror and saw his own image repeating endlessly into a dark infinity.

"You said Ballinger concluded that the energy given off at death was not the way to fuel a mirror engine," he said. "What did she use?"

"Crystals." Gwen went around another corner. "But the original stones had to be tuned frequently. Luckily, she found someone right here in town who could do that, Louise Fuller."

"The woman who makes the wind chimes?"

"Yes." Gwen glanced back over her shoulder. "Evelyn said that Louise has some kind of paranormal affinity for crystals."

"Sam will want to meet her."

"Good luck with that. Louise doesn't like people very much. She's a very odd character. Eccentric and reclusive. The locals call her the Witch of Wilby. But she does make amazing wind chimes. Even with Louise's help, however, Evelyn had a hard time keeping the mirrors working for more than a couple of hours at a time at the start of the project."

"These mirrors are plenty hot and going strong today," Judson said. "Were they tuned recently?"

"It's no longer necessary. A couple of years ago, Evelyn bought a geode online. When it arrived she cracked it open. The interior was packed with crystals that turned out to be strong enough to power the whole mirror engine. What's more, the crystals don't require tuning, either."

A chill of certainty iced Judson's senses.

"Where is that geode now?" he asked sharply.

"I assume it's still in here." Gwen went down another short hallway. "It was Evelyn's most valuable possession. She stored it in a steel box in the heart of the engine. I'm hoping that she hid whatever she wanted me to find in that container along with the geode."

"Weird hiding place."

"You wouldn't say that if you knew Evelyn. She was convinced that almost no one could get far enough into the engine to find the container. Here we go."

Judson followed Gwen around another corner and into a small, square-shaped space paneled in more mirrors. There was a small steel box in the middle of the room. The lid was closed.

Gwen unlatched the lid and raised it. Hot psi wafted out like the ominous smoke of a smoldering forest fire.

"Damn," Judson said. He walked to the box and looked down at the split halves of the geode inside. "I don't believe it."

There was something else inside the box, as well — a folded map.

He ignored the map, his whole attention riveted on the geode.

"That's the rock that fuels the mirrors?" he asked.

"Yes. It's very strange, isn't it? The interior is quite beautiful, and you can sense the power in the crystals. Evelyn told me that she had never seen anything like it."

"I have," Judson said quietly.

There was nothing about the outside of

the dull, gray geode that gave away the secrets inside. It looked like any other rock. But the glittering crystals in the heart of the stone glowed in a paranormal rainbow of colors, casting eerie shadows across the spectrum of visible and invisible light. Currents of energy rose in disturbing waves. The ring on his finger heated in response.

"That's interesting." Gwen reached down to pick up the map. "Where did you see another geode like this one?"

"In the vault in Sam's lab on Legacy Island." He held up his hand to show her the amber stone in his ring. "This crystal came from a geode like that one, and it's a good bet that both rocks came from the same place, the Phoenix Mine."

"What's the Phoenix Mine?"

"It's a long story, but the short version is that this geode belongs to my family."

Gwen frowned. "Hang on, Evelyn paid a lot of money for it and now it belongs to me."

"Don't worry, the Coppersmiths will pay you whatever you ask."

"What if I don't want to sell it?" she asked, clearly wary now.

"I'm afraid this is one of those offers you can't — and shouldn't — refuse. This geode is dangerous, Gwen. Trust me, you don't want to put it on a shelf in your living room."

"How dangerous is it?" she asked. She did not bother to conceal her skepticism and growing suspicion.

"That's the problem," Judson said. He reached down and secured the lid of the strongbox, cutting off the flow of hot energy. "No one really knows the answer to that question. But it's safe to say that it's just damn good luck that Ballinger didn't blow up this lab and everyone who happened to be inside it at the time when she ran her experiments here in the mirror chamber."

"I'm sure you're exaggerating. Evelyn was very careful."

"I doubt if she had any idea what she was dealing with," Judson said. "This geode has to go into Sam's vault for safekeeping. Like I said, we'll make it worth your while financially."

Gwen drew herself up and fixed him with a cool glare. "I'll give your offer some thought."

He was pushing her, and it was clear she didn't like it. Gwen had every right to resent his actions. He was, after all, taking possession of her inheritance.

"Look, I'm sorry," he said. "I realize I'm hitting you with a lot of information that is new to you. I give you my word that I'll explain everything later. Meanwhile this strongbox is coming with us. The energy in this chamber is hot enough as it is. If the psi levels in these mirrors go much higher, this whole place could go up in flames. It's a wonder that there hasn't been an explosion already."

"Hmm."

She did not appear convinced, but at least she was no longer arguing with him. A fresh tide of intuition was riding him hard.

"There's something else to consider," he said. "This geode is worth a fortune to certain people. Hell, it's priceless. I can guarantee you that there are folks who would kill for it."

Gwen stared at him. "Are you saying that it might have been the motive for Evelyn's murder?"

"That's exactly what I'm saying."

"Maybe that's why she left the note on the back of the photograph that sent me here. She wanted to make sure I realized that someone was after the geode. But this map has to be important, too." Gwen looked down at the folded map in her hand. "Otherwise she would never have hidden it here in the mirror engine. She was always very careful to keep this space free of any materials that could potentially interfere with her experiments."

"Let's get out of here," Judson said. He made it an order.

Gwen shot him a questioning look, but she did not argue. Without a word, she led the way back through the mirrored canyon.

They retraced their path through the shadowed lab, moving from one patch of illuminated concrete flooring to the next, leaving darkness in their wake.

At the front of the building, Gwen opened the heavy metal door and started to step outside.

Maybe he caught the small flash of light in the trees on the opposite bank of the river because his senses were spiking on high alert. Or maybe it was just dumb luck. Whatever the reason, he reacted before the logical side of his brain could present a laundry list of reasonable explanations.

He wrapped one hand around Gwen's upper arm and dragged her out of the doorway.

There was a solid *thunk* when the rifle round punched into the metal door frame. The sound of the shot echoed endlessly through the woods, audible even above the relentless roar of the falls.

THIRTEEN

"I'm guessing we aren't going to assume that shot was fired by a hunter who just happened to mistake me for a deer," Gwen said.

It wasn't easy to talk because she was flat on her back, pinned to the floor by Judson, who was on top of her. He weighed a ton, and she was pretty sure it was all muscle.

"No," he said. He rolled off of her. "We're going for worst-case scenario here. Someone just tried to kill one or both of us. Get away from the door. He may try a couple of wild shots, hoping to get lucky."

Under most circumstances, she didn't take orders well, but Judson seemed to know what he was doing. And it wasn't like she was an expert in this sort of thing, she thought.

She sat up and crawled quickly away from the partially open door, moving deeper into the lab. In the weak illumination cast by a strip of floor lighting, she watched Judson shift position in the shadows. A small shock snapped through her when she realized he had taken a gun from an ankle holster. Until that moment, it had not occurred to her that he might be armed.

Judson flattened himself on the floor and fired three fast shots. She could see from the angle of his weapon that he was firing into the thundering falls, not straight across the river into the trees. Warning shots.

The shooter in the woods did not return fire. A moment later the sound of a rapidly accelerating engine reverberated in the distance; the roar faded quickly as the vehicle sped away.

"He didn't expect me to be armed," Judson said.

Gwen exhaled the breath she did not realize she had been holding. "That makes two of us."

"You hired a security consultant," Judson said. "What made you think I didn't come with a gun?"

"I don't know," she admitted. "I suppose I was under the impression that you and your brother relied on paranormal technology for your work."

"Sam is the tech guy in the family. He likes his gadgets. But it's usually a hell of a lot easier to defend yourself with a traditional gun than it is with psi-technology, especially if the guy who is shooting at you is a long ways away. I told you, para-weapons only operate at close range."

"I see. Well, this incident certainly raises a few new questions. I can't believe that someone just tried to kill me."

"That might not have been the shooter's objective."

"Do you have another suggestion?"

"The shot was high." Judson said. "The shooter may have been trying to scare you off, not kill you."

"Okay, I'll take some comfort in that possibility. What now?"

"You're going out the back door. I'll get the car and bring it around the lab building to pick you up."

"Are you sure it's safe to go out the front door?" she asked.

"He's gone," Judson said.

"You're sure?"

"Very sure."

"But you still want me to go out the back way?"

"Humor me, okay?"

"Okay," she said. "But promise me you'll be very careful when you go out the front."

He looked mildly surprised by her concern. Then the edge of a smile appeared. He picked up the strongbox and went to the door.

"I'll be careful," he said.

She waited tensely at the rear door of the lab, listening hard until she heard the SUV's big engine fire up. She relaxed only somewhat when she did not hear any more shots.

A moment later, Judson drove around the corner of the building, braked to a halt and leaned across the passenger compartment to throw open the door. She locked the lab door and hopped up into the front seat, the map clutched in one hand.

"Are we going to report this to Oxley?" she asked, buckling her seat belt.

"Sure." Judson drove toward the road that bordered the river. "It will be interesting to see if he bothers to investigate. Even if he does go through the motions, I doubt that he'll turn up any hard evidence. But the important thing is that word will get out around town that someone took a shot at you."

"That's a good thing?"

"It will put pressure on the shooter. He'll think twice before he tries again because he knows that no cop, even a small-town one, will ignore a second hunting accident. That will buy me some time to find him."

"How do you intend to do that?" She stopped when she realized he was turning the wrong way onto the road. "Where are you going? Wilby is the other direction."

"The nearest bridge is this way. I want to get to the other side to see if I can locate the place where the shooter stood when he took the shot."

Gwen glanced at him. "You think you'll find some psi-residue at the scene that will point us toward a suspect?"

"Maybe. Sometimes I get lucky."

A hundred yards up the road, Judson drove across a narrow bridge. The lane on the far side was little more than a dirt track through the woods.

He stopped the SUV in a position directly opposite the lodge and got out.

Gwen watched him walk a few feet into the woods before she extricated herself from the front seat and followed him. The wind was sharpening. The next summer storm would be upon them by nightfall.

When she reached Judson's side, she sensed the energy in the atmosphere around him.

"Well?" she asked.

"This is where the shooter stood when he pulled the trigger." Judson studied the front of the lab. "He knew what he was doing. He aimed for the door frame, and that's what he hit."

"How do you know that?"

"He was . . . satisfied with the shot. But he was surprised when I returned fire. I was right. He didn't know that I was armed."

"Are you sure we're talking about a male?"

"No. I'm using the masculine pronoun in a generic sense, the same way I did at Ballinger's house."

"So there could be a woman involved in this thing?"

"Oh, yeah," Judson said very softly.

"Do you have any sense of the emotion that the shooter was feeling when he took the shot?"

"Angry. Scared. Desperate." Judson turned back toward the SUV. "You're wondering if it was Nicole Hudson who fired that shot, aren't you?"

"You heard her last night. She blames me for Taylor's death."

"If she was the shooter, all I can tell you now is that she wasn't trying to kill you. I need more information."

Gwen smiled. "I know what you mean. It's called context."

FOURTEEN

"Hunter." Oxley studied the scarred metal where the rifle shot had punched through the doorjamb. "Every year we get a lot of city folks up here. Most of 'em can't hit the broad side of a barn. They get excited and shoot at anything that moves."

"I can see you're not impressed," Judson said.

Gwen was initially surprised that Oxley had not kept them waiting long. His arrival at the lodge so soon after Judson made the 911 call indicated that he had been poised to spring into action if he got word that she was present at yet another crime scene. It was almost as if he had been expecting to hear more bad news, she thought. It was depressing to be the Wilby version of Typhoid Mary.

Light glinted on Oxley's dark glasses when he turned his head to look at Judson. "This kind of thing happens every season. Just glad no one was hurt."

"Gosh, so are we," Gwen said.

Oxley's heavy jaw hardened. "You think someone deliberately took a shot at you?"

"That possibility crossed my mind, yes."

"Now, why would anyone want to do that?" Oxley asked very softly.

"I don't know," Gwen said. "It occurred to me that getting the answer to that question was your job."

Oxley contemplated her for a long moment, his eyes unreadable behind the shades. "It's no secret that you made an enemy here a couple of years ago."

"You're talking about Nicole Hudson, aren't you?" Gwen said.

"Between you and me, Nicole is not real stable."

"I've heard that," Gwen said.

Oxley grunted. "I happen to know for a fact that she's still got her dad's old hunting rifle."

"Wonderful," Gwen said. "An unstable woman in possession of a weapon. What are the odds she might decide to use it?"

Oxley rubbed the back of his thick neck. "I'll have a talk with her."

"We don't think this was a hunting accident," Judson said quietly. "We wanted to report the incident in case the situation escalates."

"Escalates?" Oxley repeated in ominous tones. "Like it escalated two years ago?"

"Yes," Judson said.

"Who are you, Coppersmith, and what's your connection to Miss Frazier, here?"

"I'm a friend," Judson said. "I'm helping Gwen deal with Evelyn Ballinger's affairs."

"Friend, huh? Way I hear it, you and Miss Frazier are more than just friends, but that's your business," Oxley said. "I'd advise you to be real careful, though. Friends of Gwen Frazier have a bad habit of dying here in Wilby." He squared his cap on his head and stalked back toward the patrol car. "Call me if there are any more incidents."

"You bet," Gwen said. "Good to know you're there to serve and protect, chief."

Oxley paused before stuffing himself behind the wheel. "You want to see this situation de-escalate? Leave town. Got a hunch things will go right back to normal around here once you're gone. Just like they did last time."

FIFTEEN

"You found one of the Phoenix geodes?" Elias roared into the phone. "Just sitting around in some abandoned resort lodge?"

Wincing, Judson held the phone away from his ear. His father had built a business empire founded on rare earths and valuable ores. Elias had interests in every region of the globe. As president and CEO of Coppersmith, Inc., he did high-level deals in cosmopolitan European capitals and in hardscrabble mining camps on every continent. He had connections that stretched from Wall Street and Washington, D.C., to the farthest corners of the planet.

The strategic importance of rare earths ensured that Elias could pick up a phone and get the full and immediate attention of government officials, directors of hedge funds and the owners of a wide range of technology firms. He was the go-to man for those who wanted to know what the foreign competition was doing. In practice, Elias almost never picked up the phone. Other people wasted a lot of their valuable time and their assistants' valuable time trying to get through to him.

Elias could hold his own with anyone from an East Coast banker to a Silicon Valley engineer, but he had started out as a hard rock prospector in the deserts of the American West, and he would be a man of the Old West for the rest of his life. It was there in his voice. The drawl got thicker when he got excited. He was excited now.

"The geode was actually sitting around in a private lab here in Wilby," Judson said. He looked at the steel strongbox on the bench at the end of his bed. "The former owner cut it open. She was using it to power some of her lab equipment, a psi-reflecting engine made out of hot mirrors."

The door between his room and Gwen's stood open. Max wandered across the threshold and vaulted up onto the big bed, landing with a heavy thud. He looked at the steel box with an attentive expression for a few seconds and then he seemed to lose interest.

"You're sure it's one of the stones from the Phoenix Mine?" Elias asked.

"There's no way to be absolutely certain

of the source," Judson said. "Rocks are rocks. They don't come with tidy little stamps stating the place of origin. But this rock is definitely hot just like the others in the vault. And there's one other thing that makes me pretty sure it came from the Phoenix."

"What the hell is that?"

"I recognize the energy in it. Some of the crystals are identical to the one in my ring."

"Son of a —" Elias broke off, thinking. "Well, wherever the hell it came from, we need to get it up here to Copper Beach and into the vault as soon as possible."

"I agree, but someone is going to have to come to Wilby to pick it up. I can't leave town yet. The client insists on staying here until we find out who killed Ballinger."

"This would be the client who happens to be one of Abby's two best friends?" Elias asked.

"Gwen Frazier, right."

"Does she have any idea how the dead woman got hold of that rock?"

"Gwen says Ballinger bought it online about two years ago."

"Damn Internet," Elias growled. "Talk about the perfect black market. Anyone can sell anything and not leave a trace. Can't believe Ballinger was using that rock to fuel a bunch of hot mirrors. It's a miracle that she didn't blow up her lab and maybe the whole town."

"Gwen says that Ballinger knew the rock was powerful. That's why she kept it in a steel box. But it's obvious she didn't know what kind of fire she was playing with when she decided to use it as fuel for her engine."

"No one knows what kind of fire those rocks are capable of igniting. That's what makes 'em so damn dangerous," Elias muttered. He paused. "Huh."

"What?"

"I'm no ace detective like you, son, but it strikes me that stone would be a mighty fine motive for murder."

"That thought did occur to me."

"Wouldn't put it past Barrett to do whatever it took to get hold of one of the Phoenix rocks."

Judson suppressed a groan. He had been expecting this. His father's long-standing feud with Hank Barrett, the owner of Helicon Stone, had achieved the status of legend, not only in the family but in the global mining business. The origins of the feud were locked in secrecy. Judson was fairly certain that his mother, Willow, knew how it had all started, but she kept Elias's secrets.

"I don't think Barrett would resort to murder," Judson said patiently.

"Sure he would," Elias shot back. "But it's more likely he'd send his son to do his dirty work. Gideon Barrett is a chip off the old block, and we know that he's a powerful talent, like you and Sam and Emma."

"One thing's for sure," Judson said. "If Ballinger was killed for the stone, the murderer failed to achieve his objective. The rock is sitting here in my room at the inn. I'm looking at the box that contains it as we speak."

"Don't let it out of your sight. I'll be there tomorrow morning."

Sixteen

The storm hit just as they were finishing dinner. Gwen was very glad that Judson had insisted on driving the short distance to the restaurant. She knew that he was more concerned about security than the weather. It was easier to transport the strongbox — presently at his feet under the table — in the SUV. But when the weather turned bad in the Oregon mountains, it did so in a hurry. It would have been a very wet walk back to the inn.

"Gonna be a bad one," the young waiter said when he returned with the bill. "They're sayin' there's another one coming in tomorrow."

Judson signed the credit card receipt, got to his feet and helped Gwen into her jacket. Then he picked up the strongbox.

She glanced at him as they walked toward the door.

"I still can't believe your father thinks that

173

geode is so important that he's going to come here personally to collect it," she said.

"Dad has spent a good part of his adult life tracking down any and all rumors linked to the stones from the Phoenix," Judson said. "Under normal circumstances, he would have sent Sam or me to pick up the geode, but my brother and I are both otherwise occupied at the moment. So he's going to take charge of the mission himself."

"No offense, but your father sounds like a bit of a control freak."

"Oh, yeah." Judson smiled. "Mom says the trait runs in the family. Which is why Sam and I started our own business."

"Neither of you could work for your father?"

"Right. We reached a compromise, though. Sam and I both consult for Coppersmith, Inc. Sam handles the R-and-D lab in Seattle. I deal with company security."

"What about your sister, Emma?"

"My sister is what you might call a free spirit," Judson said. "Translated, that means she can't hold a job for long. Can't settle on a career path, either. She claims she's gaining life experience. Mom says she just needs time to find herself. Dad thinks it's time Emma got a life."

Outside in the wet night, Judson opened

the passenger-side door of the SUV. Gwen bounced up onto the seat. She watched him walk around the front of the vehicle, the collar of his jacket pulled up against the rain. The downfall plastered his dark hair to his head.

He opened the rear door, set the strongbox on the floor and then opened the driver's-side door. When he got behind the wheel, he brought a rush of the wild energy of the storm with him. Gwen's senses stirred in response.

It felt good to be here with him in the intimate confines of the darkened cab, she thought. Not just pleasant or comfortable. It was exciting, thrilling and, yes, a little dangerous.

The intense, intimate energy that had flared between them that first night in Seattle was getting more powerful and more unpredictable with every minute they spent together — at least it was on her side. She was walking an invisible psychic high wire without a net.

"Do you think there's anything to your father's theory that his competitor, Hank Barrett, might have murdered Evelyn for the rock?" she asked.

"I doubt it." Judson fired up the engine and drove out of the parking lot. "Dad and

Barrett have been fierce competitors for years, and there's no question that Barrett can be ruthless when it comes to business. But I honestly don't think he would murder a harmless, seventy-two-year-old woman to get a rock, even one as valuable as the geode."

"In other words, he would draw the line at murder?"

"Can't say for sure, but he and my father definitely have a few things in common. So, based on what I know of Dad, I think it's safe to say that while Barrett is capable of going to great lengths to achieve an objective, in the case of something like the geode, he would have used more subtle tactics."

"Such as?" she asked.

"Barrett probably would have sent his son, Gideon, to grab the rock. And if Gideon Barrett had come after the geode, he would have been successful. The fact that the stone is now sitting in that box in the back tells me that the Barretts aren't involved in this thing."

Gwen watched the rain beat a steady tattoo on the windshield. "What do you know about Gideon Barrett?"

"Not a whole lot aside from the fact that he's some kind of talent. Sam had a close encounter with him a while back. According to Sam, the one thing he learned from the experience is that Gideon is brilliant with PEC technology."

"What's that?" Gwen asked.

"Stands for psi-emitting crystals, the paranormal equivalent of light-emitting diodes and liquid crystal displays — LEDs and LCDs."

"Good grief, you mean there's another company besides Coppersmith, Inc., fooling around with para-physics and psi-technology?" Gwen shuddered. "That's a scary thought."

"Here's an even scarier thought," Judson said. His hands tightened on the wheel. "There are other folks out there fooling around with psi-tech weapon design, and some of them have been successful. Don't forget, someone made that camera that Zander Taylor used to kill all those psychics and your friends."

"You're right — that is a scarier thought. I suppose I was thinking of the camera as just a crazy one-off invention that Taylor had engineered in a basement."

"I hope that's true in this instance because it means that when we find the killer, the case will be closed. No loose ends." Judson paused. "I don't like loose ends."

Gwen thought about all the ghosts she had

seen in her life. "Neither do I. But I've got to tell you, this does make a person wonder how many psi-weapons are out there floating around the world."

"The good news is that from everything we've been able to discover at Coppersmith, there are still a whole lot of serious limitations on PEC technology."

"The distance problem you mentioned," she said.

"Right. Even for a strong talent, it's hard to focus paranormal radiation beyond twenty feet. Also any beam of psi-energy strong enough to kill has to be very narrow and intensely focused, which means that, pragmatically speaking, you can only take down one target at a time. And para-weapons tend to be fragile and unstable. Doesn't take much to set up a self-destructing oscillation pattern."

She raised her brows. "You've done a lot of thinking about crystal-based weapons, haven't you?"

"Yes," he said. "The subject has been on my mind for a while now."

"Ever since your last case?"

"Yes."

"You encountered one on the island?" she asked, probing cautiously.

"It's a long story."

"Which is another way of saying you don't want to talk about it."

"Not tonight," he said. "I've got other priorities."

"Okay, I think I get the point. Can you tell me about the Phoenix Mine instead?"

Judson pulled into the inn parking lot and shut down the engine. He sat quietly for a while. Then he seemed to come to a decision.

"You've got a right to some answers," he said. "You're in this thing pretty deep already."

"That's certainly how it appears to me."

"My father has been in mining all of his life. He's got what you might call an affinity for crystals and ores."

"Is he some kind of crystal talent like you and your brother and sister?"

"In a way, but he's not nearly as strong as the three of us. He doesn't think of himself as having any psychic ability. He calls his sensitivity old-fashioned miner's intuition. Forty years ago, he realized that the rare earths were going to become increasingly important because they are so critical to the high-tech industries."

"He called that right," she said.

"He teamed up with a couple of other miners, Quinn Knox and Ray Willis. All three of them had a feel for crystals and ores. They were all nearly broke, but they scraped up every dime they had and bought the rights to an old abandoned mine, the Phoenix. They opened it up and discovered a cache of geodes like the one in the strongbox. As soon as they split a couple open, they knew they had hit on something really big. They just didn't know what they had."

"What did they have?" Gwen asked.

"That's the problem. We still don't know. The only thing that seems clear is that the crystals inside the geodes can generate power of a paranormal nature. But modern technology isn't sufficiently advanced to harness that kind of energy."

"Are you saying that there is a whole mine full of rocks like the one in the back of this SUV?"

"No one really knows what's still down in the Phoenix because things got complicated," Judson said.

"Complicated, how?"

"Ray Willis was a mining engineer who, it turned out, had a fair amount of psychic talent, more than Dad and Knox realized until it was too late. Willis conducted some experiments and concluded that the crystals had phenomenal potential. He decided to get rid of his two partners and take full possession of the Phoenix. He rigged an explosion in the mine. Dad and Knox nearly died that day."

"Good grief, Willis tried to murder them?"

"Yes, but it was Willis who died instead. It's not clear exactly what happened that day, but Dad managed to get out of the mine with a sack full of the geodes. Those are the rocks that are in Sam's vault at Copper Beach. What Dad and Knox did not discover until years later was that in the days before he tried to murder them, Willis stole some of the geodes and hid them. No one knows where those rocks wound up."

"You think Evelyn's geode may have come from Willis's pile of stolen rocks?"

"I think that's the most likely explanation, yes," Judson said.

"What happened to the mine?"

"Following the explosion, Dad and Knox agreed to bury the secret of the Phoenix, at least for the foreseeable future. They concluded that the rocks are just too damn dangerous and modern science is not sufficiently advanced to deal with the energy in the stones. But at the same time, Dad doesn't want to destroy all records of the mine because he knows it's only a matter of time before the world hits a wall when it comes to energy resources. Sooner or later, civilization will need a new way to fuel itself."

"In other words, your family has assumed the burden of guarding the secret of the Phoenix?"

"That's what it comes down to, yes," he said.

"What happened to Knox?"

"He's dead."

"Let me get this straight," Gwen said carefully. "The members of your family are the only ones who know about the Phoenix stones and the fact that there's an abandoned mine full of paranormal crystals somewhere out in the desert?"

"We wish we were the only ones who knew about those crystals. Life for the Coppersmith family would be a whole lot simpler if that was the case. Knox is dead, but it turns out there's nothing harder to kill than rumors of a lost mine that supposedly holds a cache of priceless stones. Dad is sure that Hank Barrett, for one, is aware of the story of the Phoenix."

"But, then, your father is a tad paranoid about Hank Barrett," Gwen said.

"True, but you know the old saying: even paranoids have enemies."

"The history of the Phoenix sounds like a dangerous secret to know."

"It is," Judson said.

"Abby knows about the mine and the stones, doesn't she?"

"Yes." Judson turned in the seat to face her, one arm resting on the wheel. "And now, so do you."

SEVENTEEN

She was halfway across the state of Nevada when the ghost in the mirror stopped her.

"You need to go back to the beginning and start over," the ghost said. "You missed something important."

"I probably should have waited until tomorrow to make this road trip. I'm exhausted. It's been a very long day."

"I've got news for you," the ghost said. "It's been an even longer day for me. And tomorrow doesn't look like it's going to be any shorter. Being dead is incredibly boring when you're stuck in a mirror."

"Sorry, you're right. I'll go back to Oregon and try this again. It's just so damn frustrating."

"Yes, I know. But you need to find what you missed before you set out on this road trip."

"I'll try."

"Don't forget the names that I wrote on

the back of the map. They're important, just like the names of the cities I circled."

"Right."

"Remember how we matched things up the last time in order to find the pattern," the ghost said.

"I remember."

"And please hurry, dear. I'd really like to get out of this mirror."

"Gwen, wake up."

Judson's voice shattered the delicate threads of the trance dream. Gwen slipped into the strong, disorienting currents of the river between the underworld and the waking world and struck out for the far shore.

When she opened her eyes, she saw Judson silhouetted against a senses-dazzling fire of amber ultra-light.

She reached for his hand to lead him out of the lightning storm. "Judson," she whispered. "Come with me."

His hand closed around hers. He was very warm to the touch. She knew intuitively that the heat was paranormal in nature. She could see it in his eyes. Or was it her own temperature that was rising?

"Come with me," she said again. "You need to leave this place."

"Take it easy," he said. "Everything is okay. You're safe."

"You're the one who is in danger."

"Not now," he said. "Not tonight." He sat down on the edge of the bed and put a hand on her arm. "You're still dreaming. Time to wake up."

A heavy weight thumped down beside her on the bed. Max meowed loudly.

She realized that she was still swimming in the dark, eerie river of dreams. It wasn't the first time she had found herself trapped in the strange currents. She crossed this river every time she went into and out of one of her own trance dreams.

She always made the passage as swiftly as possible because it was a dangerous place, a scary place with unseen depths. Each time she made the treacherous passage, part of her was afraid that if she did not reach the safety of the opposite shore quickly, she would be swept over the falls into a cauldron of churning energy from which there would be no escape.

But she'd had a lot of practice making the crossing.

She took a deep steadying breath, pulled on her talent and hauled herself up out of the treacherous currents. She lowered her talent and allowed the real world to coalesce around her.

The first thing that struck her was that

she was not alone. Judson was there. She had forgotten to lock the connecting door.

She had a rule about deep dream trances. She never went into them unless she could be sure that she would be alone and undisturbed. She had learned long ago that her self-imposed lucid dreams, like her habit of talking to ghosts, unnerved others.

She was propped up against the pillows on the bed, dressed in her nightgown and the white terry cloth bathrobe and slippers provided by the inn.

Max meowed again and butted his head against her shoulder. Automatically she reached out to stroke him.

She looked at Judson. With her senses lowered, he no longer appeared enveloped in hot ultra-light. In the deep shadows, she could tell that he was wearing the crewneck T-shirt and the khakis he'd had on earlier.

"Oh, crap," she said. "Sorry about that. I should have locked the door. Didn't mean to alarm you."

Judson did not let go of her hand. "It was just a dream."

"No, it wasn't just a dream. It was a trance dream, and you don't have to act like it fell into the category of normal. People are always freaked out by the way I dream. I told you, my talent is a serious problem when it comes to relationships."

"Oh, yeah, right. You send men screaming from your bed. You know, I have to tell you, that sounds interesting."

"Okay, maybe not *screaming*. But there were some extremely awkward partings back in the days when I was trying to fall in love and pretend that I was normal."

"I know where you're coming from," he said. "I told you, my talent gets in the way of relationships, too."

She was very conscious of the feel of his strong hand wrapped around hers. His eyes still burned.

She knew that she was out of the dream, but there was a familiar, dreamlike quality in the atmosphere. An effervescent energy swirled around her, teasing and arousing her senses. A liquid heat built inside her lower body.

High wire, she reminded herself. *No net.*

"Do you always talk out loud to the ghosts in your trance dreams?" Judson asked.

He didn't sound worried. He sounded curious.

Bored by the proceedings, Max jumped down to the floor and wandered off toward the other room, tail high.

"Not always," she said. But in this case, I was talking to Evelyn again. I deliberately put myself into the dream to see if I could understand what she was trying to tell me with the map. It has to be important. Otherwise she wouldn't have hidden it inside the mirror engine. And she wouldn't have left that message on the back of the photo for me to find."

Judson looked at the map unfolded across her thighs. "Get any ideas from your dream?"

"Nothing concrete." She ran her fingers through her hair, pushing it loosely back behind her ears while she struggled to pull facts from her visions. "In my dream, I set out on a road trip. I was walking from one circled town to the next. Evelyn's ghost told me that the names she wrote on that map and the six circled towns were important. But she also told me that I should go back to the beginning."

"Back to Wilby?"

"That's just it — I'm not sure what it all means. I went into the dream assuming that the places she marked were sites of paranormal activity that she had researched online, places that she planned to check out as potential *Dead of Night* episodes. I thought one of them might be a clue to whatever is going on here in Wilby." She stabbed a finger at Reno. "I got this far before Evelyn appeared and told me I have to go back to the beginning."

"Wilby."

"I suppose so, one way or another." She tightened her hand into a frustrated fist. "Sometimes my talent is so damn frustrating."

"It's been a long day," Judson said. "You need rest."

"Probably." She sank back against the pillows. "So do you. Sorry I woke you."

"I wasn't asleep, at least not very soundly."

She gave a small sniff. "I'm not surprised, given all that psychic noise you've got going on in your aura."

He tensed. "Don't start with the therapy talk. I am not in the mood."

"Okay, okay, you've made that clear. But for the record, if you ever do decide that you'd like help getting a good night's sleep, let me know. I'm the only psychic counselor in town, and it just so happens I specialize in dream therapy. What with you being a Coppersmith and all, I'm sure you can afford me."

"I'll keep that in mind. Now, about our mutual issues with bed partners."

She stilled. "What about them?"

"I'm willing to discuss possible therapeutic solutions to that problem."

She was suddenly a little breathless. Her pulse was kicking up again but not from the rush of adrenaline and anxiety that always accompanied the crossing of the dream river. This new, unfamiliar exhilaration was a good kind of rush. There was certainly risk here, but at the moment she could not find a reason to care about the potential downside.

No net.

"Are you absolutely sure it doesn't bother you that I talk to ghosts?" she said.

"It's no big deal."

"You don't think I'm maybe borderline crazy?"

"I've met crazy. I know crazy. Trust me, you don't qualify as crazy."

"What makes you so sure of that?"

He smiled slowly, deliberately. "I'm psychic, remember?"

"Oh, yeah, right." She smiled. "I almost forgot."

He pulled her into his arms, giving her time to change her mind. But changing her mind was the last thing she planned to do.

When his mouth closed over hers, a sweeping tide of certainty crashed through her, the same kind of certainty that she got when she reached the shores of the surface world after a harrowing journey to the underworld of dreams. This was solid. This was real.

At least for tonight.

She sank her fingers into Judson's shoulders, finding the rock-hard muscle beneath warm skin. He responded with a low, husky growl that conveyed male hunger and need in the most elemental language of all. He deepened the kiss. She opened her mouth for him.

He pushed her back down onto the bed and covered her body with his own. A raging thrill flashed across her senses. She curled her leg around his thigh. The fabric of his trousers was rough against her skin. When she thrust one hand beneath his T-shirt, she discovered that his back was already damp with sweat.

She knew that he had heightened his talent. He wasn't focusing his psychic senses, she realized. He had simply opened them wide to savor all of the raw energy of the passion they were generating. She was doing the same thing.

"Judson." She twisted beneath him, threaded her fingers in his hair. "Oh my goodness, *Judson.*"

She kissed him with a ferocity that he took as a challenge, returning the embrace with the same passionate intensity. It was as if both of them had been waiting for this to happen for a very long time, and now that the moment was upon them, they were each determined to seize the opportunity.

Locked in sensual battle, they rolled together across the bed. For an exhilarating time, she was on top, glorying in her power. And then he was pinning her beneath him, and she was relishing the sensual assault he waged on her body.

He wrenched his mouth away from hers and caught her wrists on either side of her head. He was breathing hard now. There was a hot, dark energy about him that radiated across the spectrum. His ring burned in the shadows.

He got her out of the robe and the nightgown and kissed his way down the length of her. When she felt the edge of his teeth on the inside of her thigh, she gasped and twisted her fingers in his hair.

He used his hands and his tongue on her until she was melting and desperate for him. Only then did he pause to sit on the side of the bed. She heard some soft rustling sounds. There was a muffled clunk when he put the ankle holster and the gun on the bedside table.

He stood and stripped off his T-shirt, khakis and briefs. When he came back to her, she made a place for him between her legs and wrapped him close.

He thrust into her. The thrilling shock of the heavy, deep invasion was almost too much. But even as she caught her breath, her body was already adjusting, her core clenching around him. She held him prisoner, demanding that he deliver on the sexual promises he had made.

He drove slowly in and out of her until she was mindless with need, until she could not abide the sweet, piercing tension for another instant.

Her release surged through her in waves. The experience was shattering, dazzling — unlike anything she had ever known. She opened her lips on a scream of astonishment and wonder. Judson covered her mouth with his own, swallowing her cries, even as he rocked forward. His climax powered through both of them.

She could have sworn that for a timeless, joyful moment, the currents of their auras seemed to resonate together. The sensation was at once unnerving and breathtakingly intimate. It was as if for a split second they were looking into each other's very souls.

I know you, Judson Coppersmith, she thought. *I've been waiting for you.*

EIGHTEEN

The wind chimes clashed and clattered, sounding the alarm. But Louise Fuller knew that the music was not powerful enough to stop the demon from entering her house. It came and went as it pleased. It had been months since the last visit. Every time it went away, she dared to hope that it would not come back. But it was here now. She could sense its presence.

She stopped in the center of the darkened basement and swung the beam of her flashlight toward the top of the stairs. She could hear the demon coming down the hall.

The lights had gone out a few minutes earlier. She had come downstairs to check the electrical panel, but now she knew that the demon had tricked her. The only question was why had it gone to the trouble of luring her down here into the darkness tonight?

The demon had controlled her for years.

She was its slave and they both knew it. The demon laughed at her puny attempts to protect herself. In the end she always did its bidding. She would do it again tonight.

Why drive her down here into the basement?

The footsteps in the hall were closer now. The chimes rattled and thrashed in a rising crescendo. The music was frantic, desperate, ominous. Hopeless.

The demon appeared at the top of the stairs, a dark shadow silhouetted against the weak glow of the emergency nightlight that illuminated the hallway.

"Hello, Louise," the demon said. "I have to tell you that those chimes of yours have become really irritating. Good to know you won't be making any more."

The demon raised one hand. Louise felt a terrible chill, as though her heart was freezing in her chest.

Now she knew why the demon had forced her into the basement. In this place there was nowhere to run, nowhere to hide. She was trapped.

She had always known that one day the demon would kill her. Tonight was the night. A part of her welcomed the promise of release. At last the torment would end.

But a strange, unfamiliar anger surfaced

out of the depths.

She would be avenged. The other witch was in town, and she had brought a man of power with her. Sooner or later they would come around, wanting to ask questions about what had happened to Evelyn and the others.

Louise knew that she would be dead when the other witch arrived, but that was not a problem. Gwendolyn Frazier could talk to ghosts.

NINETEEN

Judson contemplated the shadowed ceiling, one arm folded behind his head, the other wrapped around Gwen's soft, sleek body. She was snuggled against him, her head nestled on his shoulder. Their bodies were still damp from the heat and energy that had gone into the lovemaking. The scent in the air was primal. He felt good, really good — satisfied in every conceivable way that a man could be satisfied.

"Okay, that was different," Gwen said.

She sounded so bemused — so serious — that he laughed, startling both of them. She levered herself up on one elbow and glared down at him.

"You think there's something amusing going on here?" she asked.

"No, absolutely not," he said, sobering fast.

"Yes, you do. I can tell."

He threaded his fingers through her

tangled hair. The tendrils felt like strands of silk. In the darkened room, her witchy eyes smoldered.

"Well, maybe a little," he conceded. "But I liked hearing you scream."

"I didn't scream."

He smiled, savoring the memories.

"You screamed," he said. "If I hadn't muffled the noise, you would have awakened the whole damn inn."

"Has anyone ever told you that you might have a problem with arrogance?" she asked.

"Just stating the facts, ma'am."

"I wasn't expecting what happened," she admitted. She flushed. "I was taken by surprise. That's all."

"Not me. I knew we would be good together."

"Hmm."

A trickle of unease feathered his senses. He cleared his throat. "Are you going to tell me it wasn't that good for you? Because I will be happy to try again."

"No, no, that's okay."

"Okay?" He sat up. "It was just okay?"

"It was more like a first."

"First what? First time with another strong talent?"

"That, too. But what I meant was that it was the first time I've ever had a climax that did not involve a small home appliance."

Relief, delight and an exultant sense of euphoria surged through him. He laughed and flopped back down on the pillows. He dragged her down across his chest.

"You had me worried there for a while, Dream Eyes," he said. "Glad I could be of service."

"That is a terribly tacky thing to say." She punched him lightly on the arm.

"Ouch. What am I supposed to say?"

"I don't know, but that definitely wasn't it."

He framed her face with both hands. "How about 'That was the best it's ever been for me, and I will remember this night for the rest of my life'?"

She looked dubious. "Would it be the truth?"

"It would be the truth."

Her soft mouth curved in a wry smile. "Okay, even if it's not the truth, it's a lot better than 'Glad I could be of service.' "

"I'll remember that. Tell me about the first guy you sent screaming into the night."

She blinked, caught off guard. "Are you sure you want to hear about my boring past life experiences?"

"I want to know everything about you."

"Well, it wasn't at night, and there were

two of them the first time."

"What the hell? *Two?*"

"I was thirteen," she said quietly. "I had just arrived at Summerlight. I was alone and vulnerable because I hadn't connected with Nick and Abby yet. Two of the older boys cornered me outside a storage room and dragged me inside."

"Bastards." Rage ripped through him.

"I was terrified and I was furious and I was desperate. I fought with everything I had, and I discovered that I had more weapons than I knew I possessed."

"You used your talent to defend yourself?"

"It was a shock to all three of us, believe me," she said. "My talent was still developing, and I was still learning to cope with it. I honestly didn't know what I could do until I realized that one of the creeps was screaming in panic and looking at me as if he was seeing a monster. I had unintentionally put him into a dream trance — a waking nightmare."

"You can do that?"

"Sure. It requires physical contact, of course. But I use my ability to put my therapy clients into a light trance all the time. It's how I work. I can make the experience very . . . unpleasant if I want."

"What happened that day when you were

attacked at the school?" he asked.

"The first creep freaked. His reaction caused his friend to freak, too. They both let go of me as if they'd been scalded and turned to run. But when they opened the door, they ran straight into Nick, who had sensed something bad was going down and decided to investigate."

"This is Nick Sawyer, the friend you've mentioned?"

"Right." She smiled. "He claims that he was born to be a really good cat burglar. He can see in the dark better than most people can see in daylight. And I'm pretty sure he's never found a lock he couldn't get through. He claims that if it hadn't been for Abby and me, he probably would have pursued a career as a jewel thief. We talked him into going into the hot books business — anti-quarian books with a paranormal prov-enance — instead."

"What did Sawyer do to the two socio-paths who tried to assault you?"

"Nick caught the first guy coming out of the storage room and slammed him into a wall with such force that the jerk's nose was broken. Nick sent the second one down the gym stairs. The result was a broken wrist and some cracked ribs."

"Did the bastards complain?"

"Sure, but the authorities didn't take them seriously. They were known bullies, and Nick was smaller and lighter. He looks more like a professional dancer than a street fighter. At any rate, from that day on, I was a member of Nick and Abby's crew. The three of us stuck together until we graduated. We're still family."

He knew it was dumb, but he couldn't suppress the flicker of jealousy that crackled through him.

"Was Nick your high school sweetheart?" he asked.

Gwen shook her head. "Nick is gay. He became my brother, not my boyfriend. I didn't go out on any real dates until I left Summerlight and went off to college."

"No high school dances? No prom night? No trips to lovers' lane?"

"Nope, nope and nope. You don't do that kind of stuff when you're attending a boarding school that has bars on the windows."

"It sounds awful."

Gwen made a face. "Summerlight was not a normal high school. The students were all there because we were considered abnormal. Some of us were more abnormal than others. And some of the kids were downright dangerous. The atmosphere was not conducive to dating, believe me. Besides, we wouldn't have been able to go off the grounds."

"Were all of the kids psychic?"

"No, a percentage were genuinely disturbed. But a surprisingly large number of students showed traits that Abby and Nick and I have come to associate with forms of psychic talent. That's what brought Evelyn to the school. She somehow discovered that there was a high proportion of talents at Summerlight. Abby and Sam found out recently that the school deliberately searched for teens with strong para-psych profiles."

"Sam mentioned that."

"I can assure you that in the course of tossing out a wide net, the school administrators managed to gather a lot of serious wack-jobs, some of whom no doubt went on to become very scary people," Gwen said.

"Like the two bastards who assaulted you. Do you know what happened to them?"

"No. They steered clear of the three of us after that. When Abby and Nick and I got out of Summerlight, the last thing we wanted to do was keep in touch with former classmates, believe me. I will give the academy credit for teaching us one very valuable lesson, though."

"What was that?"

"How to pass for normal," Gwen said.

"But it's hard to pretend you're normal when you get involved in a close relationship of any kind — friend or lover."

"Obviously, you've had some experience," Gwen said.

"Yes," he said. "But unlike you, I grew up in a family that accepted the fact that Sam and Emma and I are different." He smiled. "I should say Dad has accepted it. Mom still tries to pretend the three of us are normal, but deep down, she knows the truth."

"I'm sure that mothers always do know the truth about their offspring, whether they admit it or not."

"Probably," he agreed. "All right, the assault in the linen closet explains how you came to find out that you were capable of sending a man screaming into the night. But that was a deliberate effort on your part and done in self-defense. That doesn't explain why you would send a lover screaming from your bed."

"Not intentionally," she assured him. "Honest."

"Unintentionally?"

She grimaced. "The problem is my aura. When I sleep, I dream more intensely than most people. My dreaming aura affects anyone who happens to come into physical contact with me. If that person happens to be asleep and dreaming, my currents overpower his. The result, I'm told, is a particularly unnerving kind of nightmare."

"Well, that answers one question," he said, satisfied.

She raised her brows. "About my love life?"

"No, about how Zander Taylor happened to go over the falls. You sent him into a nightmare, didn't you? He went crazy and started running."

She closed her eyes. "I knew you would figure it out sooner or later."

"Nice work."

She opened her eyes and watched him very intently. "It doesn't bother you that I've got the ability to send someone into a nightmare landscape so intense that the victim actually leaps to his death to escape?"

He patted her bare shoulder. "We've all got baggage."

"That's very broad-minded of you, but in my case my baggage makes me a prime suspect in a few murders, past and present. And some would say that in Zander Taylor's case, I'm guilty."

"Not like he's a great loss to the world,"

Judson said.

"You're not taking this seriously, are you?"

"I'm taking you very, very seriously, Gwendolyn Frazier."

He tightened his grip on her face and pulled her mouth down to his. He kissed her until she wrapped herself around him once more.

A long time later, he awoke to the feel of someone shaking him gently.

"Judson," Gwen said.

"What?" He did not open his eyes.

"Judson, wake up."

The urgency in her voice brought him fully awake. He sat up swiftly and used his other vision to quarter the room, searching for the threat. Nothing of a dangerous nature presented itself.

"What's wrong?" he asked.

"Nothing." Gwen was on her knees amid the tumbled bedding. Excitement blazed in her eyes. "That's just it, nothing's wrong."

He sank back against the pillows. "I think I'm missing the point here. If nothing's wrong, why the hell are you acting like there is something wrong?"

"We both fell asleep."

"Yeah. Felt good. I haven't been sleeping too well lately and I needed the rest. Nothing like great sex to do the trick. Better than meds, that's for damn sure."

"Yes, you are missing the point. Judson, we both fell asleep. Side by side. I was dreaming and you didn't even twitch."

"I try not to twitch too often," he said. "It makes people nervous."

"This is no joke. You are the first person I have slept next to in my entire adult life who hasn't had a really bad reaction to my dream aura."

"Oh, that." He stretched his arms overhead. "Between you and me, I wasn't expecting to run screaming into the night."

She ignored that. "I was planning to send you back to your own room before I drifted off, but I fell asleep instead. So did you."

"Probably all that exercise," he explained.

"You were sleeping quite soundly."

"Yes, I was, wasn't I? Can I go back to sleep now?"

"I have a theory," she said. "It's just a theory, mind you, but there is a certain logic to it."

"I'm going to have to listen to this theory before I get to go back to sleep, aren't I?"

"Yes, you are." She was clearly having trouble containing her excitement. "I think that because you are a strong talent, yourself, you have a kind of immunity to me."

He raised a finger to silence her. "Now there is where you are wrong, Dream Eyes."

She frowned. "What do you mean?"

"I am anything but immune to you. Just the opposite."

He pulled her back into his arms and kissed her until she stopped talking.

TWENTY

Sometime later, he opened his eyes again when he felt Gwen slide out of bed. He knew she was trying to be discreet about it. Probably headed for the bathroom, he thought. But when he saw her put on the robe and lean down to pick up the map that had fallen to the floor, he realized something else was going on.

He levered himself up on his elbows. "Everything okay?"

"What?" Surprised, she glanced back at him. "Yes, sorry. Didn't mean to wake you. A few minutes ago, I woke up and decided to try the road trip dream again. I went back to the start, back here to Wilby, and I saw a pattern." She moved to the table and spread the map out across the surface. "But it was all wrong."

Her urgency got through to him. He shoved aside the covers, sat up and reached for his pants. Zipping his fly, he crossed the room to the desk.

"Tell me about the pattern and what's wrong with it," he said.

"I assumed going into the dream that this was a map of towns and places that Evelyn intended to visit for research purposes. But there are too many towns marked."

"There are only a half-dozen circled."

"Yes, but that's about four, maybe five too many. You see, Wesley operates with a tight budget. He doesn't like to pay for airfare and lodging for a scouting crew to check out the location unless it promises to be good. It's highly unlikely she would have selected six towns for the next episode of *Dead of Night*. And if she was working on a big project involving multiple locations, I think she would have talked it over with me and probably Wesley as well."

He flattened his hands on the table and examined the six towns. "You're thinking that there's a connection between these locations? Some paranormal significance?"

"No, well, not exactly, at least not in terms of legends about haunted houses or para-normal vortexes. In my dream, Evelyn told me to go back to the beginning. That was my intuition reminding me that this is the same kind of pattern that she and I uncov-ered after Zander Taylor went over the falls."

Judson's senses stirred. "The two of you were able to identify some of the locations of his previous kills. You concluded that he had targeted people who claimed to be psychic." He flipped the map over and looked at the six names that had been written there. "I need fifteen minutes on my computer."

Ten minutes later he shut down the obituary page of the newspaper he had been studying and checked off the last name on the list that Ballinger had made on the back of the map.

"That's it," he said. "Six towns, six deaths, all by natural causes, all within the past eighteen months or so. The names of the deceased match the names on the map. But if someone has started killing again with the camera, there's one big difference this time."

"What?" Gwen asked.

"None of the victims was a practicing psychic, real or fake. According to the obituaries, none of them was making his or her living by claiming paranormal talents."

"I don't know why the pattern is different, but someone is killing again, the same way Zander Taylor did — by paranormal means." Gwen drummed her fingers on the table. "Evelyn somehow stumbled onto the truth."

"The murderer realized she was tracking him so he killed her?"

"Yes, I think so."

Judson thought about it. "He took her computer and cell phone, hoping to get rid of any traces of her research that might lead the cops to him."

"He couldn't have known about the map and where it was hidden," Gwen said. "Either that or he was unable to get into the mirror engine to retrieve it. I told you, not everyone can handle the psi in that machine. But this doesn't make sense. Why the change in pattern?"

"We know that Taylor is dead," Judson reminded her. "Different killer, different pattern, different kind of prey. But there will be something that these six victims had in common, trust me. We just have to find the common thread."

"Whoever he is, he must be one of the locals here in Wilby," Gwen said. "Someone who knew about Zander and decided to emulate him. Maybe a copycat killer?"

"Maybe. In addition to the likelihood that the killer is a local, we know one other thing about him."

Gwen looked up from the map, understanding heating her eyes.

"The killer has enough talent to work the camera," she said. "We're looking for another psychic."

TWENTY-ONE

Elias Coppersmith arrived in a massive, shiny black SUV with heavily tinted windows. Gwen stood with Judson inside the lobby and watched the big vehicle glide into a vacant slot in front of the inn.

"Your brother, Sam, drives a black SUV, doesn't he?" she asked.

"Yes. Why?" Judson wasn't paying much attention to the question. He was watching the SUV.

"Just curious," she said. "Because you drive a black SUV, too. Same brand, I believe."

"Company discount," Judson said.

More likely something in the DNA of the Coppersmith men that inclined them toward large vehicles endowed with the souls of trucks, Gwen thought. Other rich guys drove flashy red Ferraris and Porsches.

From inside the inn, it was impossible to see the occupants of the vehicle, but she was mildly surprised when the passenger door opened. A big, lean, silver-haired man who could have been cast in the role of the town marshal in a classic western movie climbed out.

"That's Dad," Judson said. "He's early. Must have left Seattle at zero-dawn-thirty. Wonder who's behind the wheel? He probably picked up someone from Coppersmith Security before he left."

"Your father is so paranoid about that geode that he brought an armed escort?"

"Trust me, knowing Dad and his opinion of Hank Barrett, it's not just the escort who will be armed," Judson said.

She thought about the pistol strapped to Judson's ankle and wondered if going about armed was another Coppersmith family trait.

"I'd better go out and let him know he's got the right place," Judson said. "I'll be right back."

He crossed the lobby with a few long, easy strides, pushed open the glass door and went outside.

Gwen studied the family greeting scene through the lobby windows, firmly suppressing the faint, wistful sensation that fluttered through her. There was no big male hug exchanged between Judson and Elias, she noticed. But the bond between father and son was so strong that she could sense it even from where she stood. The power of a close-knit family, she thought. There was nothing else like it.

At that moment, the driver's-side door of the SUV opened. A lithe, elegantly slender, good-looking man with platinum-blond hair cut in a crisp, military style alighted from the cab with a dancer's grace. He was dressed head-to-toe in fashionable and very expensive black — black turtleneck, black trousers, black loafers. Gwen knew that all of the attire came with designer labels.

Delight spilled through her. She had family, too. The only difference was that her brother wasn't related by blood.

She rushed through the lobby, burst out of the doorway and flew across the parking lot.

"Nick," she called. "What are you doing here?"

Nick Sawyer grinned, showing a lot of very white teeth, and opened his arms. She threw herself into his embrace. He caught her with deft ease and swung her around in a circle. When he set her on her feet, she hugged him fiercely.

"I came to check up on you," he said. "The last time one of my sisters got mixed up with a Coppersmith, she nearly got killed. Are you okay?"

She laughed. "I'm fine."

Judson materialized at her side. He gave Nick an assessing look.

"You must be the cat burglar."

"That's antiquarian book dealer to you," Nick said, his eyes going cold.

"Right." Judson looked amused. "That would be the antiquarian book dealer who keeps the climbing gear stashed in the trunk of his car."

"Everyone should have a hobby," Nick said. "By the way, there's a suitcase in the back of the car. Abby packed some clothes for you, Gwen. She knew you hadn't planned to stay long here in Wilby. She figured that by now you'd be needing a few things."

Gwen smiled, aware of the warmth welling up inside. "That's my sister, always looking out for me, even while she's preparing for her own wedding."

TWENTY-TWO

"I'm telling you, somehow, somewhere, Hank Barrett is involved in this thing," Elias said. "He sent his son to do his dirty work. It's the only explanation that makes sense."

From where he stood at the window of Judson's room, he could see glimpses of the river through a thick stand of fir and pine. He had never been comfortable in heavily wooded terrain. Being surrounded by trees that blotted up the light and limited visibility made him uneasy. He had always preferred the wide open stretches of the desert where a man could see what was coming at him.

The four of them and the largest house cat Elias had ever seen were crowded into Gwen's small sitting room. The cat was stretched out alongside Gwen in one of the old-fashioned reading chairs. Judson lounged against the mantel. Nick was draped in the other wingback chair, methodically emptying the tray of fancy little sandwiches that sat on the small table. It had been a long drive from Seattle, and Elias had forbidden any food-related stops on pain of being left at the side of the road.

"No, Dad," Judson said. It was clear he was holding on to his patience with an effort of will. "It's not the only answer that works. In fact, it's not even the most likely answer."

Damn it, none of his offspring understood, Elias thought. He gripped the window ledge very tightly. Sure, they got that Barrett's Helicon Stone was serious competition. They had grown up in the hard rock business and they expected a degree of ruthlessness from a tough competitor. But they did not fully comprehend the depth of the personal hostility toward Coppersmith, Inc., that Barrett had been nursing for decades. They had not had to confront the man face-to-face and listen to him vow to destroy everything that Elias had built, everything he held dear. Nor did Judson, Sam and Emma entirely believe him when he warned them that Barrett had passed his grudge on down the line to his son, Gideon.

But, then, they did not know the whole story, Elias reminded himself. Only Willow did and she had kept his secrets.

"What makes you so sure Barrett is not involved?" he asked.

"I told you my logic," Judson said evenly. "If Gideon had gone after the stone, he would have been a lot more subtle about it, and it's a good bet that he would have been successful. But we've got the geode."

Elias grunted.

Judson's coldly determined expression was all too familiar, Elias thought. Every time he complained to Willow that none of his three offspring seemed interested in taking over the helm of Coppersmith, Inc., she reminded him that each of them had inherited not only his savvy intelligence and his feel for rocks and crystals but also his titanium-strong, mile-wide stubborn streak. *None of them could work with you for more than five minutes,* Willow always said. *You will have to step down before one of them will step up to take your place.*

But he couldn't step down, Elias thought. Not yet, not until he had made certain that Coppersmith, Inc., and his family were safe from Hank Barrett. *Should have gotten rid of him the old-fashioned way all those years ago and buried him out in the desert. No one would have found the body, and I wouldn't be dealing with this problem today.*

But a neat, tidy solution had been impossible. Willow had forbidden it. And when you got right down to it, how did you go about killing a man who had saved your ass more than once in the middle of a firefight and whose ass you had saved, in turn? Some lines could not be crossed. There was a rule about it somewhere.

"You can't know for sure that Barrett's not involved," he insisted.

But his own logic was flawed and he knew it. Judson was right. Wilby was a small town. If Gideon Barrett had come here to get the stone, he would have found it and taken it.

Gwen spoke up from her chair.

"I don't know anything more about the Barretts or Helicon Stone than what Judson has told me," she said, "but I do know a considerable amount about Evelyn Ballinger and the circumstances here in Wilby. I agree with Judson. I very much doubt that Evelyn was murdered by outsiders. This was local and it was personal."

"Yeah?" Elias rounded on her. He was aware that he was in what Willow called his bristling mode, but that was too damn bad. The situation was serious. "And just how would you know that, Ms. Frazier? Are you a trained investigator?"

"No, but I'm capable of applying common sense to a problem," Gwen said coolly.

"I find that approach so much more helpful than allowing an obsession with an old grudge to mess up my thinking."

Elias raised his brows. *Didn't see that coming,* he thought. He regarded Gwen with fresh interest and some curiosity. Very few people outside his family had the nerve to put him in his place. Willow told him that he intimidated most folks. That was fine with him. Intimidation was useful.

But Gwen Frazier looked anything but intimidated. She sat there in the big reading chair, one leg crossed over the other, radiating a calm poise that matched the *You don't scare me* message in her eyes.

He caught the brief, amused smile that edged Judson's mouth. That startled him even more than discovering that Gwen had claws. Everyone in the family knew that Judson hadn't smiled much since he had returned from the island job. He had, in fact, been ducking them all, hiding out in a little town on the Oregon coast, licking his wounds.

Elias understood. A man needed time to recover from betrayal and a close brush with death. He was pretty sure that the explosion inside the cave had done some unseen damage, as well. The family had agreed to give Judson some space. But now it was starting to look like Gwen Frazier and a small-time murder investigation were exactly what the doctor should have ordered.

Nick let out a crack of laughter and reached for the last sandwich.

"Welcome to my world," he said to Gwen. He popped the dainty sandwich into his mouth and brushed crumbs from his hands. "I had to listen to Wyatt Earp, here, carry on about those badass Barretts the whole trip down from Seattle. It gets old."

Judson looked at him. "You're bored after a few hours of listening to him obsess about Hank Barrett and son? Try listening to him harp on the subject your entire life. When we were growing up, Mom had to institute a No Barrett rule at the dinner table and on family vacations."

"No kidding?" Nick said with what appeared to be an utter lack of interest. "I can sure see how having your old man lecture you about your future business competition might ruin a trip to Disneyland, all right. Bummer."

But his air of monumental unconcern was belied by the look that he exchanged with Gwen. Their eyes met for no more than an instant, but Elias was pretty sure he could read the message that had passed between them. If these two had any memories of conversations around the family dinner table or vacations to Disneyland, they were not good ones.

"Speaking of business," Elias said, "let's get back to it." He beetled his brows at Judson. "Tell me what you found in Ballinger's house."

"It had the feel of a planned hit," Judson said. "I think the murder was done to silence a potential witness, someone who had discovered something the killer did not want her to know."

"Huh." Elias turned back to the window. "Got to admit killing an unarmed woman doesn't sound like Barrett. But I'm telling you that geode is a damn good motive for murder."

"I know," Judson said. "But there are others. Gwen and I are looking into the possibility that Ballinger's death is linked to something that happened here in Wilby a couple of years ago."

Gwen and I are looking.

Elias studied his son intently for a few beats. What was going on here? If there was a term that could be used to describe Judson's working style, that term was *lone wolf.* The trait had manifested itself early on. It had been clear from the start that of his three children Judson was the least likely to take over the family empire. Judson almost always worked alone.

Now it was *Gwen and I are looking into the possibility.*

It dawned on Elias that he had been so obsessed with the theory that Hank Barrett was involved in whatever was going down in Wilby that he hadn't been paying nearly as much attention as he should have to the energy that was crackling in the air between Judson and Gwen Frazier.

He glanced toward the open door that connected the two rooms. The sense of intimacy in the space was unmistakable.

Well, well, well, so that's how it is, he thought. Nothing like a woman to take a man's mind off a few bad memories. But he'd never been aware of this kind of intimate heat between Judson and any of his other lady friends. Gwen was different from the other women who had come and gone in Judson's life. It was as if she not only understood the dark side of Judson's moody, driven nature but also was okay with it.

"Maybe I am a little too fixated on the Barretts," he conceded. He looked at the strongbox. "We've got the geode. That's the important thing."

"It may be the most important thing to

you," Gwen said very politely. "Personally, I've got other priorities. I hired Judson to find out who murdered my friend, not to recover some dumb rock."

Elias gave her what he thought of as his most winning smile, the one he used to close multimillion-dollar deals around the world. "Tell you what, ma'am, I'll take my dumb rock and go back to Copper Beach with the cat burglar."

"Antiquarian book dealer," Nick said without inflection.

Elias ignored him to focus on Gwen, who did not seem overly impressed with his smile. "You and Judson can poke around here in Wilby and see what answers you turn up. How's that?"

"That sounds like an excellent plan," Gwen said. "When, exactly, do you intend to leave?"

Her smile was as sweet as a caramel-covered apple — the poisoned variety. Elias could tell that Judson was having trouble suppressing a laugh. It had been a while since Judson had laughed.

"We're leaving now," Elias said. He looked at the steel strongbox. "The sooner that stone gets into the vault at Copper Beach, the better."

Judson straightened away from the mantel.

"One more thing before you two take off." He looked at Nick. "Sawyer, are you as good at the urban rock climbing business as Gwen says you are?"

Elias snorted. "Urban rock climbing? That's a nice name for his line of work."

"I'm good," Nick said. There was no hint of false modesty in the words, just a statement of fact. He was starting to look intrigued. "Gwen and Abby tell me I've got a talent for it. Why?"

"I've got a job for you," Judson said. "It involves some computer work, some travel and probably a little climbing and a few locks."

"That pretty much describes my skill set," Nick said.

Gwen's eyes lit up with enthusiasm. "That's a brilliant idea, Judson."

Elias scowled, aware that he was losing the thread of the conversation. "What's this so-called brilliant idea?"

Judson looked at him. "Gwen and I need information concerning the circumstances surrounding the deaths of half a dozen people who died in various towns in the past eighteen months. We need to know how they're connected. That kind of research takes time, and we don't have a lot to spare. We can use some assistance."

"What's important about the dead people?" Nick asked.

"If we're right, they were all murdered by paranormal means," Gwen said. "We want to find out if there is a pattern, something that would make it clear that they were all killed by the same person."

Nick was definitely intrigued now. "You think there might be a connection between the dead people and what happened here in Wilby?"

"What we think," Gwen said deliberately, "is that when Zander Taylor went over the falls, he did not take the camera with him. In the past year and a half, at least six more people have died in a way that is strikingly similar to the way in which Taylor's victims were murdered."

"What do you want me to do?" Nick said.

"At the moment, all we have are names of six people who are dead,"

Judson said. "I want you to start looking into the deaths. Check out the scenes; talk to neighbors; go online. Whatever it takes. Like Gwen said, we're looking for a pattern."

"Give me what you've got," Nick said. "I'll see what I can do." He looked around. "Are there any more sandwiches?"

TWENTY-THREE

Elias stood with Judson near the front of the SUV. The rear cargo door of the vehicle was open. Nick and Gwen were back there, talking quietly, as the cat burglar secured the steel box containing the geode.

Elias cleared his throat and turned to Judson. "Your mother is going to want a report."

"Tell Mom I'm doing fine," Judson said. He was watching Gwen.

"I'll do that." Elias groped for another way to get the information Willow would demand from him. "So, you and Gwen."

Judson raised his brows. "What about me and Gwen?"

Elias felt himself turning red. He was no good at this sort of conversation. In his opinion, there were excellent reasons why someone had invented the words *personal* and *private.* But Willow was worried, and he would do anything for Willow, including embarrass himself.

"Looks like the two of you hit it off pretty good," he said, going for casual.

"Gwen is . . . different," Judson said.

"Yep, I can see that. I like her. She's got claws. That's a fine thing in a woman."

"Oh, yeah," Judson said. His mouth kicked up a little at the corner.

"About that mess on the island a while back —"

"What about it?"

"Sometimes things just go south, son. Nothin' you can do about it. You just got to walk away from a situation that can't be fixed."

Judson's eyes narrowed. He stopped smiling. "I know that, Dad."

"Believe me, I understand exactly how it feels when a man you think you can trust turns out to be a genuine diamondback rattler. It happens. You've got to let it go and move on."

Judson almost smiled again. "The way you've moved on past your issues with Hank Barrett?"

"Barrett's different."

"Yeah? How?"

"Mainly because the bastard's still alive and kickin'. But in your case, Joe Spalding is dead and good riddance."

"I agree with you." Judson stopped talking.

Elias waited, not sure how to proceed. So much for the fatherly pep talk.

Judson turned his attention back to Gwen. "I'm not staying awake at night wondering why it took me so long to figure out that Spalding had become one of the bad guys."

"Good," Elias said. "That's good." He paused. "Then why the hell are you having trouble sleeping?"

"You ever had the feeling that you saw something important, something you really need to remember?"

Elias thought about it. "Not exactly, but I know what you mean. Where did you see this thing that you can't remember?"

"First time I saw it was that day it all went to hell on the island."

Elias squinted at him. "The *first* time?"

"Now I think I see it in my dreams."

"I hear Gwen is good when it comes to figuring out dreams," Elias said.

"She says I'd have to let her walk through my dreams before she could take a crack at trying to analyze them. The process, I think, is a form of hypnosis."

Elias squinted at Gwen. She was animated and sparkling in the sunlight as she chatted with Nick.

"Strikes me that a man would have to be absolutely sure he could trust a woman all the way to hell and back before he let her put him into a trance," Elias said.

"Yes," Judson said. "But that's not the hardest part."

"What is the hardest part?"

"Gwen sees herself as a kind of healer," Judson said.

Now, at last, I understand, Elias thought. "You don't want her to see you as a man who might need a nurse."

"No," Judson said.

"Seems to me," Elias said, "that a man who wants respect from a woman needs to show the lady that he respects her talents and abilities in return."

"I know it's none of my business, but I couldn't help but notice that the door between your room and Coppersmith's was unlocked from both sides," Nick said. "Would that be for, ah, security purposes?"

"It would." Gwen handed Nick the box lunch that she had asked the inn's cook to prepare. "And you're right, it's none of your business. Here you go, road food and coffee."

"Thanks." Nick took the sack from her. "I appreciate this. I'll be lucky if Wyatt Earp allows a pit stop along the way. For sure, there won't be any restaurant breaks. The old man is obsessed with this damn rock."

"Thanks for helping us check out the names on that list we gave you," Gwen said.

"Yeah, sure, no problem," Nick said. "The job sounds interesting. Something different."

"Don't tell me you're getting bored with the hot books market. You've made a lot of money in that line."

To her surprise, Nick shrugged. "The money's good, but to tell you the truth, I'm not all that interested in the books or the wack-jobs who collect them. If you and Abby hadn't convinced me to go into the business, I probably would have found another career."

Gwen smiled. "International jewel thief?"

"We've all got a talent."

"Given the nature of your talent, Abby and I thought you were better suited to the book business."

Nick grinned. "You were just looking after me, trying to keep your brother out of jail."

"That, too. Don't get me wrong — it was wonderful to see you, Nick — but how in the world did you and Mr. Coppersmith end up driving down here together?"

"Abby introduced us yesterday when I

went to the island to get my marching orders."

"What marching orders?"

"Didn't Abby tell you? No, she probably hasn't had a chance. She asked me to walk her down the aisle."

Gwen smiled. "Of course. No surprise there. You're her brother."

"Well, technically speaking, she does have a father."

"Even if she had asked him to walk her down the aisle, I think the odds are good that he would have declined at the last minute due to some schedule conflict. I hear his latest divorce is not going well. Evidently, the most recent Mrs. Radwell is making things as difficult as possible, and word has it that the future Mrs. Radwell is getting impatient."

Of the three of them, Abby was the only one who belonged to what — from the outside — passed for a real family. But appearances were deceiving, Gwen thought. Abby's father, Dr. Brandon C. Radwell, was notoriously unreliable. *Two-faced* was another term that came to mind. Radwell was the author of the bestselling *Families by Choice: A Guide to Creating the Modern Blended Family.* The best that could be said about him, in Gwen's and Nick's opinion, was that the man practiced what he preached. Radwell was currently in the process of extricating himself from his third marriage. Wife Number Four was waiting in the wings. In the process of making and breaking families, Radwell had left Abby with a step brother and two half sisters. In spite of the charming family portrait on the back of Radwell's book, Abby was not close to anyone in her legal family.

Gwen glanced toward the front of the SUV where Judson and his father were still deep in a quiet conversation. "One thing's for sure, Abby is marrying into a real family. The Coppersmiths have wrapped themselves around her. She's one of them now."

Nick nodded. "Yeah, they'll take good care of her."

"And you do look fantastic in a tux."

"Sure." Nick winked. "But the really good news is that Girard, the wedding planner, is smokin' hot."

Gwen laughed. At the other end of the SUV, Judson and Elias broke off their conversation to look at her. Judson smiled as if seeing her laugh pleased him. Elias squinted a little against the sun and nodded once, to himself, as if whatever he had seen satisfied him. Then he took out a set of keys and tossed them to Nick.

"Time to hit the road, son," Elias said. He yanked open the passenger-side door. "You drive. I'll ride shotgun."

Nick looked at Gwen. "The scary thing is that he means that part about the shotgun."

Gwen stood with Judson and watched the big SUV pull out of the inn parking lot. She waved one last time to Nick and then turned to go back into the lobby.

"What's next on our agenda?" she asked.

"Next, we start talking to the people who were most closely acquainted with Evelyn," Judson said. "Got some names?"

"Not a lot, but there is one person who is at the top of the list. Louise Fuller. I'm not saying she and Evelyn were close, because Louise wasn't close to anyone. But they worked together on the mirrors, and in a weird sort of way, I think they understood each other. Evelyn was probably the only person in town who realized that Louise had some true paranormal talent. Everyone else thinks she's crazy."

"In that case, we'll start with Fuller."

Judson pushed open the glass door. Gwen went past him into the lobby. Riley Duncan looked at her across the front desk.

"The boss wants to talk to you, Miss Frazier," he said. "It's about your cat."

Gwen stopped. "What now?"

Trisha emerged from the office, an apologetic expression on her face.

"I'm sorry, Gwen," she said. "But my housekeeper reports that Max has taken to clawing the drapes and the bedding while you're out."

"Oh, dear, I didn't realize that," Gwen said. "By all means put the damage on my bill. I'll start putting Max into his carrier when I'm out of the room. He's not going to like that, but if he's destroying the furniture —"

Trisha sighed. "I'm afraid that won't work. Sara says she will not go in there again as long there is a cat in the room. She's allergic. You'll have to take Max with you when you go out."

TWENTY-FOUR

The eerie music of the wind chimes rattled Gwen's senses and sent slivers of ice across the back of her neck. She stood beside the open door of the SUV and looked at Louise Fuller's small house.

The wind was kicking up in advance of the incoming storm. The sharp breeze stirred the dozens of crystal-and-metal sculptures suspended from the porch roof. The ghostly notes echoed all the way across the spectrum. Gwen glanced at Judson, who had just gotten out from behind the wheel. She knew that he was picking up the same vibes.

In the rear seat of the SUV, Max crouched in his carrier and lashed his tail, making it clear that he was not a happy camper.

"I see what you mean about the wind chimes," Judson said. He studied the weather-beaten old Victorian. "Weird."

"I told you, Evelyn always said that Louise has a paranormal sensitivity for tuning crystal and glass."

She started to close the door of the vehicle, but Max yowled and flattened his ears. Gwen looked at him through the space between the two front seats.

"It's your own fault that you had to go into the carrier and come with us," she reminded him. "You were scaring the house-keeper."

Max bared his fangs.

"It's okay, take it easy." Gwen softened her tone. "We're not going to abandon you. We'll be back in a few minutes."

The chimes clashed and tinkled on the rising currents of air. Max meowed, plaintively this time. He clawed at the mesh door of the carrier.

"I think I'd better bring him with us," Gwen said. "He seems very agitated."

"He doesn't like being stuffed into that carrier," Judson said. "I don't blame him."

She opened the rear door of the vehicle and hauled out the heavy carrier with both hands.

"I think he's putting on weight," she said.

Judson came around the front of the vehicle. "Here, I'll take the carrier."

He grasped the handle. Max did not look any happier, but he stopped complaining.

They started toward the front door.

"I'll warn you before we go inside — assuming Louise invites us inside, which is not a sure thing — the indoor chimes are even stranger than the ones hanging from the porch roof," Gwen said. "They pretty much guarantee that none of Louise's visitors hangs around long."

"Was Louise one of the subjects in Ballinger's study?" Judson asked.

"No. Evelyn asked her to participate, but Louise refused. All she cares about are her chimes. Be prepared for her to refuse to talk to us." Gwen paused. "Two years ago, she accused me of being a witch like her."

Judson's eyes went cold. "I'm assuming that wasn't intended as a compliment?"

"I'm not sure what she meant, to be honest. That's the thing about Louise. She lives in her own world and interprets reality through her own crystal ball, so to speak. I don't think she intended to insult me. In her own way she was trying to warn me."

"Did she say why you needed to be careful?"

Gwen hunched her shoulders a little against the wind and the unnerving music of the outdoor chimes.

"Something about the demon," she said. "I asked her for an explanation, but she wouldn't give me one."

"Sounds like this is going to be a complicated interview."

"It won't be straightforward, that's for sure."

They went up the front steps. Judson stopped to examine one of the musical sculptures more closely. It was a large piece, consisting of several thin crystals of varying sizes and shapes. Each was wrapped in a strip of silvery metal.

"This is incredible," he said. "At least some of the sound is coming from the paranormal end of the spectrum. I can hear it with all my senses."

"Evelyn's theory was that the wavelengths of music move through both the normal and the paranormal zones," Gwen said. "That's why it has the ability to affect us so profoundly on the emotional level. Most people, including those with no obvious paranormal ability, respond to music on the psychic level."

"You know, I think one of these sculptures might make a great wedding gift for Sam and Abby."

"If you want to give them one of Louise's sculptures, you'll have to buy it in a local shop. Louise makes her living creating and selling what she calls her tourist chimes.

But her personal wind chimes are different. They're not for sale. She calls them wards."

Judson glanced at her, frowning. "As in magical wards? The kind used to ward off demons?"

"I think that's what she means, yes. She worries a lot about demons. That's why she surrounds the house with the wind chimes."

Judson reached out to catch hold of one of the chimes. "I wonder what kind of alloy she used to wrap these crystals."

"I wouldn't touch that if I were you," Gwen said quickly.

But it was too late. Judson had already snagged one of the metal strips between his fingers.

Max hissed.

"Damn." Judson released the metal chime as if it were red-hot, wincing. "I see what you mean. That had a lot in common with touching a live electrical wire." He surveyed the sculpture more closely, careful not to make physical contact. "But the shock was to my psychic senses."

"The one time I tried it, I got a bit of a jolt, too."

He looked down the long row of chime sculptures clashing and tinkling in the charged air of the fast-approaching storm. "Do they all have that effect on the senses?"

"I don't know," Gwen said. "After the first go-round, I decided not to carry out any more experiments. But my guess would be that the chimes out here are all a little hot. And I'd advise you to be very, very careful inside because I'm pretty sure those are even hotter."

"I wonder how she does it?"

"I asked her that once." Gwen rapped on the front door. "She said something about tuning the frequencies of the stones and a lot of other stuff I didn't quite understand."

"Sam is very interested in techniques for tuning paranormal crystals. I wonder if Louise would be willing . . . Huh."

She turned to look at Judson over her shoulder. "What?"

She realized he was looking down at his ring. The amber-gold crystal was glowing ever so faintly.

"My ring," he said. He looked grim. "I think it's responding to the chimes."

"Or maybe it's picking up on your psychic response to the music."

"Maybe."

Max pawed the door of the carrier, meowing softly.

Gwen turned back to the door and knocked again, more forcefully this time. No one responded.

Judson abruptly set the cat carrier down on the porch.

"Get away from the door, Gwen," he ordered.

She did not argue. Now she, too, could sense the darker currents swirling beneath the exotic energy of the chimes. The music of the sculptures had initially masked some of the violent energy that was seeping out of the house.

"Oh, damn." Her hand froze in mid-rap. She backed away. "Not again. This can't be happening."

Judson was already at the door. The gun had materialized in his hand as if by magic.

He opened the screen door and tried the doorknob. It turned easily. Gwen knew that was not right. Louise always kept her doors locked.

When he opened the door, the draft stirred the chimes in the hallway. The spectral music sounded like the wailing of doomed souls.

There was a sudden clattering somewhere deep inside the house. It was followed by the thud-thud-thud of running footsteps.

"That's not Louise," Gwen said. "She had severe arthritis. She could never move that fast."

"Stay here," Judson said.

He raced down the hall.

Max snarled and began attacking the door of the carrier with his claws and teeth. The spitting, hissing and scratching grew increasingly violent.

"Stop that, Max," Gwen said. "Please."

The door of the carrier flew open. Max shot out. He dashed across the porch and into the house.

Before Gwen could react, she heard a familiar voice screaming in panic somewhere inside the house.

"Let me go, let me go," Nicole Hudson shouted. "Please, I swear I won't tell anyone —"

"Take it easy." Judson's voice echoed along a hallway. "No one's going to hurt you."

To Gwen's surprise, Nicole obeyed. At least she stopped the hysterical shrieking and subsided, instead, into jerky, frightened sobs.

"Please don't hurt me," she whimpered. "I won't tell Chief Oxley."

"Tell him what?" Judson asked.

"About what I saw in the basement," Nicole whispered. "Please."

"Let's go see what it is you're not going to tell anyone about," Judson said. He raised his voice. "Come on in, Gwen."

Gwen moved through the doorway. She groped for the hall light switch and found it. But when she flipped it, nothing happened.

Judson appeared at the end of the hall. The gun was no longer in sight. He had a firm grip on Nicole's arm.

"I just tried the switch at the other end of the hall," Judson said. "The power is out. Looks like someone got to the electrical panel."

"It wasn't me," Nicole whimpered.

"What's going on?" Gwen said. But she knew.

"Where's the body?" Judson asked Nicole.

"Downstairs in the basement," Nicole said. She gave him a pleading look. "Someone killed Louise."

"What makes you think she was murdered?" Gwen asked quietly. "Was there blood?"

"I don't know. I didn't go down there."

"But you're sure she's dead?" Gwen asked.

"I think so. She died the way the others did." Nicole looked at Gwen with an expression of veiled horror and then looked away very quickly. "Just like the others. Everyone will think it was a heart attack or that she tripped on the basement stairs. Or something. No one will be able to prove that it was murder."

"Let's go take a look," Judson said.

"Please, I don't want to go down there," Nicole whispered.

"Where are the basement stairs?" Judson asked.

"That way," Nicole muttered. She gestured toward a hall.

Judson steered her in the direction that she had indicated. Gwen followed. Max appeared at her feet, crowding close. His ears were flat and his tail was high.

"There you are," Gwen said quietly. "I wondered where you went."

They halted in front of an open door midway along the hall. Concrete steps descended into an inky darkness split by a sharp beam of bright light that angled across the concrete floor.

"A flashlight," Judson said. "She took it with her when she went downstairs to check the electrical panel."

Max wove a restless path between Gwen's legs and muttered urgently in the mysterious language of felines. The sepulchral music of the sculptures that hung from the ceiling seemed to grow louder. *Should have closed the front door,* Gwen thought. The draft was getting stronger.

Nicole froze at the top of the steps. "I

don't want to go down."

"We're all going down together," Judson said. "And remind me to ask you later what the hell you were doing here in the first place."

Nicole started reluctantly down the steps. "I just wanted to talk to her."

"Did you bring your father's old hunting rifle along for the chat?" Judson asked."

"No, I swear, I didn't bring it." Nicole stopped, gripped the railing and stared back at him. "I know what you're thinking. Oxley came by the shop. He said you thought I took a shot at you out at the old lodge yesterday, but that wasn't me. He asked me to show him Dad's old rifle but I couldn't find it. Someone stole it."

"Yeah?" Judson made it clear he didn't believe a word Nicole was saying. "When did that happen?"

"How should I know?" Nicole wailed. "I keep it in my grandmother's cedar chest. I haven't had any reason to open that chest in months."

"You're lying," Judson said. "We can go over the details later."

Halfway down the steps, another unsettling shiver of awareness stirred Gwen's senses. She realized that Max was no longer talking to her. She glanced back and saw that the cat was not following her down into the basement. She could see him silhouetted in the doorway. He had gone very still, very alert, at the top of the steps. But he was not watching her and the others. His attention was fixed on something only he could see.

The dark music of the chimes was growing more intense, almost painful. The wind keened through the old house. The shadows in the hallway lengthened as the storm gathered outside.

The light shifted abruptly down below in the basement. Startled, Gwen turned quickly and saw that Judson had picked up the flashlight. She made herself take a deep, steadying breath.

Judson played the light beam across the body. Louise was sprawled faceup on the cold concrete. The ropes of her long gray braids were tumbled around her head. She had always been thin, but in death she appeared gaunt, almost skeletal. Her sharp features were so starkly etched that it was as if her skin had been drawn tight over her skull.

The violent energy pooling in the room left no doubt as to the cause of death. She knew from the way Judson was studying the body that he was picking up the same vibes and probably a lot more information than she could.

"Poor Louise," Gwen whispered.

"This was murder," Judson said.

Nicole cringed and turned away from the body. "You can't blame this on me."

Judson ignored her to sweep the beam of the flashlight around the small space. The light raked across crates and boxes filled with crystals, mirrors, and the metals that Louise used in her sculptures.

Judson shifted the light again, aiming in another direction. "The electrical panel is over there on that wall. But she was here, near this crate when she died. If she came downstairs to check the panel, why did she end up over here?"

The light danced across a handful of palm-sized crystals in the shape of teardrops that lay on the floor near the body. Gwen followed the ray of light and was not surprised when a ghost appeared in one of the crystals.

"I knew you would get here sooner or later," the specter said. "Took you long enough."

Judson moved the light past the crystal. The ghostly image disappeared.

"Wait," Gwen said. "Move the light back to those crystals on the floor."

Judson did not ask any questions. He

swept the beam back to the stones.

"See a ghost?" he asked matter-of-factly.

"Yes." Gwen went toward the crystals.

"Ghost?" Nicole yelped, beyond terrified now. "You two are crazier than the old witch was."

Gwen did not bother to respond to that. Neither did Judson. He kept the beam of light aimed at the crystals

Gwen crouched down to take a closer look. The ghost snorted in disgust.

"So much for that psychic talent of yours," the ghost said. "What good does it do you? You're always too late. Now you'll have to live with the knowledge that you couldn't save me from the demon, just like you couldn't save Evelyn."

"Don't start with me," Gwen said. "You're the one who claimed to be a witch. Shouldn't you have seen this coming? You knew I was in town. You could have picked up the phone. Except you don't have a phone, do you? Or anything else in the way of technology."

"Oh, shit," Nicole whispered. "Does she really think she's talking to Louise's ghost?"

"Something like that," Judson said. He kept the flashlight aimed at the crystals. "Keep quiet."

"You want me to shut up?" Nicole was

incensed. "She's the one talking to a dead woman's ghost."

"You think that makes her weird?" Judson said. "You're the one who had an affair with a serial killer."

"What?" Nicole gasped. "No, no, that's not right. It can't be right. Zander couldn't have been the killer. Gwen's the one who murdered those people two years ago and now Evelyn and Louise."

"Quiet, both of you," Gwen said. "I need to concentrate. What were you doing here, Louise?"

"I knew all about your little problem with seeing ghosts at crime scenes, remember," the ghost said.

"I remember," Gwen said.

"Obviously, I came down here to see what was wrong with the electrical panel, but then the demon appeared. I knew that he had come to kill me. I was about to be murdered. I did my best to leave you a message."

"You managed to open this box of crystals before you died," Gwen said, looking the scene over.

"The demon didn't understand that I was trying to leave a message for you."

"Just like Evelyn did with the photo." Gwen studied the scene, thinking. "Very few people know about my thing with ghosts."

"No, you've kept that quiet all of your life, haven't you?" the vision said.

"It's awkward."

"Tell me about it. I see demons, remember? At least I used to see them."

Gwen opened her senses a little further, deepening the trance as she sought to see the unseen. "Tell me something I don't already know."

"I would if I could, but you know it doesn't work that way. All I can do is lay a heavy guilt trip on you so that you'll feel compelled to find the person who did this," the ghost said.

"The first step is to figure out why someone would want to kill you."

"Witches have never been popular, but we have our uses. Evelyn had need of my talents, remember?"

"How were you involved in this thing?" Gwen asked.

"Obviously, I knew something that Evelyn knew. After the demon got rid of her, he had to get rid of me, as well."

"But why now?"

A violent series of hellish musical chords crashed through house. The explosion of wild notes charged the atmosphere with a fierce, painful energy. At the top of the stairs, Max screeched.

The dream-trance shattered, Gwen whirled around.

"Max," she said.

The big cat was silhouetted against an ambient glow of ultra-light energy. His back was arched, his tail rigid. He snarled at something that could not be seen from the basement.

Nicole shrieked.

"What's happening?" she yelped.

Gwen grabbed her shoulder. "Hush," she whispered. She used a little energy to drive home the message.

Nicole stopped the ear splitting scream, but she started to shake uncontrollably. "There's something here in this house, isn't there? It's going to kill us just like it killed Louise."

Judson was at the top of the stairs, flattened against the wall. He looked down the hallway in the same direction that Max was staring.

"There's no one in the house," he said. "But there's too much energy building in the atmosphere. We're getting out of here now."

Gwen gave Nicole a firm push toward the stairs. "Go."

Nicole rushed up the steps. Gwen followed.

The ghostly music of the clashing chimes howled and shrieked through the house, penetrating the very walls. The floorboards shuddered under Gwen's feet.

Judson led the way back toward the front door. For the first time, Gwen noticed that his ring was hot.

"What's going on?" she asked.

"I'm not sure," he said. "But these damn wind chimes are churning up some serious energy. It feels like the music has reached a critical point and now the currents are oscillating out of control."

Nicole reached the top of the stairs. "I don't understand. The music is horrible, but how could it be dangerous?"

"I don't think any of us wants to hang around to find out," Judson said. He looked at Gwen. "You two go first. Head for the car and do not stop running until you're both inside. Got that?"

"Yes," Gwen said.

Nicole was hysterical now. Gwen half dragged, half pushed her through the house. Max stayed close, so close that Gwen was afraid she or Nicole would trip over him. That was the last thing they needed.

The clashing and clanging and rattling of

the chimes grew more wildly discordant. The sense of rising energy was thick in the air.

The chimes rose to a senses-shocking crescendo just as they reached the living room. A paranormal storm exploded around them. The raging currents of fiery music crashed like powerful waves, churning the atmosphere.

Instinctively, Gwen fought the onslaught by heightening her talent. It worked to some degree, shielding her senses from the worst of the energy, but she knew she could not keep up such a high level of counterforce for long.

Nicole gave a choked scream and fainted. The suddenness of her collapse caused Gwen to lose her grip on the other woman. Nicole crumpled to the floor in an untidy heap. Max screeched.

The path to the front door was blocked by a cascade of searing energy.

Judson reached up and grabbed the nearest sculpture suspended from the ceiling. Gwen saw the shudder that went through him when he made physical contact with the dancing wind chimes. He gritted his teeth against what she knew had to be a sharp jolt to his senses. He yanked the chimes from the hook and smashed the device on the floor.

The green crystals, each framed in a strip of dark metal, clattered and thrashed and then fell silent. But the dark music in the house grew louder and more ferocious. The paranormal flames flared higher.

"So much for that tactic," Judson said. "The energy storm is blocking every route out of the house. We're going to have to run through it."

"I'm not sure that's possible." Gwen looked down at Nicole. "I think we might lose consciousness like she did."

"We've got a better chance of getting out of here if we maintain physical contact," Judson said.

She wanted to ask him why he believed that to be true but concluded that it was not the best time to discuss his theory of para-physics. They had no choice but to run the experiment. Neither of them would be able to sustain much more of the assault on their senses.

"All right," she said. "Plan B it is."

She reached down to grasp one of Nicole's wrists. Judson grabbed the other.

"Whatever you do, don't let go," Judson said.

Max hissed.

Judson scooped him up into the crook of

his arm. To Gwen's amazement the dazed cat did not attempt to scratch or claw his way to freedom.

The music rose and fell in nerve-shattering waves as if the sculptures were engaged in some demonic orchestral battle. The energy was growing hotter and more intense by the second.

But now there was another kind of fire igniting the atmosphere of the small space around the four of them. Gwen realized that the fresh tide of energy came from the stone in Judson's ring. It glowed like a miniature sun.

The countercurrent of psi flooded the atmosphere. The chimes trembled and shook violently in response. Gwen heard glass and crystal fracture.

In the next instant, the terrible music was suddenly muted. Gwen could still hear the chimes, but it was as if the sound was coming from another room or even another dimension. The paranormal firewall blocking the path to the door receded. The relief was almost overwhelming.

"I can dampen the wavelengths in a narrow space around us," Judson said. "But not for long. Let's go."

Together they hauled Nicole toward the front door. The amber ring burned with astonishing energy. Gwen sensed the raw power that Judson was controlling and knew that such an extraordinary expenditure of psychic power would exact a cost later. At the very least, Judson would be exhausted.

They made it through the door. Gwen grabbed the cat carrier when they dashed across the porch, and then they were out in the driving rainstorm. The explosion came seconds later. The currents of paranormal energy generated by the chimes swept outward like tentacles seeking to draw the intended prey back into the house.

There was a low, heavy *whoosh* followed by a great roar. Gwen looked over her shoulder and saw that the house was on fire.

Judson turned his head to look. "Damn it to hell and back. There goes whatever evidence the killer might have left. Fire usually destroys most traces of psi."

"I don't understand." Gwen stared at the blaze, her heart pounding. "There was no fire, just a lot of paranormal energy. How could it explode like that?"

"As Dad discovered one day forty years ago at the Phoenix Mine, if you get enough psi burning in a confined space, it can explode across the spectrum into the normal range." Judson dropped Nicole's wrist and unclipped his cell phone. "Oxley is not going to like this."

"How are we going to explain it to him?"

"No problem," Judson said.

Gwen blinked. "Really?"

Judson's mouth twisted humorlessly. "The thing about paranormal events is that if you think about it, you can usually come up with a perfectly logical, perfectly normal explanation."

"Is that so?"

"In my experience," he said, punching in the emergency number, "no one ever wants the truth, anyway."

TWENTY-FIVE

"A gas explosion," Gwen said. She smiled, coolly appreciative. "You know, that actually sounded like a very plausible explanation."

"Thanks," Judson said. For some reason — probably because he was still in the post-burn buzz — he liked that she was impressed with how smoothly he had pulled a rabbit out of a hat for Oxley. "Got to admit, I've had practice."

She glanced at him, curiosity shadowing her eyes. "In your consulting work for that government agency you mentioned?"

"Government agencies are really good when it comes to cover-ups. It's an art form. I learned a lot working for Joe Spalding."

"The director of the agency?"

"Yes."

"Abby mentioned that the agency — your client, I believe — was closed down due to funding cuts?" Gwen said.

"Funding is always a problem with government agencies."

"Did Spalding become a lobbyist? That's what usually happens, isn't it? Those guys always land on their feet."

"Spalding did not land on his feet. Spalding is dead."

"Ah." Gwen fell silent.

He drank some wine and lowered the glass, aware of the exhaustion that was settling into his bones. They were sitting in front of the fireplace in Gwen's little parlor, their feet propped on the needlepoint hassock. There was a bottle of generic red from the Wilby General Store and the remains of a takeout pizza on the table between them.

The bio-cocktail of adrenaline and psi that always followed a heavy drain on the psychic senses was still washing through him. He was edgy and restless. What he really needed was some fast, over heated sex with Gwen, but it wouldn't be chivalrous to suggest it, given what she had been through today. Instead, he was using alcohol to bring him self down harder and faster. Soon he would crash. Maybe tonight he would not dream.

Max was crouched on the windowsill, staring out into the night. Gwen said he looked depressed, but in Judson's opinion the cat looked ready for revenge.

I'm with you, cat, Judson thought.

"I wonder if Nicole will remember anything about what happened," Gwen said.

Judson rested his head against the back of the chair. Nicole had regained consciousness just as the first fire truck arrived. The medics had treated her and concluded that she did not need to go to the emergency room. One of Oxley's officers had driven her home.

"Probably not much," he said. "Loss of consciousness, regardless of the reason, usually results in some memory loss. I doubt if she'll ever recall exactly what happened in the minutes leading up to that explosion. But she should be able to tell us why she went to see Louise today. We need that information."

Gwen turned her head to look at him "What the heck did happen at Louise's house today? She's had those chimes hanging inside and out on the porch for years. Why did they go crazy this afternoon?"

"I'm no para-physicist like Sam, but I've got a hunch that the explosion was the final event in a chain reaction that started a few hours earlier when the killer used some kind of paranormal crystal to murder Louise Fuller. Hell, maybe it started decades ago."

"What do you mean?" Gwen asked.

"The energy must have been building

inside Louise Fuller's house for years, thanks to those sculptures. The situation was probably already very unstable. When the killer used his weapon to murder Fuller, there would have been a lot of hot psi involved. That added to the instability. The whole place was a smoldering fire waiting to go up in flames. Then along came the storm. That could have been the spark that ignited the blaze."

Gwen looked at him. "There was more than just a storm involved. There was you and me, and we were both running very hot while we were inside that house."

"Yes," he said, keeping his voice very neutral.

"Do you think that maybe we were the sparks that lit the fuse or whatever it was that set that house on fire?"

"Maybe."

"Geez."

"Like I said, there was a hell of a lot of energy buildup in that house before you and I arrived."

Gwen nodded thoughtfully. "What, exactly, did you do with your ring?"

He looked down at the stone. It was no longer infused with power, but in the firelight it still glowed like liquid amber.

"Damned if I know," he said.

"Good grief." She stared at him. "Seriously? You don't know how that stone does what it does?"

"I've only performed that particular trick on one other occasion." He drank more of the wine. "Someone was trying to kill me at the time."

"You're talking about your last case again, aren't you?"

"Yes." He lowered the glass.

"How did you know that the three of us and Max needed to make physical contact in order to stay inside the safe zone you created?" Gwen asked.

"You want the truth? I wasn't sure it would work. Just figured that the physics made sense. And there didn't seem to be a lot of other options."

"What physics?" Gwen asked. "You must have some theory about how the stone works."

He studied the ring. "I can focus psychic energy through it, but it feels like I'm trying to control summer lightning when I do it. There's a lot of wild power in the crystal, but as far as I can tell, all it seems to do is dampen other paranormal currents in the vicinity." He paused. "Including human auras."

"You mean you can use it like a weapon?"

"Over a short distance, yes."

"How do you tune it?"

"What?" It was getting hard to concentrate. The deep weariness was getting heavier.

"You said that paranormal crystals that are used in high-tech ways require frequent tuning," Gwen reminded him. "How do you tune that stone?"

"I have no idea."

"Hmm."

He watched the firelight blaze in the ring. "I've only used it at full throttle twice — today and on my last case. I won't know if there's any juice left in it until I've had a chance to get some rest."

"You're exhausted," Gwen said. "You pulled a lot of firepower today shielding all of us."

"I just need sleep."

She drank her wine in a speculative silence for a time. He felt energy shift in the space and knew she had slipped into a trance. Max meowed softly and jumped down from the windowsill. He trotted across the room, bounded up onto the chair beside Gwen and settled down. She stroked him absently.

Judson closed his eyes and savored the gently charged atmosphere.

"Go ahead," he said. "Take a look. But I'll

warn you, it makes me hot."

"You're too tired to get hot."

"Shows how much you know." He opened his eyes. "What do you see?"

She blinked and slipped out of the trance. He felt the psi levels go back to what passed for normal between them. *Nothing will ever be normal for us, Gwen Frazier,* he thought.

"Okay, I'm no expert on the subject of crystal physics, but based on what I see in your aura and what I observed today when you used the ring, I think that you are actually tuning the ring automatically simply by wearing it," she said.

He studied the ring. "Usually you have to use one crystal to tune another. And usually the process requires someone with a special talent for the work, the psychic equivalent of a person with perfect pitch."

"Maybe it works in your case because your aura generates some wavelengths that resonate naturally with the stone. That would explain your affinity for it."

"Huh." He tried to think about the physics involved, but he was too far gone.

"Go to bed," Gwen said gently.

"Good idea." He set the unfinished wine aside. "I will do that right now. Keep the door between our rooms open. Security reasons."

"Okay," she said.

He could feel her watching him as he went through the doorway into his room.

"Stop worrying," he said. "I've been here before. I'll be fine after a little sleep."

"Okay," she said again.

But he could tell that she was worried. He knew she would not get any rest until she was certain that he was going to be okay. He wanted to tell her that there was no need for her to keep a vigil. He wasn't ill. And he sure as hell didn't need therapy. He just needed some sleep.

He fell onto the bed, closed his eyes and tumbled into the darkness before he could think of a way to reassure her.

Twenty-Six

Really, he had been born for a life of crime.

Nick Sawyer stood in the darkened house and listened to the currents of emptiness that resonated from the shadows. The dead woman's family had put the house on the market a couple of weeks back. The For Sale sign in the front yard read "Motivated Seller."

The house was almost empty. There were a few odd pieces of furniture and some pictures left, but the heirs had sold off most of the contents shortly after the old lady's death. There was probably nothing to discover in the way of clues to the mystery he had been sent to solve, but he had wanted to get a feel for the victim. Standing here, in her front room, somehow gave him a sense of her that he had not been able to obtain with his online research or his chats with the neighbors.

He moved through the heavily draped living room until the traces of seething energy on the floor brought him to a halt.

"Hello," he said to the shadows. "This is where he whacked you, isn't it? You were watching television. They said your body was found in a big easy chair. The guy next door said your son helped himself to your big-screen TV on the day of the funeral. Let's see what else you can tell me."

He went upstairs to the bedroom, noting the little elevator that had been installed at some point in the past.

"Too frail to make it up the stairs under your own steam," he said. "You were an easy target, weren't you? You couldn't have run, even if you had tried. But you didn't."

At the top of the stairs, he went down the hall to the master bedroom, savoring the chill of intense awareness and the adrenaline rush.

This business of poking around in the private affairs of other people was a lot more fun than the hot books business. He had gotten a kick out of chatting up the old woman's neighbors earlier that day, too. He was almost as good a con as he was a burglar. Not that it had taken any real skill to get people to talk. Folks had been only too willing to tell him how the old lady's son and daughter-in-law had ignored her for the most part, except when they had come around looking for money.

He studied the bedroom. There was an ancient chest of drawers standing against one wall, but everything else had been cleared out.

He crossed the room and started opening the drawers.

It was weird how a person's entire future could get changed by a small twist of fate, he thought. If he hadn't met Gwen and Abby in that hellhole of an institution that went by the name of the Summerlight Academy, he would have become a happy world-class jewel thief by now. His ability to see in the dark was superior to the latest and greatest in high-tech military night-vision goggles. And he was very, very good with locks and computers.

But Gwen and Abby had insisted that he make his living in a semi-legitimate manner. To avoid the endless nagging of his sisters, he had allowed Abby to teach him the ropes of the paranormal books business. It had been a good gig for the past few years. He had made a lot of money because he worked what Abby called the deep end of the market — the dangerous underworld of paranoid, obsessive collectors who would pay any amount of money to obtain the volumes they coveted.

Although he had an affinity for hot books — he figured that was no big deal because he had a natural sensitivity for just about anything that had serious value — he was not particularly interested in the rare volumes he brokered. When you got right down to it, he was just a go-between — a well-paid go-between, but a go-between nonetheless. The only part he actually enjoyed was the night work. So he craved the illicit thrill of sneaking around in the dark, learning other people's secrets. *So sue me. But first you have to catch me. Not gonna happen.*

Gwen said he got his kicks from this kind of thing because it allowed him to use his senses to the max. She claimed he would have been just as happy if he had engaged his psychic talents as a cop. But he knew the truth. He liked rummaging around in other people's secrets because his own past was concealed behind a locked door, one that he had never been able to open — and he was damn good at getting through locked doors. Thus far, every key he had tried had failed to open the door to his past.

The sperm donor bank his mother had used to conceive him had burned to the ground years ago. Half of his family history — the part pertaining to his father — had been destroyed in the fire. He had lost most of the other half of his past when his mother, a single woman who had been orphaned when she was an infant, died in a car accident the year he turned ten. There had followed a series of foster homes and, finally, the Summerlight Academy.

It was there that he had met his real family, his sisters, Gwen and Abby. They were the reason he had stayed at Summerlight. It would have been a simple matter to bail from the school using his rapidly developing talents, but he could not leave Gwen and Abby behind. They had needed him to protect them from the crazies and the bullies. It was the first time anyone had ever needed him. It was like he suddenly had a job to do. He had made sure the three of them had stuck together until graduation.

After leaving Summerlight, Gwen and Abby had reversed their roles, becoming the protectors. They had done their best to keep him from taking up a life of crime, even though he had assured them he would be brilliant at the business. He'd gone along with the more legit gig to keep peace in the family. But at times like this, when he was standing alone in the dark inside someone else's house, he knew that he had missed his true calling.

He closed the last drawer and went to the closet. It was empty except for a pair of sturdy white walking shoes of the style that they sold to little old ladies who were unsteady on their feet.

He found the small safe concealed behind a wall panel. It was still locked, but it required less than forty seconds to get it open. The stack of bills inside told him everything he needed to know about the old lady.

"A little paranoid, weren't you, Granny?" he said to the emptiness. "You didn't trust anyone, not even your own son. Well, you knew him better than anyone else, didn't you? After all, you were his mother."

There was one other item in the safe, an old-fashioned checkbook register.

He shoved the cash and the checkbook into the small black backpack he wore and went downstairs. He exited the house the same way he had entered, through a rear window.

He found the car where he had left it several blocks away in a parking lot behind a grocery store. He drove the nondescript vehicle back to the airport and turned it in at the rental counter. He had used one of his spare sets of identification to rent the car. He liked to keep a lot of extras on hand, not only for himself, but also for Gwen and Abby. Just in case.

It occurred to him that Abby probably wouldn't need that kind of security backup anymore now that she was marrying into the Coppersmith family. That clan took care of its own. And something about the energy between Gwen and Judson Coppersmith told him that she might not need her brother much longer, either.

The thought of losing his sisters to the Coppersmiths threatened to stir up the dark waters deep inside. Since their days at Summerlight, Abby and Gwen had been there for him. Abby had taught him the ropes of the hot books business. Gwen had always been around to drive the nightmare monsters back into the depths. The bad dreams hadn't surfaced in a while, but he knew they were still swimming around down there in the bottomless pit.

Okay, so Gwen and Judson were sleeping together. No problem. At this point it probably didn't amount to anything more than a one-night stand. Maybe two or three nights. Whatever. It didn't mean he would lose her, too. What was happening between the pair was just the natural result of a lot of adrenaline, excitement, danger and mutual physical attraction mixed up together. He'd been there often enough to know how the chemistry worked.

But a chill went through him. Gwen didn't do casual sex, and while the relationship between her and Judson had ignited quickly, it did not look like it would burn out fast. Even Wyatt Earp had noticed the heat between those two.

He did not want to think about what his nights would be like if the dream monsters returned. He did not want to think about what his world would be like if he lost both of his sisters to the Coppersmith family. So he got some coffee and found a private space in which to suck up the caffeine while he went through the bankbook that he had found in the wall safe. Numbers were always interesting, especially when they were linked to money.

After a while he took the small computer out of the backpack and went online. It didn't take long to find what he was looking for. He was as good at finding interesting stuff hidden in cyberspace as he was opening concealed wall safes.

Really, he had been born for a life of crime.

Twenty-Seven

She sensed the dark energy of Judson's psi-charged dreamscape just as she was about to slip into a lucid dream of her own.

She was in her robe, nightgown and slippers, curled up in the chair in front of the fire with her feet tucked under her. She was orchestrating the delicate trance-like state, summoning images from the scene of Louise's murder, when the currents whispered to her from the other room.

Her first thought was that the unfamiliar tendrils of dreamlight had been generated by her own self-induced hallucination. As often as she had gone into the waking dreamstate, she could never be sure of what she would experience. Trances were, by their very nature, unpredictable.

But when she heard Judson utter an urgent, half-choked shout, she was jolted out of the trance.

She stood quickly. Max was awake, too.

He sat up on the bed and gazed fixedly toward the doorway into the other room.

Judson groaned.

Gwen hurried to the doorway. In the faint light from the fireplace behind her, she could see Judson sprawled on the bed. His ring was infused with sun-hot light.

Max jumped down from the bed and joined her in the doorway, meowing in a low, uneasy manner.

Gwen heightened her talent and slid into a waking trance to get a sense of what was going on in Judson's dreamscape. She was not surprised by the explosion of amber lightning that crackled in the atmosphere, but she was stunned by the dark, seething energy of violence that pooled around the bed. With her dreamer's intuition, she knew that Judson was living through whatever had caused the nightmare. His unnaturally deep sleep had intensified the effects.

"Good grief," she whispered. "How long have you been dealing with this dream, Judson?"

She walked slowly toward the bed. She had never dealt with a sleeper so profoundly asleep. Normally she worked with clients who were awake. The therapeutic process involved putting clients into a light trance and then summoning their dreamscapes to a level just below that of conscious awareness. But her intuition warned her that it would not be a good idea to try to shake Judson awake. In his present condition, it would take him some time to distinguish between his dreamscape and the waking world. In effect, he would wake up in the midst of a vivid hallucination. It might take him a few seconds — as long as a minute, perhaps — to sort things out. In those circumstances, a strong psychic wearing a ring infused with unknown paranormal energy could do a lot of damage in even a short period of time.

Although she dared not bring him out of the dreamscape too abruptly, she had to make physical contact in order to help him. She was not sure how he would respond to even the lightest touch. He was trapped deep in the underworld. That was never a good thing.

"Really, Max, the first lesson everyone with psychic abilities should be taught is how to control their own dreams," she said softly.

Max meowed again. It was an aren't-you-going-to-do-something-about-this-situation sort of meow. He twitched his tail a few times, expressing his growing impatience, and came to sit very close to her feet, pressing his big body against her leg.

On the bed Judson uttered another low, guttural sound. The energy whipping around him grew darker and more dangerous. The sunlight stirring in his ring got hotter.

There was no option, Gwen thought. She could not let him slide deeper into the dreamscape.

She gathered herself and pulled hard on her talent. At her feet, Max pressed more firmly against her leg as if to offer support.

Cautiously, she reached out and touched two fingertips to the palm of one of Judson's out-flung hands.

Although she thought she was braced for the physical connection, it was all she could do not to scream aloud when the electrifying shock zapped across her senses.

She walked straight into the heart of his nightmare.

Amber lightning arced and flashed in the darkness that enveloped her. She sensed the ghastly fog that was the hallmark of violence and death. A dreadful miasma infused with a terrible violet-hued light seethed around her feet. She thought she heard a cat meow.

"Judson," she said quietly. "Where are you?"

"Welcome to my world," he said. "You

281

shouldn't have come here."

She turned, searching for him in the lightning-streaked darkness.

. . . And saw him watching her from the shadows, a churning pool of ultraviolet energy at his feet. His eyes burned with a heat that matched the molten fires that flared in his ring.

He did not look like a man trapped in hell — in this dark underworld, he reigned.

"You should not be here, either," she said. "It's just a bad dreamscape. Come with me."

Conversations conducted in other people's dreamscapes were no different than those she had with ghosts in her own trances. The dialogue came to her as feedback from her dreamer's intuition based on what she sensed in the client's aura.

"I can't leave," Judson said.

"Why not?"

"I lost something here. I have to find it."

"What did you lose?" she asked.

"I don't know yet, but I'll recognize it when I find it."

"I understand. This is a recurring dream for you, isn't it?"

"Oh, yeah. I come here often."

"You come here to search for whatever it is you lost, but tonight you've gone down too deep," she said. "I was afraid of this. You're here now because of what happened at Louise Fuller's house today. You need to return to the surface with me. You must let your senses recover before you dream this dream again."

That seemed to amuse him. "You don't get it, do you? This is my world. It's where I belong."

"No, it's your dreamscape, and you can change it. I can show you how."

"It may be a dreamscape, but it's also my past," he said. "No changing that, is there, Miss Psychic Counselor?"

"You can't change the past, but you can find a better way to deal with it."

"Damn. You sound like a real therapist," he said. "The expensive kind. But you're not a real one, are you?"

"No, I'm just a psychic counselor, but I do know something about how to find things that are lost in dreamscapes. You're going about it the wrong way."

"Yeah?" He was starting to sound bored.

She was losing him.

"Come back to the surface with me," she said. "Later, when you're fully rested, I'll help you search this dreamscape."

"I don't think so."

"Why not?"

"You're right," he said. "I've come down too far this time. Never been this deep before. But I can see things here that I've never seen before. Maybe tonight I'll find what I'm looking for."

"It won't do you any good if you can't get back to the surface. I was afraid of this. Listen up, Coppersmith. You went too deep into your dreamscape tonight because of that psi-burn at Louise's house today."

"You were there, too. Why didn't you crash and burn the way I did? Have you got some special psychic superpower?"

"No, I'm okay tonight because you protected me from the worst effects of the storm in Louise's house," she said. "But you were also shielding Nicole and Max and yourself, as well. Heaven only knows how much energy you had to focus through your ring to save us all. But you temporarily exhausted your senses in the process. You need to be sleeping soundly now, not visiting this dreamscape."

"You should leave before you get trapped here with me."

"I'm not leaving without you," she said. "Come back with me, Judson."

"I don't think that's possible. Too late."

There was no emotion in the words — neither regret nor despair. Judson sounded as if he was making an observation about the weather, detached. *Like one of the ghosts,* she thought. Another chill shivered through her. This was not going well. She had never dealt with anyone who had fallen this far down the rabbit hole of a dreamscape. She was out of her depth, as well, but she was very sure of one thing. She had to get Judson back to the surface before he went any deeper.

"No, it is not too late," she said. "We can get out of here, but we have to do this together. You're not the only one who went too deep tonight. I had to come this far down to find you. I am trapped with you."

"I told you that you should not have come here."

This time she thought she heard a flicker of emotional intensity in Judson's dreamscape voice. He sounded angry. She told herself that was a good sign.

"Well, I did come here and now I'm stuck," she said. "If you don't come with me, I won't be able to leave this place."

"You're the psychic dreamer. Get out of this hell while you still can."

"Not without you. Stop arguing with me. This isn't just an ordinary dream. This could become a coma. We have to leave. Now."

It was weird, but she was starting to lose her temper, too. That wasn't supposed to happen to her in a dreamscape. She had trained herself to be the clinical observer and guide. It was her job to gently lead the client out of the closed loop of a recurring nightmare. Any strong emotion on her part caused distortions and confusion in the world of dreams — a world that was constructed of distorted and confusing images.

"You don't give up easily, do you?" Judson asked. He sounded intrigued by her stubbornness.

"No," she said. "Not when it comes to my clients."

"Is that what I am? A client?"

"That's what you are tonight. Take my hand, Judson." She made it a command.

For a harrowing eternity in dreamtime, she thought that he would not respond. Then, to her overwhelming relief, he reached for her hand. She knew the action was just her mind's way of interpreting what was happening. In a very real sense she was dreaming, too. Judson was resurfacing. He wasn't really reaching for her hand. She knew that. The hand-holding was a dream metaphor.

Which was why it came as a physical as well as a psychic jolt when she felt his powerful fingers lock fiercely around her wrist in the waking world. The shock brought her instantly out of the dreamscape. Judson came with her.

He opened his eyes. Simultaneously he tightened his hand around her wrist.

"It's okay, Judson, you're awake." She gave him what she hoped was a reassuring smile, assuming that, with his preternatural night vision he could see it. Delicately, she wriggled her fingers, trying to free her manacled wrist. He did not release her. Instead, he continued to shackle her while he watched her with eyes that burned.

"I'm not one of your clients," he rasped.

"You're awake. It was just a bad dream. I was afraid you might be sleeping a little too deeply, you see."

"I'm not one of your damned clients."

"What?"

"I said I'm not your *client*."

She reminded herself that after awakening from a deep dream, the dreamer often continued to be confused by images from the underworld for a time. The goal was to soothe and reassure and guide the dreamer all the way back to the shore of the normal.

"You're not a client," she said soothingly.

"Damn right."

He used his hold on her wrist to pull her

off her feet and down onto the bed. The maneuver was conducted with the precision of a judo throw. One instant she was upright, the next she was flat on her back. The shadowy bedroom spun around her.

Okay, this was a new experience in the uncharted waters of psychic dream counseling, she thought. She had lost control of the session. That was not supposed to happen.

Before she could reorient herself and come up with a game plan for dealing with the situation, Judson was on top of her, one muscled thigh pinning her leg to the quilt. He captured her other wrist, anchored it beside her head, and took her mouth with a ruthlessness that stunned her senses.

The kiss was incendiary, literally. Hot energy burned in the atmosphere. She was mildly astonished that they did not set fire to the drapes. But unlike the terrible energy of the dream, this was the fiercely exhilarating fire of turbocharged passion.

Judson was running hot. She was still fully jacked from the dream therapy work. That made for a lot of heat. But it was the return of the breathtaking sensation of psychic intimacy that shocked and thrilled her. Something very strange had happened between them last night and it was happening again tonight. Her intuition warned her that the more time that she and Judson spent together — not just having super-heated sex but within range of each other's auras — the more powerful the bond would become — at least on her end.

Judson freed one of her wrists so he could untie the sash of her robe. His palm closed over her breast. He moved his mouth down to her throat.

She slid her hand up under his T-shirt and clawed at his muscled back. He was burning up with a psi-fever.

"Judson," she whispered.

"Not a client," he growled. "Say it. Not a client."

"Not a client," she gasped. "You can't be a client, because I never sleep with clients."

"That's right. You don't sleep with clients. You sleep with me now. Only me."

He yanked opened the top of her night-gown and kissed her breasts with a hungry, desperate reverence. At the touch of his tongue on her sensitive nipples, she cried out. He released her other wrist to unzip his trousers. He fumbled the hem of her night-gown up to her waist. Then his hand was between her thighs.

"Wet and hot," he said against her throat. "That's how I like you."

She reached down and circled him with

her fingers. "Hard and hot. That's how I like you."

His laughter was low and dark and wicked. "We were made for each other, Dream Eyes."

Maybe, she thought, but probably not. This wasn't love. They hadn't had time to fall in love. This was raw passion fueled by the bond that had been forged in the paranormal fires of shared danger and the dream therapy experience. She knew she could not trust her emotions tonight, but in the heat of the moment she did not care.

Judson got his pants off and then he was back on top of her, driving into her hard and deep. She pulled him close and wrapped herself fiercely around him.

Her release swept through her in seconds. She heard Judson groan as he followed her over the edge and into the effervescent seas that awaited them.

TWENTY-EIGHT

It had been a good night at the online fishing hole. The grooming of the new client was coming along nicely. The woman's ninety-two-year-old father-in-law was in excellent health and showed every indication of making it to a hundred. Unfortunately for the heirs, the old man was burning through the inheritance at a fast clip. At the rate he was going he would outlive his money. The daughter-in-law had a problem with that. She and her husband had been counting on her father-in-law's money to finance their own retirement.

It was all so unfair. Sundew understood that. And it wasn't as if the old man enjoyed a good quality of life, after all. He had been forced to give up both driving and his beloved golf a few years ago. Now he spent his days playing cards and watching television with the other residents at his very expensive retirement community while he whined that no one ever came to visit him. Meanwhile his son and daughter-in-law were watching their inheritance go down the drain.

The old man's death would change everything.

Back at the start, Sundew had been obliged to spend months drumming up business. The process involved hours of online research just to identify potential clients. Then followed the laborious task of introducing them to the notion that their inheritance problems could be made to go away as if by magic — for a price.

The business was more streamlined these days, requiring less research and less risk. As always, word of mouth had proved to be the best form of advertising. The online whispers were so effective that Sundew had no shortage of potential clients dropping into the chat room.

Money was no longer the object. Now Sundew worked to support a habit.

Somewhere along the line, the murder-for-hire game had become a total rush.

Until recently, Wilby, Oregon, had been the perfect lair in which to hide between hunts. True, the brouhaha two years ago had been a near disaster but things had settled down after Gwen Frazier left town. Then

Sundew had discovered that Evelyn Ballinger had become suspicious. The problem had been resolved easily enough, but now the situation had begun to disintegrate.

The bitch was back in town, and she was not alone.

On her own, Frazier wouldn't have been a problem. She was nobody, just a low-level talent who could view auras — not exactly a weapon of mass destruction. In spite of what had happened two years ago, it was hard to see her as a serious threat. One way or another, she could be dealt with.

But Coppersmith's presence complicated the situation. His family was powerful and would no doubt make a lot of waves if one of the sons and heirs to the business empire turned up dead in a small town like Wilby. Questions would be asked.

The Coppersmiths also appeared to be a family with a lot of secrets. What's more, they were very good at concealing those secrets.

Secrets were always interesting. Sundew's own family kept a lot of them. And they were just as good at hiding them as the Coppersmiths were.

Twenty-Nine

Judson awoke just before dawn to a sure and certain knowledge of the killer's mind.

I know what you are and why you're killing, you bastard. I'm one step closer. Not much longer now.

He shoved aside the quilt and sat up on the edge of the bed. He was wearing only his briefs. Memories of the night slammed through him. He'd gone back into the damn dream — maybe too far into it this time — but Gwen had pulled him out. Like it or not, for a time he had become her client.

He reached for the holster and gun. What mattered, he concluded, was that after she had yanked him out of the dream, they had gone back to being lovers.

The door between the two rooms was open.

He pulled on his trousers and went to the doorway. Gwen was still in her nightgown and robe, but she was not in bed. She was curled up in the chair, her head resting on a pillow. Her eyes were closed. Max was ensconced alongside her thigh. The cat glared at him through half-closed eyes.

"Tough luck, pal," Judson mouthed. "Just because you got to her first, don't think you've got claiming rights."

Max did not look impressed. Judson was deliberating between scooping up Gwen and putting her on the bed or covering her with a blanket when she opened her eyes.

"You're awake," she said.

"So are you."

"How are you feeling?"

"Good." He paused and then did what had to be done. "Thanks to you. I'm not real sure we'd be having this conversation this morning if you hadn't pulled me out of that dream last night. I owe you."

She raised her brows. "No, you don't owe me any more than I owe you. We're partners in this thing. Yesterday you saved me as well as Nicole and Max. Last night I was able to help you. That's what partners do. You have my back; I have yours. Neither of us would leave the other behind. That's how it works."

He moved closer to the fire. "You know about that kind of thing because of your time with Abby and Nick at Summerlight, don't you?"

"Yes," she said.

He looked at her, understanding sleeting through him. Partners. Lovers. *Not client.* He could work with that.

"No," he said. "Neither one of us would leave the other behind. Not ever."

"Glad we got that settled." She smiled and stretched. "I did some thinking while you were out."

"I had a few thoughts of my own when I woke up." The cold thrill of the hunt was riding him now. "I know him, Gwen. Not his name and identity — not yet — but I *know* him and I know why he's killing."

Excitement illuminated her eyes. He knew then that she comprehended what he was feeling. He also knew that she didn't have a problem with knowing that he was a little addicted to the rush. Make that a lot addicted.

"You woke up with a flash of intuition?" she asked. "Tell me."

"We've been working on the assumption that we're dealing with a copycat killer who managed to get hold of Taylor's camera. But that's not what's going on here. This guy is a pro."

"A professional?" Gwen uncurled her legs, her expression sharpening. "Are you talking about a hit man?"

The suddenness of her movement disturbed Max. He grumbled, rose and vacated the chair. He landed on the floor with an audible thud and stalked across the room. He vaulted up onto the windowsill and glowered out at the dawn-lit world.

"The way he got rid of Evelyn Ballinger and Louise Fuller feels like the work of a pro who is cleaning up," Judson said. He dropped into the chair across from Gwen. "It explains the controlled energy I picked up at the scenes. Pros get an adrenaline rush when they take out the target, but they know how to handle it. They're crazy in their own way, but they leave a different calling card."

"A psychic hit man armed with a crystal that can kill without a trace." Gwen leaned forward and folded her arms on her knees. She looked into the fire. "I don't know which scares me more, the thought that we're dealing with a wack-job of a serial killer or a hit man who kills for money."

"I'll take the wack-job any day," Judson said.

She glanced at him. "Why?"

"Because the wack-job is more likely to screw up. The pros tend to disappear fast when the heat comes down, and they know how to stay disappeared as long as necessary. Pros have several sets of IDs and rent houses on no-name islands in the Caribbean. Pros are very hard to catch."

Gwen frowned. "But this pro is evidently living in a no-name town in the Pacific Northwest."

"Principle is the same."

"But pros don't go around murdering people at random," Gwen said. "Or do they?"

"No. By definition, they do it for the money or to protect their own secrets. Motives tell you a lot. If we're right, he murdered Evelyn because she stumbled onto the truth about his day job. Now we need to find out why he killed Louise."

Gwen unfolded her arms, leaned back and drummed her fingers on the arm of her chair. "I'm no psi-techie, but you said that the weapon the killer is using is probably crystal-based technology of some kind, right?"

"That's my working assumption based on where the killer was standing when the victims died. Can't think of any other way the hits could have gone down."

"You also mentioned that most high-tech paranormal crystal gadgets, with the possible exception of that ring you are wearing, require periodic tuning if they are to maintain optimum power."

Adrenaline spilled into Judson's blood-stream.

"The bastard needed someone who could tune crystals," he said softly. "Louise was his para-tech IT department. She tuned the crystal in his weapon. Is that what you're thinking?"

"Yes."

"That's brilliant, Gwen. I like it. I like it a lot."

"Okay, slow down," Gwen said. "There is one flaw in my logic. If the killer needed Louise to keep him in business, why would he murder her?"

"He concluded that he had no choice. Like I said, this guy is a pro and he thinks like a pro. He's cutting his losses. Louise knew way too much about him. He had to get rid of her before we talked to her."

"He'll probably leave town now that he's covered his tracks. Maybe he's already gone."

Judson watched the dancing flames, thinking about what he had learned at the death scenes. "I don't think so. He'll leave eventually once the heat has died down, but he would prefer not to disappear while we're here, not unless he feels he has no other option."

"Why not?"

"This is one very small town. If the killer is living here as a pillar of the community, so to speak, and he suddenly vanishes, everyone, including Oxley, will notice. Questions will be asked. A pro would prefer to avoid that, if possible." Judson shook his head, rerunning the insights he'd gleaned at the kill sites. "No, he's hoping that with Ballinger and Fuller both dead, we'll hit a brick wall."

"In that case, what do we do next?" Gwen asked.

"Try to think like he does. One thing we know for sure." "Yes?"

"Sooner or later, he will need another crystal tuner," Judson said.

THIRTY

Judson's phone rang. He snapped it off his belt, glanced at the coded number and took the call.

"What have you got for me, Sawyer?" he said.

"He's a pro," Nick said. "He's getting paid."

"Believe it or not, I got that far."

"Gee, aren't you Mr. Sherlock Holmes."

"Given your astonishing skill and talent, I expect a little more information," Judson said. "Anything else?"

"I've got lots more, thanks to my astonishing skill and talent. First off, you were right, he wasn't targeting psychics. None of the victims showed any interest in the paranormal. None of them claimed any kind of psychic ability."

Judson smiled a little at the hum of excitement in Nick's voice. Sawyer and he had more in common than either one of them would ever admit, he thought.

"So, what did all the hits have in common?" he asked.

"That greatest of all motivators — money. Four of the six definitely qualified as elderly. The other two were suffering long-term chronic illnesses. All six were standing in the way of very healthy inheritances and/or insurance policies."

"We look to the heirs," Judson said.

"I'm way ahead of you on account of my astonishing skill and talent," Nick said. "I checked out a couple of them already. The forty-two-year-old son of the last victim recently transferred a very large amount of money into an offshore account. A similar amount was paid to the same account by a nephew of one of the other hits."

"You know what? You're good at this, Sawyer. I think you and my mother should spend some quality time together."

"I've spent some time with your mother," Nick said. "I'm in the wedding, remember? Nice lady. Turns out she and Girard both think I have excellent taste. I'm the one who suggested deep violet and gold for the color theme."

"Glad to hear it, but that's not why I think you and Mom should talk. Mom knows how to follow the money better than anyone else

I've ever met. I'd say she has a psychic talent for it, but she doesn't believe in the paranormal."

"You're kidding?" Nick snorted. "After raising you and your brother and sister?"

"Mom prefers to think we're all just highly intuitive."

"Oh, right. That sounds so much more pleasant than thinking that her kids are freaks."

"Something like that."

"That's a mom for you, always looking on the positive side when it comes to her little ones," Nick said. His voice had gone utterly flat.

Judson pushed past the sudden silence on the other end of the connection. "What I'm trying to say here is that it would be extremely helpful if you and Mom could get together for an afternoon, like today, and figure out if anyone connected to this case who is still here in Wilby has been moving large amounts of money around."

"You want us to vet an entire town full of aging hippies, chronic underachievers, failed artists and assorted misfits? That would take days, not an afternoon." But Nick was sounding interested again.

"I'll have Gwen put together a list of folks who were connected to the Ballinger Study.

I'll call you as soon as I've got the names."

"I'll await your call with bated breath. Meanwhile, I've got one other factoid that might interest you. It's true that none of the victims was into the paranormal, but in the case of at least two of them, I can tell you that about a month before the hits were made, the heirs — a nephew in one case and a daughter-in-law in the other — spent some time in a chat room run by an online psychic counselor. Until that point, neither the nephew nor the daughter-in-law had shown any interest in psychics or fortune-tellers or tarot cards."

Judson tightened his grip on the phone. "You could have mentioned that sooner."

"I wanted to save the best for last."

"Got a name for this online psychic counselor?" Judson asked.

Gwen's eyes widened.

"The online psychic goes by the name of Sundew," Nick said. "And before you ask, I looked it up. Sundews are carnivorous plants. Cute, huh? I'm thinking that it would be interesting to find out if any of the other lucky heirs contacted Sundew prior to the murders."

"Yes," Judson said. "It would be very interesting. How the hell did you come across the info on Sundew?"

"I spent a little time on the computers of the two heirs I just mentioned," Nick said smoothly. "It's amazing how many people leave their passwords lying around."

"You know, it would be very inconvenient if you happened to get arrested in the course of this investigation," Judson said.

"You don't need to spell it out." Nick's tone went cold and flat again. "I'm aware that if I get picked up, I will discover that the Coppersmiths have never heard of me."

"Much as we might like to pretend we've never heard of you, that's not an option."

"No?"

"No. For better or worse, you now fall into the friends-and-family category. Mom would brain me if you weren't around to walk Abby down the aisle. If you run into trouble with the authorities, you keep your mouth shut and you call me."

"What will you do?" Nick said, reluctantly curious.

"Coppersmith, Inc., has a herd of lawyers, very good lawyers. They will take care of the pesky details. You won't sit in jail long."

"Good to know."

"But my life would be vastly simplified if you did not get picked up in the first place," Judson warned.

"Relax, I've never been caught. I'm not

about to spoil my perfect record of non-arrest now. Send me that list of people you want your mom and me to vet, and be sure you take good care of Gwen. Anything happens to her, you'll answer to me."

"Understood."

Judson ended the call and looked at Gwen. "Evidently not all psychic counselors conduct themselves according to your own high ethical standards."

"Damn," Gwen said. "Nothing like a killer psychic counselor to give the profession a bad name."

THIRTY-ONE

Gwen watched Judson pick up the coffeepot and move through the bathroom doorway to fill the pot with water. Max followed him on the off chance that Judson might also refill the food dish.

"You think this Sundew is using the chat room to troll for business, is that it?" Gwen asked.

"That's my best guess," Judson said through the doorway. "Online rumors probably send prospects his way. He can check them out anonymously in the chat room, select those who look like serious prospects and contact them privately to offer his services."

"We may have put a glitch in his business model here in Wilby, but if we don't stop him, he will continue to kill, won't he?"

"Sure." Judson emerged from the bathroom and poured the water into the coffeemaker. He put the pot on the hot plate and dropped the pre-measured bag of coffee into the machine. "He's addicted by now, probably has been for a long time."

Gwen shuddered. "But you said he was a pro, that he does it for the money."

"Doesn't mean he's not addicted to his work, specifically the feeling of power that it gives him."

Max abandoned hope of another meal and vaulted up onto the bed. He settled down and half closed his eyes.

Gwen tried to suppress the chill that iced her nerves. "If Sundew is addicted to murder, he's simply another kind of serial killer, even if he does consider himself a pro."

Judson flipped the switch on the coffee-maker. "Just another one of the monsters."

"Okay, say he will need another crystal tuner," Gwen said. "How would he go about replacing Louise? It's not like you can look up crystal tuners online or find one in a phonebook. At least I don't think you can."

Judson watched the coffee drip into the pot as if the machine was a crystal ball that would reveal secrets. "If I were the killer, it might occur to me that the best source of leads would be Evelyn's files."

Gwen raised her brows. "It *might* occur to you?"

He winced. "Sorry about that. I've been

thinking like the bad guys for a while now. Over time it becomes a habit."

"No need to apologize," she said briskly. "You aren't really thinking like the bad guys when you try to get inside their heads."

"No?" He sounded amused.

"No. You're thinking like a good investigator. You're doing what you were born to do — hunt bad guys."

"Thanks. I'll cling to that theory. How did Evelyn find her test subjects two years ago?"

"I see where you're going here." Gwen took a deep breath and exhaled slowly. "Evelyn had her own counseling records from the time she worked at the Summerlight Academy. They were stored on her computer. Her files would provide a nice, neatly categorized list of people with talents. It's horrible to think that Sundew is going to stalk some poor innocent crystal tuner and force her to tune his weapon for him."

"He's not going to get the chance to do that because we're going to stop him," Judson said.

"Do you really think we can do that?"

"Yes," he said. "I really think we can do it. And soon."

The coffee finished brewing, and they drank it in silence for a time. After a while, Gwen lowered her cup.

"It wouldn't be all that easy to find them, you know," she said.

Judson looked at her. "You're talking about the talents in the Summerlight files?"

"Yes. I told you that the one thing most of us learned was how to keep a low profile and pass for normal. The truly dangerous talents really excelled when it came to learning those lessons. But there were also the students who were overwhelmed by the onset of their abilities or too fragile psychologically to handle them. Some of them ended up in institutions. Some ended up on the streets. Some simply disappeared. This Sundew will have his work cut out for him trying to find a crystal tuner in those files."

"You're good at passing for normal," Judson said. "Why didn't you go into the mainstream professional world? With your talent you could have done brilliantly. I'll bet you could easily be pulling in several hundred bucks an hour as a high-end shrink. No one would have to know that it was your psychic talent that made you so good at your work."

She smiled faintly. "In other words, you want to know why I bill myself as a low-rent psychic counselor when I could have a string of letters after my name?"

"For the record, I never used the term *low-rent*."

"Right. Well, the answer is two fold. First, it's hard to outrun your past when that past includes a place like Summerlight."

"All you needed was a new identity," Judson said.

"It's true that Nick could have set me up with a false identity, complete with transcripts from some respectable school," she agreed. "He's offered to do it on several occasions."

"He's versatile."

"Certainly." She was aware of a flash of genuine pride. "Nick is very talented. And to tell you the truth, I have considered taking him up on his offer from time to time. But I didn't want to spend the rest of my life pretending to be something or, rather, someone I'm not."

"It would have been hard work."

"In order to maintain the lie, I would have had to deceive everyone around me twenty-four hours a day, seven days a week, year in and year out. I think that would have become intolerable over time."

"Sort of like going into the witness protection program," Judson said.

"Just imagine not being able to confide the truth about your own past to a close friend or a lover without running the risk of losing the person's friendship or love. Imagine not being able to trust anyone with the truth about yourself."

"My family has been keeping secrets for two generations," he said. "We expect to have to keep them a while longer."

The quiet comment caught her by surprise.

"Yes," she said. "You and your family do know what it's like to keep secrets, don't you? Those crystals from the Phoenix Mine —"

"It's not just about the crystals. Sam is getting married. He and Abby will want children. Both of them have powerful paranormal profiles. We don't know much about psychic genetics, but it's a good bet their offspring will be talented, too. We'll have to protect the kids and help them cope with their psychic sides."

"I hadn't thought about it, but I suppose even a member of the wealthy and powerful Coppersmith family who possesses some talent has to learn to pass for normal."

"You do if you want to operate in the normal business world. And Coppersmith, Inc., is a very big business."

She smiled. "I've heard that."

"The bottom line for all of us is that we're

going to need to stay at least partly in the shadows all of our lives, and our descendants will, too. There's no telling if or when the public will learn to treat the paranormal as normal."

"But at least you've got a family around you to help you guard those secrets."

"What do you know about your own family?" he asked.

"My family by DNA? Not much. I was raised by my aunt who took me in after my parents were killed in a car crash. Aunt Beth was a very good person, but she was also very religious. When my talents started to emerge, she was . . . horrified. I think she truly believed that I was possessed. She took me to church a lot. I finally got the point and pretended to be cured. But I'm pretty sure she knew that I was still having visions. On her deathbed her last words to me were, *Don't tell anyone.*"

"Not bad advice, under the circumstances."

"No, it wasn't," Gwen said. "And I tried to follow it. But I wound up in Summerlight, anyway."

Judson frowned, looking suddenly thoughtful. "How did that happen? It was an expensive boarding school, by all accounts. Abby told Sam that her family paid a fortune to send her there."

"I got in the same way Nick did. We were informed that our expenses were covered by a special charity fund. Lucky us. Evelyn told me the truth, though. She said that social workers and shrinks and others who dealt with troubled youth who displayed certain symptoms were encouraged to send the kids to Summerlight for evaluation. If they met the criteria for admission, they would be accepted, all expenses paid. Sam said at least one, maybe more, of the counselors at the school actively searched for students who displayed evidence of talent."

"When this job is over, I'm going to try to find out if there are other copies of those old school files floating around," Judson said. "I don't like the idea that someone can use them to go on a talent hunt."

The words acted like a dash of icy water on Gwen's senses. She straightened in her chair and shoved her fingers through her hair.

"If you'll excuse me, I'm going to take a quick shower," she said. "It's been a long night. I'm ready for breakfast."

She pushed herself up out of the chair. But Judson was already on his feet, blocking her path. His jaw was steel-hard and his eyes burned.

"What the hell did I say?" he asked.

She held her ground. *Show no weakness.*

She gave him a blandly polite smile. "I don't know what you're talking about."

"Don't give me that." Judson wrapped his hands around her shoulders. "I said something just now that sent you straight into deep freeze. *What did I say?*"

"Sorry." She kept her tone light and polite. "It was nothing. Just a reality check."

He tightened his grip and pulled her closer. "Talk to me, Gwendolyn Frazier. I may be psychic, but I can't read your mind."

"It's all right," she said, softening her words because she could see that he had absolutely no idea why she was offended. The truth was that she had no reason to be hurt. "You reminded me that this is just a short-term job for you, that's all. You're here as a favor to Sam and Abby. That you'll be moving on after you've closed the case."

Comprehension hit him with visible force. His eyes narrowed.

"So that's it," he said. He moved his hands up to cup her face. "Let's get something straight here. The job is supposed to be short-term. I hope to hell it is because there's a killer running around. But I don't want *us* to be short-term. As far as I'm concerned, this is not a weekend hookup."

The wave of relief that swept through her was so strong that she would have collapsed back into the chair if he had not been holding her. Don't get too excited, she warned herself. Just take it one day at a time.

She cleared her throat. "I wasn't quite sure what you meant. Things have been a little intense lately. In situations like this, emotions can get overheated. Judgment can be impaired. Intuition is unreliable."

"Is that right? You've had a lot of experience in situations like this?"

Her temper flared — much too quickly, she realized. Talk about overreacting.

"You know what I'm trying to say," she said. "For heaven's sake, we're practically strangers."

"You said we were partners."

"That, too," she said quickly. "At least for now."

"Partners who sleep together. Do you know what that makes us?"

"No," she said.

"It makes us lovers."

She caught her breath. *"Lovers?"*

"Yes. Lovers."

He kissed her before she could say another word. It was a thorough-going kiss. He did not let up until she sighed and softened against him. By the time he freed her, they were both breathing hard.

"Lovers," he said again, making it a statement of fact.

"Okay," she said. She took a deep breath and then she took a step back. "Lovers."

He looked satisfied. "Glad we got that cleared up."

"You bet." She headed for the bathroom. "Who says men don't know how to communicate?"

She closed the door very firmly and locked it.

THIRTY-TWO

Max's soft meow alerted Judson when he emerged from the bathroom after his own morning shower. The cat was in Gwen's room.

A faint trickle of energy shifted in the atmosphere, reminding Judson of the light current of the underground river that had guided him out of the flooded cave. He heard soft footsteps out in the hall and checked the time. It was just going on seven.

He heard the muffled sound of the stairwell door closing outside in the hall.

Max meowed again, more urgently.

Judson took a clean shirt out of the closet and went to the doorway between the two rooms. On the far side of the big bed he saw Max crouched in front of the hall door of Gwen's room.

Gwen came out of the dressing room area, fastening the waistband of her jeans.

"What's Max complaining about?" Judson asked.

"I don't know." Gwen looked toward the door. "He just started making noise a couple of minutes ago while you were in the shower. He's probably hungry. I'll feed him before we go downstairs to breakfast."

Max abruptly lost interest in whatever had attracted him to the door. He rose and trotted across the room to greet Gwen with a demanding purr. She reached down and scratched him behind the ears.

"He heard someone out in the hall a moment ago," Judson said.

"How do you know that?"

"Because I heard someone, too. Whoever it was went down the emergency stairs at the back of the inn."

Gwen straightened. "Probably a guest going out for an early morning run."

"Maybe. I'm going to take a look."

Judson turned, crossed his room, opened the door and went out into the hall. The wall sconces lit the scene in a warm, golden glow. He glanced at the muddy footprints on the floor and then he followed them to the stairwell door.

He opened the emergency door just in time to hear the first floor door open and close at the bottom of the stairwell.

He went back along the hall and let himself into his own room. Gwen was waiting.

"Well?" she asked.

"Our visitor came from outside. She left a little mud on the carpet and the stairs."

Gwen was impressed. "Did your para-senses tell you that the person was a woman?"

"No, I cheated and used my normal senses. The footprints belong to a woman. She came up the emergency stairwell, went to your door and then turned around and went back down the same stairs. Let's take a look in your room."

He went through the connecting doorway and walked around the bed to take a closer look at the place where Max had been crouched earlier. From that angle, he could see what had not been visible from the other side of the room.

An envelope lay on the floor.

He picked it up.

"Looks like she left a message," he said.

"Probably the bill for room charges here at the inn," Gwen said. "I'll take care of it at breakfast."

"It's not the bill for the room." There was no name or address on the outside of the envelope, but he could sense the anxiety that stained the paper.

He slit the seal and took out the photograph.

Gwen came to stand beside him.

"It's a copy of the same group shot that I found on the floor near Evelyn's body," she said. "The picture of the seven research study subjects." She took a closer look. "Someone drew a circle around my face."

Judson turned the picture over and read the scrawled message on the back aloud. *"You are next."*

Thirty-Three

"You're sure about this?" Gwen asked.

"Almost positive," Judson said.

Gwen opened her senses a little and watched his aura as he shut down the SUV's engine. He was definitely running hot with a mix of adrenaline and psi — he had been ever since he had opened the envelope that contained the unpleasantly marked-up photo. But, as usual, he was fully in control.

He sat quietly for a moment studying the thick stand of mist-shrouded trees that stood between the vehicle and the rear door of Hudson Floral Design.

In the backseat, Max glowered through the recently repaired door of his carrier.

It had stopped raining, but an early morning fog had rolled in off the river, muffling sound and limiting visibility. At least, Gwen thought, the fog had that effect on those like her who possessed merely normal hearing and vision.

"What do you see?" she asked Judson.

"What?" He glanced at her. His eyes glowed with a low level of psi.

"Just wondered if you could see through the fog."

"Sometimes I forget that you see things differently than I do. Don't worry, I won't blunder into a tree and brain myself."

"That possibility never occurred to me." She turned back around to study the scene. "I have to tell you that knowing that you're *almost* positive you know what we're doing here is not the most reassuring thing you could say under the circumstances. Remember, she's got that old rifle."

"I gave you the option of staying behind at the inn," Judson reminded her.

She ignored that. "Maybe we should talk to Oxley first."

"That won't do any good."

"Things could get awkward if you get caught."

"I won't get caught. But if I do, get on the phone to Dad."

She almost smiled. "That sounds similar to the advice you gave Nick."

"Because it's the best advice under the circumstances."

"Wow." She snapped her fingers. "Must be nice to come from a family that can make every little problem go away."

"The Coppersmiths can't make every problem go away, but we're pretty good when it comes to the annoying legal stuff." He unfastened his seat belt and opened the door. "I won't be long."

"Forget it." Gwen got out, too. "You're not going in without backup, partner."

He gave that a few seconds of consideration. Then he nodded once. Decision made.

"Okay," he said.

"Glad we got that settled," she said. She told herself that she was pleased that he seemed to be treating her as an equal partner in the investigation.

"All things considered, I'd rather have you where I can keep an eye on you," Judson added.

So much for the partnership, she thought.

"You do need me, Judson Coppersmith," she said. "I'm the one who knows this town and the people in it. Without me, you wouldn't have a clue where to start investigating. What's more, I'm in charge here. I'm the one paying the bills, remember?"

"Paying the bills doesn't mean you're in charge. It makes you the client."

"Semantics."

They wove a path through the trees to the

narrow strip of paved parking area behind the shop. Gwen waited for Judson to crack the old lock. To her surprise, he knocked on the door instead. The sharp rap of his knuckles on wood gave her a start. But she was even more astonished when he wrapped his hand around the knob and opened the door.

"We know you're in there, Nicole," he said calmly.

Gwen glanced at him, startled. It was certainly news to her.

"Uh, Judson, I'm not so sure a confrontation would be wise."

She stopped talking when she heard reluctant footsteps on the other side of the door.

Nicole appeared in the opening. She was dressed in faded jeans, a long-sleeved denim shirt and a light down vest. Her hair was scraped back in a ponytail.

"I should have known you'd figure out that I was the one who left the photo under Gwen's door," Nicole said. Her mouth twisted in a humorless smile. "You're both psychic, after all. Me, I'm just a fool who was dumb enough to fall for one of your kind. Don't worry, I learned my lesson."

A chill whispered through Gwen. She remembered something Evelyn had said once, long ago. *The risk in proving to others that the paranormal is real is that there will be those who will view people of talent not only as different but also as dangerous. And what people fear, they try to control, isolate or even destroy. Remember the Salem witch trials.*

"Zander Taylor was not one of our kind," Gwen said quietly. "He was a monster."

"No shit," Nicole said. "I finally figured that out for myself yesterday."

"It's time to talk," Judson said.

"Yeah, sure." Nicole turned on her heel and walked away into the shadows. "Guess it doesn't matter much anymore."

Judson moved through the doorway. Gwen knew from the shiver of energy in the atmosphere that he had kicked up his talent. She followed him into the back room of the shop. A dark, earthy perfume of freshly cut flowers, potted plants and decaying foliage assailed her senses.

Rows of decorative vases lined the shelves of the back room. Dried floral materials stood in large metal containers. A glass-fronted refrigerator hummed quietly in one corner. Several pairs of gardening shears and an assortment of other tools were neatly arranged on a nearby workbench.

Nicole went into the front of the shop. Large pots filled with chrysanthemums, orchids, daisies and lilies loomed in the shadows. Baskets of herbs and flowering plants hung from the ceiling.

Nicole moved behind the counter and opened the door of a small office. She flipped a light switch on the wall, illuminating the interior.

Gwen looked at the photos that covered the walls and shuddered. Trisha Montgomery's description was right. The small space was a shrine to Zander Taylor.

There was a large floral calendar tacked over the desk. The month of August was illustrated with a scenic shot of Oregon wildflowers. There were neatly written notes in several of the squares around various dates. *Carter wedding. Feed dogs. Order new vases for inn.* But aside from that single, cheerful exception, every inch of wall space was covered with photographs of Zander Taylor.

The pictures were various sizes. In most of the images, Taylor posed for the camera alone, smiling his charming psychopath's smile. Nicole was with him in a few of the shots, leaning into him, her arm wrapped around his waist, looking happy and thrilled to be in love.

But the Zander Taylor shrine had been vandalized. Each of the pictures had been savagely sliced, not once but over and over again. A pair of sharp gardening shears lay on the desk. The only untouched image in the room was the calendar illustration.

"People tell me I should move on," Nicole said. "They say I need to get past losing Zander." She studied one of the ripped photos. "But I can't seem to do that. For two years, every time I walked into this room it was like I had just lost him yesterday. I was okay with that."

"You didn't want to be free of him," Gwen said gently.

"No." Nicole's smile was bitter. "But now that I know the truth about him, I want to escape more than anything else in the world. That's not going to be possible."

"Why did you leave the photo under Gwen's door this morning?" Judson asked.

"I wanted to warn her." Nicole hugged herself and looked at Gwen. "Figured it was the least I could do after all the things I've said to you and about you, all the accusations I made. I felt bad about taking that shot at you, too."

"You're the one?" Gwen asked.

"I wasn't trying to hit you. I just wanted to scare you, make you leave Wilby."

"What were you trying to warn me about when you left that picture under my door this morning?" Gwen asked.

Nicole surveyed the pictures. "It's Zander. He's come back, you see. And now he's going to kill all of us. But I'm pretty sure he'll take you out first."

Judson watched her intently. "Zander Taylor is dead. They found his body in the river two years ago."

"You were one of the people who identified him," Gwen said.

Nicole shook her head. "He was a very powerful psychic. He could fool anyone. I wouldn't put it past him to fake his own death. I'm telling you, he has come back to take his revenge and then he'll complete his mission."

"What mission?" Judson asked.

"Two years ago, he told me he was some kind of undercover investigator. He said that because he was the real deal — a genuine psychic — the FBI had hired him to hunt down and expose the frauds and fakes and scam artists who pretended to be psychic. He said criminals like that took advantage of the elderly and folks who were in mourning. He said every year the con artists stole millions and got away with it because there was no one who could stop them."

"Except him," Judson said.

Nicole sniffed and reached for a tissue. "He told me that he was like a modern-day

Harry Houdini who traveled around the country, exposing the frauds. He claimed that he had joined Evelyn's research study here in Wilby to gather evidence against her."

"Did he say why he wanted to expose Evelyn?" Gwen asked. "She never worked as a storefront psychic. She never told fortunes or pretended to contact the dead. All she ever did was study the paranormal."

"He claimed that Evelyn's research study was just a cover," Nicole said. "He told me that in reality she was operating a school to teach con artists how to pose as psychics. But he said that in the course of his investigation, he had discovered that there was a real psychic in the study group, a very dangerous killer who could commit murder without leaving any trace."

"He was describing himself," Judson said.

"Yes, I know that now." Tears of pain and rage glittered in Nicole's eyes. She blew into the tissue. "I was such a gullible fool."

"No," Gwen said. "Taylor fooled all of us."

"But you and Evelyn Ballinger eventually realized what was going on," Nicole whispered. "I didn't. Not until yesterday."

"What did Zander tell you after the first two people in the study died?" Gwen asked.

Nicole shivered and started to rock back

and forth in the chair. "He said that he was in grave danger because he was closing in on the killer. He said he might have to disappear without warning, but if that happened, he would come back for me."

"He realized that Evelyn and I were on his trail," Gwen said. "He knew that even though we could never come up with hard proof that he was the killer, we would know the truth about him. He couldn't have that. He decided that he had to get rid of both of us. He intended to start with me."

"The day before he went over the falls, he said that you were the most dangerous person in the study group," Nicole whispered. "He said he was positive that you were the murderer."

"So when they pulled his body out of the river, you assumed that he had confronted me and that I had killed him," Gwen said.

"It all seemed to fit." Nicole unfolded her arms and scrubbed the tears from her eyes with the back of one hand. "Chief Oxley said that you were the last one to see him alive. Oxley doesn't believe in the paranormal, but I could tell he had his suspicions, too. When Evelyn shut down the study and you and most of the others left town, I was convinced that you were the killer that Zander had been hunting. I thought no one would ever catch you and that Zander would never be avenged."

"Then, two years later, Evelyn is found dead and I'm back in town," Gwen concluded. "You and Oxley and a lot of other people are wondering if the killing has started again because I'm here."

"Yes. But it's been two years and I've had some time to think." Nicole stared at one of the pictures on the wall. "I've asked myself a lot of questions since Zander died. I haven't been able to find many answers. That was why I went to see Louise yesterday."

Judson examined the photos. "What questions have you been asking yourself?"

"Mostly about his precious camera," Nicole said. "Zander never let it out of his sight. He said it was a special hand made camera that had come out of a secret government lab and that only someone like him — a real psychic — could operate it. He told me that the focus was paranormal in nature and had to be adjusted frequently. He called it a tune-up and said that Louise was one of the few people in the world who knew how to do it."

"How did he explain her knowledge of the workings of a paranormal camera?" Judson asked.

Nicole shrugged. "Something to do with her ability to tune her wind chimes. He said she had the magic touch because she was a genuine witch. He laughed when he told me that. At the time, I thought he was teasing me. I knew he believed in the paranormal, but he had always made it clear that he didn't believe in magic and witchcraft. I assumed he meant that Louise had some psychic talent that allowed her to adjust the focus of the camera."

"The camera disappeared after Zander died," Gwen said. "Evelyn and I looked for it."

"So did I," Nicole said. "In fact I went back to the falls to search for it. When I couldn't find it there, I went to the house that Zander had rented to look for it. I even asked Louise if she knew what had happened to it."

"What did she say?" Judson asked.

"Nothing helpful. Something about the demon taking it. She said it wouldn't have done me any good because I didn't have the kind of power it took to make the camera work. She was having one of her bad days that day. You know how it was with her. She was always walking a fine line between semi-crazy and real crazy. On that day she was definitely on the wrong side of the line."

"Why did you want the camera?" Gwen asked.

"I just wanted a keepsake," Nicole said. "Something that had been important to Zander. He had made it clear that the camera was his most valuable possession. When I couldn't find it, I assumed you had stolen it or else it had gone into the river."

"Evelyn and I convinced ourselves that it had gone over the falls with Zander," Gwen said. "But now that Evelyn and Louise are both dead by paranormal means, it's looking like someone else found the camera that day, someone who has the talent to use it."

Nicole looked at her. "I was afraid you were going to say that."

"It's possible that there were two crystal-based weapons all along," Judson said. "We don't have all the answers yet. You said that you went to Louise's house to ask her a question."

"Yes."

"What was it you wanted to ask her?" Judson asked.

"I remembered what Zander had said about Louise having the ability to adjust the camera focus. He called her a witch, but he told me that very few people had her kind of talent. It occurred to me that if Gwen was using the camera, she would need to get it refocused periodically and that maybe she knew that Louise could do that kind of magic."

"That was very good thinking," Gwen said. "The same thing had occurred to me. Now that Louise is dead, Judson and I are going on the theory that whoever has the camera was using Louise to tune it but then decided that she had become a liability and killed her before we could talk to her."

"Yes, I think that is exactly what happened," Nicole said. "When I found her body, I was terrified. Those damn chimes. I think I'll hear them in my nightmares for the rest of my life."

"The chimes were sounding when you got there?" Judson asked.

"Yes," Nicole said. She unfolded her arms and massaged her temples. "It was like a ghost was causing them to make that terrible music. It seemed to be getting louder and louder. I wanted to run. But then I heard your car in the driveway. I thought maybe the two of you were working together. You had murdered Evelyn and Louise and now you were going to kill me, too. The chimes made it impossible to think clearly." Nicole paused to take a deep breath. "But last night I realized I had been wrong about you, Gwen, and probably everything else, as well."

"What convinced you that I wasn't the killer?" Gwen asked.

Nicole moved one hand in a small gesture. "You and Mr. Coppersmith saved me from the fire."

"That's it?" Gwen frowned. "You decided we were the good guys just because we didn't leave you behind when the house went up in flames?"

"The kind of monster Zander described to me would have left me in that house." Nicole shook her head. "How could I have been so wrong about Zander?"

"The ability to charm those around him was part of his talent," Gwen said. "You know that he was psychic. Well, think of him as a kind of hypnotist. He could make people believe just about anything. Evelyn and I were fooled for a while, too. So was everyone else in town."

"I wonder if he fooled Louise," Nicole said quietly. "That poor crazy old witch. Do you suppose she ever realized that she was aiding and abetting a serial killer?"

THIRTY-FOUR

"We need some deep background on Zander Taylor," Judson said. "And we need it fast. How much did you and Evelyn find out about him when you realized that he might be the killer?"

"Not much," Gwen said. "All we had to go on were the forms that he filled out for Evelyn's files when he joined the study. He claimed that his mother gave him up for adoption shortly after he was born. Evidently something terrible happened to his adoptive parents. Zander told us they were murdered in the course of a home invasion. Afterward he ended up in the foster care system. But who knows? With Zander, you could never be sure when you were getting the truth."

Judson thought about that while he pried off the lid of his coffee cup. Gwen's cup of tea sat untouched in the console between the two front seats. They had picked up the coffee and tea at Wilby's lone fast-food restaurant after leaving Nicole's shop. At Gwen's suggestion, he had driven out along a narrow road that dead-ended on a tree-studded bluff overlooking the falls.

From where they were parked, they could see the old lodge that Evelyn had converted into a lab on the opposite side of the river. The windowless structure sat shrouded in gloom and shadow, another sad monument to the futility of pursuing paranormal research, Judson thought.

Gwen contemplated the dark lodge through the windshield. "Every dime Evelyn ever got went into that lab. I asked her once why she had wasted so much of her life trying to prove the paranormal was normal."

"Did she give you an answer?"

"She said she had been saddled with the ability to perceive just far enough beyond the normal to know that the paranormal existed. She said that a little knowledge was always a dangerous thing because it made you want more. She yearned for answers."

"So does my brother, Sam. He says he can't abandon the research when the reality of the paranormal confronts him every time he looks into a mirror. And now he's talking about doing the research for the sake of his future children."

"I've met Sam, and it's obvious that he's fascinated with crystals and para-physics," Gwen said. "But that's not what compels you, is it?"

"No. Don't get me wrong. I'm always interested in what comes out of the lab — everyone in the Coppersmith family is curious about the research — but I'm not obsessed with the latest crystal theories or the results of some new experiment." He shrugged, drank some of the coffee and lowered the cup. "Not unless I can figure out how to use it."

Gwen smiled her knowing smile. "In the course of one of your investigations."

"Sam is my partner in Coppersmith Consulting because he likes the scientific and technical end of the security business — the forensics. But me, I like the hunt."

"Yes, I know." She picked up her tea and removed the lid. "I also get the feeling that you like to work alone."

"I can work with Sam," he said, feeling oddly defensive.

"Sure," she said. "Because he's family. You can trust him."

He breathed deep and exhaled slowly. "I trust you, Gwen."

She looked startled. Then she positively glowed.

"Why, thank you," she said. "I'm honored. As it happens, I trust you, too."

"Good. That's good." He shifted slightly, searching for a path into the difficult conversation he wanted to have. "There's something else I want to say. I respect what you do with your talent."

Her eyes widened. "Really? I'm thrilled. I have to tell you there's just not a lot of respect out there for those of us in the psychic counseling profession."

"Okay, maybe I need to qualify my statement. I respect you. Not sure about the other psychic counselors. Lot of phonies out there."

"Sadly, that is all too true." She took a cautious sip of the tea. "Which is why I'm thinking of changing careers."

"What?"

"I like this detecting business."

"I can tell," he growled.

"All modesty aside, I feel I have a certain flair for it."

"You do," he agreed. "But where, exactly, are you going with this?"

"I've been solving historical murder cases in a fictional sense for the past two years for *Dead of Night.* In the process, I've learned a

lot about researching cold cases from Evelyn. I've learned a lot from you, too. In fact,
I've picked up several very helpful pointers
in the course of our partnership."

"Gwen, if this is going where I think it's
going —"

"And then there's my dream therapy
work." Gwen's enthusiasm was growing
stronger by the second. Her eyes sparkled.
"When you think about it, that has a lot in
common with what you do — searching for
clues, understanding motives. It's like I've
been serving an apprenticeship all these
years. Now I'm ready to come out of the
shadows."

He was getting a bad feeling, a real deer-
in-the-headlights kind of feeling.

"What are you planning to do when this
case is over?" he asked.

"I'm going to open a psychic detective
agency," Gwen announced.

She was damn near incandescent now, he
thought.

"I was afraid you were going to say that."
He set his cup down in the holder. "Gwen,
listen to me, this business isn't what you
think it is."

"Don't worry, I don't plan to compete
with Coppersmith Consulting," she said
quickly. "I'm not interested in industrial

espionage or secret agent work."

"Okay, that's a good thing because —"

"I'm thinking more along the lines of small, quiet murder cases and missing persons work."

"There are no quiet cases of murder, and when people go missing it's usually for a reason — often a dangerous reason."

"Don't worry, I'll be careful."

"That's supposed to reassure me? Gwen, you read auras for a living. You fix bad dreams, remember?"

"I just explained that background will be very helpful in my investigations." Excitement and energy heated her eyes. "This feels right, Judson. It's like I've been floundering around all my life trying to find myself and figure out what I ought to be doing."

"You sound like my sister, Emma."

"I've found my passion, Judson, just as you have. I'm sure your sister will find hers, too, eventually."

For a nightmarish instant, he was back in the flooded caves, sucking up the last of the air in the tank. It took him a couple of seconds to breathe again.

He wanted her to feel passion for him, he realized, not for the investigation business. But she had a point. He did have a passion for the work that he did. How could he argue that she shouldn't feel something similar? Because it could be dangerous. That was the reason. The thought of Gwen going off on her own to investigate *small, quiet murder cases* scared the living daylights out of him. But he also had to admit that he understood.

They sat quietly for a time, the rain drizzling steadily on the windshield. The surging energy of the falls was a palpable force that penetrated the SUV. Something deep inside Judson responded to the wild currents. The steady, unrelenting roar was muffled by the closed windows, but it was always there in the background. He wondered absently how many eons the water had been cascading over the cliff. You didn't have to be psychic to know that there was such a thing as the paranormal. You only had to look at the forces of nature to realize that energy existed across a vast — perhaps an endless — spectrum that extended far beyond what people, with their limited senses and puny machines, could measure.

"Sometimes the hunt doesn't end well," he said after a while. "Sometimes I get the answer too late to do anyone any good. Sometimes people won't accept the answers I come up with. Sometimes I don't find any answers."

"Sometimes I can't fix a dreamscape," Gwen said. "Sometimes my clients won't accept the answers I come up with. Sometimes I can't find the answers, either. But at least as a private investigator I'll be able to find some of them."

"The major drawback to investigation work is that you have to deal with the clients," he said.

"They can't be any more frustrating or difficult than my dream therapy clients."

"Maybe not, but they can be more dangerous. My last client tried to kill me."

"Good grief." She swallowed hard. "Well, I promise I'll be careful."

"You keep saying that."

"No offense, but given your career path, you aren't in a position to lecture anyone else about the importance of not taking chances. Neither of us can ignore our talent, Judson."

"This conversation isn't going well, is it?" he said. "Maybe we should get back to the investigation that we're trying to work on here."

"Okay."

He settled into the corner and rested one arm along the back of the seat. "It occurs to me that Zander Taylor may have given you more hard facts than you realize."

Gwen's brows elevated slightly. "What makes you say that?"

"A skilled liar is usually smart enough to mix in as much of the truth as possible. It makes for a more convincing story."

"One thing I do know about Zander is that he was an excellent liar," Gwen said.

"In which case, it's possible that at least some of the information he gave Evelyn when he applied to the study was true," Judson said.

"Even if you're right, how do we sort the wheat from the chaff?"

Judson closed his eyes and summoned up a little energy, putting himself into the zone — into the head of the dead psychopath.

"Got a hunch that when we go looking, we'll find out that Taylor really was adopted and that his adoptive parents were murdered — maybe by Taylor himself, given what I know of his para-psych profile — but that's not our problem now."

"Sometimes I wonder how many people he did kill, but I suppose we'll never know," Gwen said somberly. "Maybe I don't want to know."

Judson opened his eyes. "He was probably also telling the truth when he said he wound up in the foster care system. Those are all facts that could be verified. They are also facts that make him look somewhat sympathetic. That would be key to the impression he wanted to make."

"I'm inclined to agree with you if only because when he talked about the system, it was clear that he had an intimate, working knowledge of it."

"Like you?"

"Yes," she said evenly. "But even if those particular facts are true, where does it get us?"

"I'm not sure yet," he admitted. "Still asking questions. Turning over rocks. That's how I work. But we need to move faster. I don't have time to do the research. I'm going to put Sawyer on Zander Taylor's backstory and see what he can find." Judson reached for his phone. "Damn. It would be so useful to have those old files from Ballinger's time as a counselor at Summerlight."

"Why?" Gwen asked,

He started to key in Sawyer's phone number. "They might give us a better handle on Taylor, for one thing. The school must have had some data on his past."

"But Zander didn't attend Summerlight."

Judson stilled just as he was about to punch in Sawyer's number. "Are you sure?"

"Positive."

"I thought all of the subjects in the Ballinger Study were drawn from the Summerlight files."

"Evelyn found most of us in her Summerlight records but not all of us," Gwen said. "Back at the start, she also advertised briefly online. She gave up that approach after only a few days because she got flooded with replies from fantasy game players, fake psychics, and the alien-abduction and tinfoil-helmet crowd. She said there was no way to sort through all the wacky claims to try to find the one or two genuine talents who might have applied."

"How did she find Taylor?"

"He told us that he saw one of those online ads that Evelyn ran at the start of the project. He contacted her online and charmed her by appealing to her academic pride. He posed as a serious researcher. Claimed he'd heard about her work in the field and that he had read some of the papers she had published in an online journal. When he offered to come to Wilby to meet with her at his own expense, she jumped at the chance. After she talked to him, she was convinced that he had some real talent."

"That works." Judson looked out at the thundering falls, the phone gripped in his hand. "It definitely works."

"What are you talking about?" Gwen demanded. "Why is it important that Zander got involved in Evelyn's study through an online ad?"

Judson turned back to her. "Think about it. Evelyn runs a short series of ads on the Internet and then cancels that recruitment approach in favor of relying on the Summerlight files. Yet in that brief span of time, she somehow attracts the attention of a psychic serial killer."

Gwen nodded slowly. "There are a gazillion phony psychics advertising online. What are the odds that Taylor just happened to see Evelyn's little ad? Is that what you're asking?"

"Yes."

"If you're asking me, I have no idea what the odds are," Gwen said. "I avoid math whenever possible."

"This isn't math — this is my intuition talking."

Gwen smiled. "You mean your talent."

"I think Zander Taylor found out about Evelyn and her study two years ago because he had a tripwire already in place."

"Tripwire?"

"An alert system designed to make sure that any and all news out of Wilby, Oregon, popped up on his computer."

"For heaven's sake, why would he monitor news from this little dot on the map?"

"There's only one reason that I can think of," Judson said. "He kept track of Wilby because he had a personal connection here."

"But no one here in town knew him — I'm sure of that. Someone would have said something at some point."

"You told me that Louise Fuller wasn't exactly the communicative type."

"Louise." Gwen's eyes tightened a little at the corners. "Good heavens, you're right. Nicole said that she tuned the crystal for him. That means he could have known about Louise before he came here to Wilby. Maybe he was using her all along to tune his camera. But none of his kills was in the vicinity of this town, at least none that we could identify."

"A smart psychopath doesn't foul his own nest, at least not unless he loses control or decides to get rid of witnesses. Why take the risk of killing locally?" Judson paused a beat. "Unless the challenge is downright irresistible."

"Evelyn's group of study subjects was an irresistible attraction," Gwen whispered. "Zander's addiction got the better of his control."

349

"Taylor paid attention to events in Wilby because Louise Fuller, his tuner, was here. That leaves us with the question of how he found Louise in the first place."

"And why no one in town knew him until he joined the study," Gwen added.

Judson looked at the lab on the other side of the falls. "Just winging it here, but a couple of things I know for sure. Psychic talent seems to have a strong genetic component. If the Coppersmiths are any example, the ability to perceive and manipulate the paranormal can go down through the bloodline. The other thing I know is that family secrets are always the most tightly held."

"Family secrets?" Gwen was dumbfounded.

"We need confirmation. I'll call Sawyer."

He keyed in the coded number.

Nick answered on the third ring. Judson could hear muffled voices in the background. One of them was his mother's.

"This had better be important," Nick said. "I'm a little busy at the moment, Coppersmith."

"Doing what?" Judson asked.

"Getting fitted for my tux. By the way, your mother says that you had better show up for a fitting soon or you're going to be in big trouble. You're Sam's best man, remember?"

"What I remember is that you're supposed to be working on my case."

"Some of us — those of us with true talent — are capable of multitasking. Your mother and me, for instance. By the way, Mrs. Coppersmith says to tell you that she hasn't turned up any odd financial maneuvers on the part of anyone on the list of suspects you gave me."

"I'll add some more names to the list," Judson said.

"Pink?" Outrage vibrated in Nick's voice. "I'm walking the bride down the aisle. I can't wear a pink shirt. This is a classic wedding. I wear a white shirt."

"Damn it, Sawyer," Judson said. "Pay attention."

"Turns out that a couple of other heirs also spent some time in Sundew's online chat room," Nick said. "Neither had ever indicated any previous interest in psychic counseling. No, not pleats. Think Armani, not your high school prom rental."

"Forget the damn fitting, Sawyer," Judson said. "I'm pulling you off the psychic chat room project for now. Something more urgent has come up."

Nick uttered a long-suffering sigh. "What

do you want now?"

"Deep background on a woman named Louise Fuller."

"What am I looking for?"

"Family history. I'm looking for a bloodline link between Louise and Zander Taylor."

"The psycho who tried to murder Gwen? Shit. Think that son of a bitch is still alive after all?"

"You tell me."

"Give me everything you've got on her," Nick said.

Judson rattled off the few facts they had.

"I'll get back to you as soon as I've got something," Nick promised, cold and serious now.

Judson ended the call.

"Now what?" Gwen asked.

"Now we wait," Judson said. He hated this part. "I don't think it's going to take Sawyer long to find the answers, because I doubt if Louise knew how to bury her own past."

Gwen watched him. "You already know the answer, don't you?"

Judson hesitated. "I've learned the hard way not to leap to conclusions."

"But you know, don't you?"

"Yes," he said. "It's the only answer that fits."

■ ■ ■ ■

Nick called back fifteen minutes later. Judson could hear the energy in his voice. *We're more alike than you think, Sawyer,* he thought. *We both thrive on the hunt.*

He put the call on speakerphone so that Gwen could hear the conversation.

"I may have something and it's not good," Nick said. "Thirty-four years ago, Louise Fuller was living in L.A. Got caught up in a cult that was heavily into psychoactive drugs. The cult was really a cover for a well-organized criminal gang. The leader controlled his followers with drugs and sex. He used his male followers to sell the drugs, and he pimped out his female followers. Louise was one of the prostitutes. She got pregnant. Gave the baby up for adoption."

"Any leads on the father?"

"No. That's a brick wall. Louise was living in a drug haze at the time. The cult leader was sending her out onto the streets every night to sleep with anyone who had the cash. According to the caseworker, Louise was delusional and incapable of handling motherhood due to addiction and mental health issues. The baby went to a childless couple who —"

"Were later murdered in the course of a home invasion," Judson concluded.

"You're thinking Louise's baby was the future Zander Taylor, aren't you?" Nick asked.

"It explains a lot. Wouldn't be surprised if he was the one who murdered his adoptive parents."

"Yeah, struck me as a possibility, too," Nick said. "At the time, young Zander was in therapy. Actually, he had been for years because he was exhibiting the usual warning signs — torturing small animals and setting fires — at an early age. He was thirteen when the so-called home invasion took place. He told police he came home from school and found the bodies. Afterward he went into foster care for a couple of years, bounced around in the system creating havoc wherever he landed and, eventually, to everyone's great relief, disappeared."

"What about Louise?"

"The cult eventually broke up," Nick said. "The leader vanished. Louise moved to Wilby and started making her wind chimes for fun and profit."

"Looks like Taylor tracked her down at some point. By then he had a handle on his own talent. By all accounts, he was an expert when it came to charming people.

Louise would have been an especially easy target because she was psychologically fragile."

Gwen spoke up from the other seat. "And because she was his mother, for heaven's sake. Part of her would have wanted to be reunited with her only child."

"You're usually right when it comes to that kind of stuff, Gwen," Nick said.

"I'm guessing that Louise gave the crystal that powered the camera to her son," Gwen continued. "She was always worried about demons. Maybe she gave him the crystal as a sort of personal protection device."

"Taylor came back to Wilby periodically to get his weapon refocused," Judson said. "Louise probably never knew what he was doing with it."

"The problem with that theory is that no one there in Wilby had even met Taylor until he showed up to take part in Evelyn's study," Gwen said. "If he was visiting Louise occasionally to get the camera crystal tuned, why didn't someone notice?"

"Louise lived in the middle of the woods, a few miles outside of town," Judson reminded her. "It would have been easy for Taylor to visit her without being seen by any of the locals. It wasn't like he would have had to see her very often to get the camera retuned. His kills were probably months apart."

"And the camera might have been good for two or three kills before it needed tuning," Gwen said quietly.

"If that's true, Taylor wouldn't have had to visit good old Mom more than two or three times a year, at most," Nick said. "So maybe he could keep his visits to her secret. But if you're right, it means that she kept those visits secret, too. Why? What would be the point?"

"I don't have all the answers yet," Judson said.

"No kidding?" Nick snorted. "Sounds to me like you've got most of 'em. Why call me?"

"I had to get as much of the backstory as possible because someone else with Taylor's talent is using his camera to murder people for profit. Whoever he is, he was using Louise to retune the camera. But Zander Taylor didn't kill for the money. He did it for kicks."

"Psychos like that don't usually change their M.O., so we can forget the theory that Taylor is still alive," Nick said.

"Yes," Judson said. "We're dealing with a different killer who happens to have the same kind of talent. And if you believe in genetics —"

Gwen went very still. "Family."

"What did she say?" Nick asked.

"She's thinking what I'm thinking," Judson said. The deep thrill of intuition heated his blood. "Based on what little we know of psychic genetics, there is at least a possibility that the killer we're hunting is related to Zander Taylor."

"Louise Fuller might have given up more than one baby," Gwen suggested.

"Ah, yes, the ever-popular twins, separated-at-birth scenario," Nick intoned. He voice lightened. "Afraid that won't fly in this case. According to the file, Louise had no other children. Her son was delivered by cesarean section. She had her tubes tied at that time. She told the caseworker that she couldn't risk giving birth to another baby."

Gwen leaned forward. "Did she tell the caseworker why she didn't want another child?"

"According to the notes, Fuller explained that her baby was the offspring of a demon," Nick said. "She didn't want to take the chance of repeating that mistake."

"Damn," Judson felt his intuition crystallizing into certainty. "We need to find him."

"Who?" Nick asked.

"The demon father," Judson said. "He's

the key to this whole thing."

"Not a chance in hell I could track down one of what was evidently a very large number of customers that Fuller slept with thirty-four years ago," Nick said. "I'm good, but not that good. That kind of street prostitution is a cash business. There is no money trail. And after all this time, there won't be anyone left who will remember names and faces. It's a dead end."

Gwen leaned forward to speak into the phone. "The demon wasn't one of the customers," she said. "The demon is the bastard who pimped her out. That's why she feared him. He controlled her, body and soul."

"We're looking for the cult leader," Judson said. "He made a career change at some time in the past. He became a free lance contract killer. Go back to your computer, Sawyer. Find Sundew."

Thirty-Five

Gwen waited impatiently until Judson ended the call. Energy, excitement and anticipation were sleeting through her.

"I know why Louise gave her son the crystal camera," she said.

"Yeah?" Judson clipped his phone to his belt. "I'm assuming you don't think it was because she planned to set him up in the serial killer business."

"No, she gave it to him so that he could use it to protect himself from his father, the demon."

"Huh." Judson considered that with a coolly thoughtful air. "You know, that works in a twisted kind of way."

"Maybe she even dared to hope that Zander would do what she could not do herself — destroy the man who had abused her for so long."

"She wanted her son to be her avenger. Yes, that works, too. You know, talking to you is useful. It helps me clarify things. You're good at this profiling stuff."

She was surprised by how much his praise warmed her. "Thanks. Side effect of my talent, I guess. You can get into the heads of the bad guys. Me, I sort of get into the heads of the victims."

"The talking-to-ghosts thing."

"Right. That's what it's really all about, I think. I'm profiling the victims when I do that."

"Yes," Judson said. He looked intrigued by that notion. "You do seem to have a talent for that."

"We make a good team."

"Looks like it."

"Well, whoever the demon is, the bastard has a lot to answer for."

"He does," Judson agreed. "One thing is certain, everything points to the demon being a resident of Wilby. He's right here in town. He's been here all along. But Louise would have known that he was here. If she was terrified of him, why did she move here in the first place?"

"She was a psychologically and psychically damaged woman," Gwen said. "Any bastard who could run a cult would have found it a snap to control her. He would have wanted her here, not only because it was convenient but also so that he could keep an eye on her to make sure she didn't get any ideas about going to the cops."

"And if we're right, this particular demon bastard has some serious talent," Judson said. "That would make it even easier to manipulate a fragile woman like Fuller."

"Poor Louise. No wonder she was such a basket case. The next question is, did father and son know each other?"

Judson tapped one finger on the steering wheel. "Maybe not back at the beginning when Taylor first tracked down his mother here in Wilby. But at some point along the way, yes, they discovered each other. Maybe Louise told Taylor about his father, or maybe the demon discovered there had been a mother-and-son reunion and introduced himself. The father now has the camera or at least he's got the crystal inside it. He's been using it for the past year and a half."

"That confirms the motive for Evelyn's murder. She stumbled onto the identity of the demon."

"Yes."

"We're back to waiting again, aren't we?"

"Unfortunately, yes."

THIRTY-SIX

Gwen suppressed a small groan when she saw Wesley Lancaster pacing in front of the entrance to the inn. His blond mane fluttered in the soft breeze. He glanced impatiently at the expensive black watch on his wrist. When he looked up, he spotted Judson's SUV pulling into the parking lot. His relief and impatience were plain on his handsome face.

"I knew he wouldn't give up easily," Gwen said. "But I was hoping he would wait a while before he started pestering me again."

Judson eased the SUV into one of the empty slots and shut down the engine. "Are you going to talk to him?"

"Are you kidding? Of course I'll talk to him. It will take a while to get a psychic investigation agency up and running. In the meantime I need the income from those *Dead of Night* scripts." Gwen unbuckled the seat belt, opened the door and hopped out of the front seat. "It's just that I'm a little busy at the moment. With luck I can convince him to be patient."

"I don't think so," Judson said.

He was not looking at her. His attention was fixed on the entrance to the inn. She followed his gaze and saw Wesley striding toward the SUV.

"It's about time you showed up, Gwen," Wesley said. "I need to talk to you. "It's important. I've come up with a dynamite concept for *Dead.* It will take the series in a new direction."

"Okay, give me a minute," she said.

She opened the rear-seat door and reached inside with both hands to haul the cat carrier out of the vehicle. Max grumbled and flattened his ears.

"It's your own fault you didn't get to stay here and enjoy room service while we went out," Gwen reminded him. "This is what you get for frightening housekeepers."

Judson came around the front of the SUV, somehow managing to make it appear that he was unaware of Wesley's presence.

"I'll take Max," Judson said.

"Thanks." Gwen gave him the heavy carrier. "I'll talk to Wesley in the lobby."

"I'll escort Max upstairs," Judson said. "Don't leave the inn."

"I won't," she promised.

Judson finally deigned to acknowledge Wesley's existence with a fractional inclination of his head.

"Lancaster," Judson said evenly.

Wesley frowned impatiently. "I see you're still around, Coppersmith."

Judson ignored him. Instead, he angled his head and gave Gwen a quick, possessive kiss that caught her by surprise. He didn't bother to wait for a response. Instead, he straightened and gave her a narrow-eyed look.

"Don't be long," he said. "Got a lot to do this afternoon."

He headed for the lobby entrance, gripping the cat carrier in one hand as though it was weightless. Gwen watched him with a mix of irritation and amusement.

Wesley watched Judson, too, his jaw very tight. "Someday you'll have to tell me what you see in Coppersmith." He paused deliberately. "Besides the Coppersmith family money, that is."

"You know, insulting me and the man I'm currently dating is probably not the best way to start this conversation."

Wesley grimaced. "I know. Sorry about that. It's just that I really need your help at the moment, and I'm getting the feeling that

Coppersmith is doing his best to stand in my way."

"You and I have a business relationship," she said. "Judson understands that. The tearoom is empty at this time of day. Why don't we talk in there? I'm sure the staff won't mind if we use one of the tables for a private conversation."

"Fine."

She led the way through the lobby and into the quiet tearoom. She took a seat at a table near the window. Wesley sat down across from her.

"Where have you been?" he asked. "I waited nearly an hour and a half for you to show up."

"I had no idea that you were back in Wilby. Why didn't you call to make an appointment?"

"I tried. Your phone was off."

Belatedly she remembered she had turned off her phone when they went to Nicole's shop.

"Sorry, my fault," she said. "We've been busy." She dove into the tote, took out the phone and switched it back on. She glanced at the list of missed calls. "You called six times?"

"I was starting to get worried, if you want to know the truth." She dropped the phone back into the bag. "About what?"

"In case you've forgotten, two women were recently found dead in this very small town within the past forty-eight hours. This morning you went missing."

"I wasn't missing."

"No one here at the inn knew where you were. All anyone could say for sure was that you were last seen in the company of Judson Coppersmith."

She took a breath and let it out slowly. "Sorry. It never dawned on me that anyone would be worried."

"I don't think anyone else except me was concerned," Wesley said. "But I have to tell you Evelyn's death shook me. And now the local witch is dead in a house fire. Maybe I've done one too many *Dead of Night* episodes, but the town of Wilby is starting to give me the creeps. When you didn't answer your phone this morning, I guess I overreacted."

"Louise," Gwen said. She spoke quietly but firmly.

"What?"

"The dead woman's name is Louise Fuller. And for the record, she was not into witchcraft. She was a troubled soul who was plagued with some serious mental health issues."

Wesley reddened. "Sorry. I seem to be doing a great job of offending you today, and believe me, that's the last thing I want to do."

"Tell me why you tried to call me six times today and why you waited an hour and a half for me to show up here."

Excitement transformed Wesley's handsome face.

He leaned forward, braced his arms on the table and started talking in low, urgent tones.

"It's the perfect way to revitalize the series," he said. "Don't know why I didn't think of it right away. It was the shock of hearing that Evelyn was dead, I guess. At first all I could think of was finding her files."

"Oh, for pity's sake, I should have guessed. You were the one who searched Evelyn's office after her body was removed, weren't you?"

"Now, Gwen, it wasn't like that. I didn't take anything."

"How could you do such a thing? Talk about invading the privacy of the dead. Talk about illegal as hell. It's called breaking and entering, you know. People go to jail for stuff like that."

Wesley's eyes darkened with outrage.

"You're accusing me of breaking into Evelyn's house?"

"It wasn't an accusation," Gwen said. "More like a statement of fact."

"Based on *what*?"

"Intuition."

"You can't go around accusing people of illegal actions based on intuition."

"It was you. Don't bother to deny it."

"All right, I dropped by her house that day, but I swear I didn't take a damn thing. And I didn't break in. The back door was unlocked when I got there. All I did was take a look through her files. I was her employer. I have a right to whatever she was working on at the time of her death."

"That house belongs to me now. Don't go near it again without my permission."

"Calm down. I apologize." Wesley slumped into his chair. "I've got no reason to go back there, anyway. And just to be absolutely clear, I repeat, I didn't take anything."

"Why did you make such a mess?"

"Because I was in a hurry," Wesley said. "I was afraid someone might come along and find me inside the house and think I was one of those people who robs empty houses after the owner dies. I didn't want to get caught, that's all. But I didn't steal anything."

"I believe you," she said. "Not that it makes any difference when it comes to the underlying ethical issues involved."

Wesley watched her for a long moment. He drummed his fingers on the table. "You really think she was murdered, don't you?"

"Yes."

"Like the others two years ago?"

"Yes."

"I knew it. It's perfect." Wesley used both hands to rake his blond hair back behind his ears. Excitement lit his eyes again. "If you're right, this could be huge."

"I doubt it. If I'm right, all the victims were killed by paranormal means and that will be impossible to prove."

"But that's exactly what you're trying to do, isn't it? Prove that Evelyn was murdered by paranormal means. That's why you're hanging around Wilby. This isn't about taking care of Evelyn's estate. It's about trying to find out what really happened to her and to that witch."

"Louise Fuller."

"Louise Fuller," Wesley repeated obediently.

Gwen exhaled slowly. "It's true — I'd like to find some answers."

"Where does Coppersmith fit into this?"

"He's a friend."

"You're sleeping together — I know that much," Wesley said. "Hell, everyone in town knows it. But that's not the whole story. I've known you for two years. You haven't had a serious relationship in all that time."

"I didn't realize you'd been paying such close attention to my personal life."

"I admit that after my divorce last year, I asked Evelyn about you from time to time," Wesley said. "She made it clear that you were not interested in an intimate relationship with a man. I got the message."

"Did you?"

"Well, I thought I got it. I assumed that you just didn't like men in that way, that you were more interested in women." Wesley frowned. "But when you showed up here with Coppersmith, it was obvious that something had changed."

"And you're wondering why him and not you? For heaven's sake, Wesley, you've never had any deep feelings for me. We both know that. Two years ago I was a curiosity to you — a woman who claimed to have some paranormal talent. You wonder what it would be like to go to bed with me, that's all. You're looking at this through the lens of your ego. Give it a rest. Sometimes two people just don't click."

"But you and Coppersmith have clicked, is that it?"

"I think we're getting a little off topic here."

Wesley grunted. "Yeah, you're right. Believe it or not, I'm here to offer you a business proposition."

"I'm listening."

"I have had an absolute brainstorm. Wait until you hear my new concept for the show. It's going to take *Dead of Night* into the big leagues."

"Let's hear it," Gwen said, trying to sound enthusiastic.

"Up until now we've focused on old legends that involve haunted houses and reports of mysterious paranormal events." Wesley was very intent now. "But that's gone stale. What the show needs is a new edge."

"How do you plan to get that?"

"We're going to refocus the series. We'll investigate cold cases, crimes that have never been solved."

"I hate to break this to you, but that's not a new concept."

"No, no, no, we've been doing historical murders. I'm talking about recent murders that have gone cold due to lack of evidence.

Maybe some missing-person's stuff, too."

"Wesley —"

"Here's the twist." Wesley leaned forward and lowered his voice. "We will solve the cold cases using real psychic investigators."

He threw himself back in his chair and spread his hands wide apart in a *Voilà* gesture. He waited for a reaction, smiling in expectation.

Gwen tried to think of something encouraging to say.

"I see," she said. "This is a fictional series, right?"

"No, no, no. Don't you get it? We'll work with genuine psychic investigators to reopen cold cases and solve real crimes."

"Where do you plan to find these psychic investigators?" she asked.

"It pains me to say it, but there are a lot of fakes and frauds in that line."

He winked. "But you and I know where to find the real deal — genuine psychics — don't we?"

She sat very still. "Evelyn's records?"

"I envision a small team of investigators composed of people like you and some of the others who participated in the Ballinger Study."

"As I recall, you were never convinced that there is such a thing as the paranormal, let alone that people could use that kind of talent to solve crimes."

"Between you and me, I'm still not entirely convinced," Wesley said. "But that isn't important. This is television. This will work. I know it in my gut. With Evelyn gone, I'm going to need your help putting the show together. The first step is to track down the psychics who participated in Evelyn's study two years ago."

"That's why you searched her house, isn't it? You weren't looking for her last ideas for a new *Dead of Night* episode. You wanted to find her records relating to the Ballinger Study."

"You want the truth, Gwen? I'm desperate and I need your help. Ratings are in the toilet. They're threatening to cancel *Dead of Night.* What's more, this isn't just about me. If I don't come up with a new concept and fast, we're both going to be out of a job."

"I'm sorry, but I don't think this is a good idea, Wesley. I was okay with writing up scripts based on Evelyn's research of historical crimes, but you're talking about taking the show in a whole different direction, one that could cause a lot of legal problems."

"What do you mean?" he demanded.

"Stop and think about what might happen if you go around the country trying to reopen murder investigations in a reality TV format. Law enforcement isn't going to be at all cooperative. The families of the deceased will be upset. And even if you did uncover a for-real case of murder using psychic investigation techniques, how on earth would you go about proving it?"

"This is television," Wesley said. "We don't have to prove anything. All we need to do is come up with a convincing theory of the crime that's strong enough to cast doubt on the original findings. Hell, we'll be doing a public service. At the very least, we can force regular law enforcement to take a closer look at some cold cases."

"How do you intend to decide what cases warrant a *Dead of Night* investigation?"

"That's where you come in. Your job will be to come up with the right cases. Shouldn't be too hard. Once the word gets out online that I'm looking for reports of deaths that are unexplained or are in some way suspicious, we'll be flooded with leads."

"I can't help you, Wesley."

But he was not paying attention now. Dazzled by his own brilliance, he plowed forward.

"We'll start right here in Wilby," he announced. "We'll investigate Evelyn's death."

Gwen stared at him. "What?"

"It's perfect." He flung up both hands, palms out. *"Paranormal researcher slain by dark forces unleashed in her secret lab."*

"Forget it." Evelyn's ghost had been right, she thought. Wesley wanted to use her death as an episode on the show.

"After the first show, the lab will become the permanent set for *Dead of Night,*" he continued. "All of our future investigations will launch from there. I have to get back inside the lodge as soon as possible and take a closer look. Word in town is that you inherited that as well as her house. We could run over there right now."

"No."

That stopped Wesley. His face fell. "She didn't leave the lab to you? But everyone is saying —"

Gwen got to her feet. "The lab is mine, but I won't allow you turn Evelyn's death into an episode for your series."

Wesley stood. "You think she was murdered. This is your chance to prove it."

"Law enforcement and courts require hard evidence. No one is going to pay any attention to an investigation run by a bunch of television psychics."

She started toward the door.

Wesley lunged after her. He seized her upper arm, forcing her to stop.

"I need Evelyn's list of psychics," he said. "I'll pay you for it. Name your price."

She glanced down at his hand. "Let me go."

"Listen to me, damn it, you can't walk away. There's too much at stake here."

Gwen sensed the flood of icy energy an instant before she heard Judson's cold voice.

"Take your hands off her," he said.

Gwen felt the shock that snapped through Wesley. His hand dropped away. He stepped back so quickly he bumped into a nearby table. He glared at Judson.

"Don't you dare threaten me, Copper-smith," he said. "I'm trying to talk to Gwen. She works for me, damn it. I've got a right."

Judson ignored him. He looked at Gwen.

"Finished in here?" he asked.

The banked embers of a glacial fire still burned in his eyes. Heads were turning in the lobby. At the front desk, Riley Duncan was frowning.

Trisha Montgomery appeared from the back office. "Is there a problem?" she asked. The question was coolly polite, but there was steel in her eyes. "Gwen?"

"It's all right, Trisha," Gwen said quickly.

The situation was deteriorating. She knew that she had to separate the two men as fast as possible.

"Wesley and I have finished our business discussion," she said to Judson. "And the last thing we need is a scene," she added in low tones as she whisked past him.

She held her breath, but in the end Judson reluctantly turned away from his prey and followed her. They climbed the stairs in silence. Wesley stalked out of the tearoom, crossed the lobby and went outside to get into his car. Trisha returned to her office. Riley went back to work. The guests picked up their books and magazines.

On the third floor, Judson unlocked Gwen's door. She walked into the room. Max was ensconced in the center of the bed. He got to his feet to greet her. She crossed the room to rub his head.

Judson closed the door and stood with his back to it.

"What was going on down there?" he asked.

"Don't look now, but we may have some competition in the psychic detective business." Gwen sank down onto the side of the bed. "Wesley wants to fire up a new TV series focused on solving real cold case crimes using a team of genuine psychics as investigators. But you know how hard it is to find real talent."

Comprehension heated Judson's eyes. "He

wants Evelyn's records of the Ballinger Study so that he can use them to find genuine psychics. He was the one who searched her study before we got there."

"Yes." Gwen planted her hands behind her on the quilt and braced herself. "I didn't have the heart to tell him that I was planning to go into the psychic investigation business myself."

"The field is getting crowded," Judson said. He glanced at his watch and went to stand at the window, looking out into the woods. "We have some time. How long would it take?"

"How long would what take?" she asked.

He turned his head to look at her. "You said you could help me find what I'm looking for in my recurring dream. How long would it take?"

She stilled. "Not long."

"Let's do it."

"Are you sure?"

His eyes burned. "Dad said that a man would really have to trust a woman before he let her put him into a trance. I told you earlier that I trust you."

"But you still don't like the idea of needing dream therapy."

His smile was rueful. "You know me well, don't you, Dream Eyes?"

"Think of me as a repair person. Some people fix plumbing. I fix dreams."

"You have a gift, an incredible talent," he said. "What you do is amazing."

"Why, thank you."

"Walk through my dreams, partner. Help me find what I need to find."

"All right, but I have to warn you, I need context first," she said.

"I knew you were going to say that. Am I good or what?"

"You're good. Talk to me, Judson."

THIRTY-SEVEN

He needed answers, and it wasn't like he was having any luck getting them on his own, Judson thought. Time to call in the services of an expert. Gwen was one hell of a talent. And he trusted her.

He turned back to the window.

"What, exactly, do you mean by context?" he asked.

"I know that your dream is connected to whatever happened on that last job with your no-name-agency client, but that's all I've got. I need more if you want me to guide you through a trance."

"All right," he said. "I'll tell you what happened. But I don't see how it will help you interpret my dream."

"Take your time."

He fell silent for a moment, gathering his thoughts and memories. After a while, he started talking. He knew that he would not stop until he had told her everything.

"You know that Sam and I do — did — some investigative work for an off-the-books government agency," he said. "What you don't know is how we got the client."

"I assume you don't advertise Coppersmith Consulting services online."

"No. The director of the agency, Joe Spalding, recruited me and two other guys, Burns and Elland, in our senior year in college. Spalding was a quietly powerful figure in the intelligence community. He had been green-lighted to set up an experimental covert ops department staffed with agents he believed had some paranormal talent. It was supposed to be an updated version of the old CIA remote viewing project."

"How in the world did he identify potential agents like you?" Gwen asked.

"Spalding's real secret asset was that he was a talent himself," Judson said. "A strong one. He could recognize other people with similar psychic profiles if he got close enough to pick up the energy of their auras. He set up shop on a handful of college campuses, offering to pay students to take what he called an experimental psychology test that was designed to determine if a person had any psychic talent. I signed up out of curiosity to see if his test really worked."

"You knew you had some talent, so you were testing his test," Gwen said.

"Yes. The test, as it turned out, was a fraud. It was the old tell-me-what-card-I'm-holding-up-now experiment."

"Useless, according to Evelyn."

"Right. But Spalding wasn't depending on the results of his test. He was trying to find other people with what he called hot auras. A lot of nontalents showed up to take the test, of course, but he also got a few people who, like me, were drawn to the experiment because we wanted to know more about the psychic side of our natures."

"Spalding recognized you when he saw you," Gwen said.

"Yes. He found Burns and Elland at another campus. He offered all three of us a thrilling career filled with action and adventure as well as the opportunity to use our psychic talents in the service of our country."

"I gather you couldn't resist the offer," Gwen said.

"Hell, no." He turned around to face her. "I was twenty-one and looking for all the things Spalding promised. Mom tried to talk me out of joining the agency. But Dad was all for it. He said it would be good experience since I seemed fated for a career in the security field. And it was good experience. For a while."

Gwen smiled. "You were living every young man's dream. You were a real psychic secret agent. Very cool."

"Good times, yeah. Spalding understood that I preferred to work alone, and he let me run with my assignments. He didn't ask questions. All he cared about was results. I always got results. But after a couple of years, I realized that I wasn't cut out to work for someone else. I liked the investigation process, though."

"Because it suited your talents," Gwen said. "It was satisfying work."

"Yes. But I knew that I didn't want to work for Spalding or anyone else forever. I wanted to be my own boss. In the meantime, Sam had finished getting his fancy degrees in geology and engineering. We all knew that he was destined to head up the Coppersmith R-and-D lab, but like Emma and me, he didn't — couldn't — work directly for Dad."

"You Coppersmiths care a lot about each other, but you're all too strong willed to take orders from each other," Gwen said.

"Like Mom says, we're all chips off the old rock and Dad is a very hard chunk of stone. As it happened, Sam was thinking about setting up his own consulting firm, but there's not a lot of demand for paranormal crystal consultants outside the Coppersmith R-and-D lab. Spalding, however, saw a use for Sam's talents in the field. It was Spalding who suggested that Sam and I set up a private investigation business and work for him on a contract basis."

"Coppersmith Consulting."

"Trust me, the word *consulting* covers a lot of gray territory. Spalding liked the idea of a contract arrangement because it was so easy to hide off-the-record investigations that way. Sam and I went into business. Spalding was our main client. Things went along swell for quite a while. But about a year ago, things started to change."

"What happened?" Gwen asked.

"The changes were subtle at first. As contract consultants, we realized we were out of the need-to-know loop on a lot of stuff. But we had our intuition. We started to get uneasy about some of the jobs. Started turning down work from Spalding unless we could get enough background out of him."

Gwen smiled. "You and Sam wanted to know what you were getting involved in when you agreed to take a job. You wanted context."

"Sounds familiar?"

"Yep. So, to recap, I'm getting the impression that over time your relationship with Spalding and his little agency became somewhat strained."

"Right." He started to prowl the room. "But we all managed to make it work for a while. The bottom line for Spalding was that he needed us. We were the strongest talents he could put on a case and he knew it. If he wanted results, he used us, and if he used us, we demanded context."

"What about the other agents?"

"Burns and Elland turned out to be the canaries in the coal mine. I noticed the changes in them first."

"What kind of changes?"

"I had worked with both of them long enough to have a sense of their paranormal strengths as well as their limitations. Their abilities were similar to your friend Sawyer's — preternatural night vision and hearing, lightning-fast reflexes. They could disappear into the shadows."

"What happened?" Gwen asked.

"I went into the office one day to get a briefing from Spalding on a new investigation. Spalding was on the phone when I arrived. Burns was there. He offered to pour a cup of coffee for me. When I took the mug from his hand, I sensed something in his energy that just seemed somehow wrong."

"Define wrong," Gwen said.

"Unstable. Unhealthy. Unwholesome. He looked bigger, too, like he'd been lifting weights. There was some kind of heat in his eyes that I'd never noticed before. I asked him if he felt okay. I wondered if he might be coming down with a heavy-duty virus."

"How did he respond?

"It was as if I'd flipped a light switch. He went from calm and friendly to furious, like I'd insulted him. I thought he was going to take a swing at me. Then Elland came into the room and said something like, *Take it easy, buddy.* Burns turned around and stomped out of the room. After he left, I saw that Elland was suffering the same kind of fever, but he was a little more in control."

"Were they sick?"

Judson paused again in front of the window.

"Damned if I know," he said. "If it was an illness, it was a fever that affected their paranormal senses. All I knew for sure was that I didn't want to spend any time around either Burns or Elland. We Coppersmiths are a healthy bunch, but that day in Spalding's agency I started wondering if people like us — people of talent — might be vulnerable to fevers of the senses that normal people don't have to worry about."

"A reasonable concern. When did you run into Burns and Elland again?

"When they tried to kill me on that Caribbean island," he said.

"Wow. Okay. Go on."

"Shortly after that small scene at the agency, Spalding contacted me about an urgent, high-priority investigation. An intelligence analyst from another agency was missing. The working theory was that either he had gone rogue with some extremely sensitive information or else he'd been murdered. Spalding wanted me to find out what had happened. As usual, my job was to get answers. Sam and I don't do apprehension or arrests."

"You're just the consultants."

"Just the consultants," he agreed quietly.

"This was that final job that Coppersmith Consulting took for the no-name agency?" Gwen said. "The one where you went off the radar for a while?"

He glanced at her, surprised. "You know about that?"

"I didn't at the time. I was in Hawaii. But when I got back, Abby said that you had dropped out of sight for a while in the course of your last case and that something had gone wrong but that you had returned safely. Everyone said that you were taking some time off over on the coast to come up with a new business plan for Coppersmith Consulting."

"All true," he said.

"Except for the part about the recurring dreams."

"Except for that part."

"Tell me what happened on the island," Gwen said.

"I followed the missing analyst there. The story was that he had gone on a cave-diving trip. The islands in that part of the Caribbean are riddled with underwater caves. They attract a certain breed of diver."

"The thought of going into an aboveground cave is more than enough to give me the jitters. I can't even imagine going into one that is filled with water. Panic-attack city."

"It's not for everyone or even every diver," he said. "At any rate, it didn't take me long to discover that the analyst had disappeared shortly after arriving on the island. The local police had conducted a brief investigation, discovered he'd gone cave diving and concluded that he had drowned attempting to swim through a flooded cave system the locals called the Monster. I was told that he was not the first reckless tourist who had vanished that way."

"But you were suspicious?"

"I'd done some research on the missing analyst," Judson said. "He was an experienced diver, but he had never been into cave diving. It seemed unlikely that he would have attempted to dive the Monster, even less likely that he would have gone in alone. There's adrenaline junkie and there's dumb adrenaline junkie. Based on what I had learned about him, the analyst was not dumb."

"Did you find him?" Gwen asked.

"I found the place where he had been murdered. It was inside a cave at the entrance to the Monster. But his body was gone. I was pretty sure that whoever had killed him had taken the corpse down into the flooded part of the cave and wedged it there so that if it was ever discovered, the death would look like an accident."

"You decided to search for the body, didn't you?"

"That was the plan." Judson resumed his prowling. "But I never got the chance to put together a search-and-rescue operation because Burns and Elland arrived. They had been tailing me. They intended to get rid of me the same way they did the analyst. I was going to disappear into the Monster. Just another adrenaline junkie diver who took one too many chances."

"How did you survive?"

"The old-fashioned way. I had a gun. I used it."

"Yes, I suppose that approach still works." Gwen exhaled slowly. "You shot them both?"

"Yes, but here's the thing, Gwen, I didn't kill them." Judson stopped. "I got the information I wanted out of them and then I called the local cops. I waited until the emergency responders had arrived on the scene and explained that Burns and Elland had murdered the man who had disappeared into the sea caves. I flashed the fancy agency ID Spalding had given me, and the locals were satisfied. I swear, the last time I saw Burns and Elland, they were still alive and on the way to the hospital. Neither of them had life-threatening injuries."

Gwen frowned. "They didn't make it?"

"No. I wasn't around to witness what happened, but I found out later that both men went crazy after about a day and a half in the hospital. They both died within forty-eight hours. Suicide. Burns hung himself. Elland slashed his own wrists. Big medical mystery as far as the local authorities were concerned."

"Hmm. You have no idea what happened?"

"The nurses said the two men kept screaming for their special meds. They said their boss had the drugs they needed. They gave the hospital staff a number to call, but no one ever answered."

"Because by then their boss, Spalding, was dead?" Gwen said gently.

"Yes. Before they were taken away in an ambulance, Burns told me that the plan was to dump my body in the same underwater cave that they had used to conceal the analyst. They knew they had to make my death look very, very good."

"They were obviously aware that your father and your brother would tear Spalding's agency and the whole island apart looking for you if they had any suspicions about how you had died."

"Don't forget Emma and my mother," he said dryly. "They've both got claws, trust me."

"I believe you," Gwen said.

"But Burns and Elland had convinced themselves that if my body was found strapped into a full set of diving gear, everyone would be forced to conclude that I had tried to retrieve the analyst's body on my own and died in the attempt. It wasn't long before I found out that Spalding was laboring under the same assumption. He was very sure of himself there at the end when he told me how the plan was going to work."

"Back up," Gwen said. "How did you happen to run into Spalding?"

"He was waiting for me in the cave. I went there with my own dive gear, planning to take a look around just under the surface of the cave pool. I knew I had to find the analyst's body as quickly as possible. Evidence, including the paranormal kind, vanishes fast in the water. I had just gotten into my wetsuit when Spalding showed up."

"He was on the island, too?"

"He had followed Burns and Elland to make sure everything went as planned. He said he knew I might turn out to be more of a problem than they could handle. He also said this was his last agency operation. He was closing down the store."

"Did he know that Burns and Elland were in the hospital?" Gwen asked.

"Yes. He also knew that if they were still alive, I had probably gotten enough information out of them to find the analyst's body."

"He tried to kill you?" Gwen asked.

"Sure. But first I asked him what the hell was going on. He talked. Told me that he was going to take a new position as the director of security for an ultra-classified division of a pharmaceutical firm. He said the company was developing a line of designer drugs aimed at enhancing psychic talents in individuals. He said that the firm had a version of an effective formula but there were still a number of side effects."

"The kind that caused Burns and Elland to go mad and take their own lives?"

"They were on the drug," Judson said. "Evidently it is highly addictive. Withdrawal leads to insanity, followed by death. In any event, the CEO of the firm had determined that an experienced security expert who not only had some real talent of his own, but who also possessed a working knowledge of the U.S. intelligence community, would be invaluable to the organization."

"That description obviously fit your old boss like a glove. Was Spalding on the drug, too?"

"Yes."

"What else did he tell you?"

"Not much." Judson gripped the edge of the window and looked out at the river. "He was in a hurry. He said he couldn't afford to waste any more time. He intended to stage his own death after he got rid of me. He planned to start his new career in the private sector with a new identity."

"But first he had to kill you without leaving any evidence. How in the world did he plan to do that?"

"He had a weapon. It was crystal-based technology. Looked like a flashlight. He said it was a gift from the CEO who had hired him. Next thing I know, he's aiming the device at me. I felt a jolt of icy energy. I thought it would freeze my heart, literally."

"Like the wind chime storm at Louise's house?"

"No, that energy was chaotic and discordant — unfocused. The radiation from Spalding's little crystal gun was very focused and very powerful."

"What did you do?"

Judson touched his ring. "That was when I found out what I could do with this crystal. I used it instinctively, intuitively. I pushed energy through the ring. The wavelengths somehow neutralized the forces of Spalding's weapon. But that wasn't the end of it. The currents of the flashlight gun were reversed. Sam says the effect would have been similar to a wave of water hitting a swimming pool wall and rebounding back in the opposite direction."

"The reversed currents overwhelmed Spalding's aura," Gwen said. "That's what killed him."

"Yes. I wasn't thinking about the science at the time because that was when I realized I'd maxed out whatever luck I'd been running on up to that point."

"For heaven's sake, what else could go wrong?" Gwen asked.

"On that last job? Everything. Energy started building fast inside the cave. I got a few seconds' warning because I could feel the rising psi levels. A weird aura formed. I grabbed my gear and went into the cave pool to ride out the blast. But when I surfaced a short time later, I saw that there had been a massive fall of rock. The cave entrance was sealed by several tons of stone. The explosion had released some toxic gasses. There was only one way out."

"Oh, my," Gwen whispered. Her eyes were stark. "You swam out through the underwater cave?"

Judson crossed the room and lowered himself into one of the wingback chairs. "I'd talked to some of the locals about that particular cave system because I knew I was going to have to dive it to look for the body. I was told that there were indications that there was an exit to the sea. But the system had never been fully explored or mapped. There were no cave lines from previous dives."

Gwen shuddered. "Trapped in an underwater cave system would be my worst nightmare."

"No," he said. He met her eyes. "Your worst nightmare — my worst nightmare — would have been spending what was left of my life buried alive, inhaling toxic fumes and knowing that no one knew where I was."

She took a deep breath and nodded once. "Okay, I stand corrected. Being buried alive might be a tad worse than getting trapped in an underwater cave. But still."

"But still. I sure as hell wouldn't want to repeat the experience on my next vacation. I survived thanks to the dead analyst. He'll never know it, but I owe him my life."

"What do you mean?"

"Burns and Elland didn't bother to drain his tank after they killed him. They left the flashlight on the body, too. They wanted to make the accident look real just in case someone did come looking."

"No wonder you have nightmares," Gwen whispered.

"Sometimes I dream about that swim through the cave system, but the bad dream, the one you found me in last night, takes place just before I went into the water to try to swim out to the sea. I catch a glimpse of something small out of the corner of my eye. At the time I don't think about it. I've got other priorities." He tightened one hand into a fist. "But later, in my dreams, I relive that moment, and I know that whatever I saw or thought I saw is important."

"Do you have any idea what you're looking for in the dream?"

"No." He shook his head. "Believe me, I've thought about it a million times."

He leaned forward and rested his forearms on his knees, his fingers lightly linked. "Do you really think you can help me find whatever it is I'm searching for in that damn dream?"

"I can help you look for it," she said. "But there's no guarantee that there is anything to find. Your nightly search might be merely a manifestation of the stress of what happened to you that day. One way or another, I should be able to help you break the endless dreamscape loop, though. That should give you some closure to the dream."

"Do it," he said. "Now."

THIRTY-EIGHT

She walked toward him through the seething fog of dreamlight.

"Don't trip over the body," he said.

"Where is it?" Gwen looked around.

"At your feet."

She glanced down and then raised her fathomless eyes. "Yes, I see it now. That's the trouble with entering someone else's dream. I can usually grasp the big picture, but I have to depend on the dreamer for the little details."

For some reason that amused him. "Little details like dead bodies?"

"Right. Okay, I've frozen the scene for us so that you can take your time examining events. Now, it would be very helpful if you gave me a tour."

"Things don't look quite the same as they do in the usual version of this dream," he said. "I don't feel the same, either."

"That's because this is a lucid version of

the dream. You are aware that you're dreaming. You can exert some control. Because of that perspective, the experience feels different than it would under normal dream conditions."

"If you say so."

"The tour, Judson," she prompted quietly.

He looked around, getting his own bearings in the eerie dreamscape. The scene was frozen, just as Gwen said, but he knew exactly where he was. The timeline was clear. The explosion had not yet occurred. If it had not been for his para-vision, he would not have been able to see anything except the beams of light radiating from the two flashlights, his own and Spalding's. The dead man's flashlight had fallen from his hand. So had the crystal weapon.

The interior of the cavern was spacious. It stretched up into the darkness as far as twenty or thirty feet. But the entrance from the outside world was a tight, twisted passage barely large enough to allow a man to pass through.

With his senses heightened, he could see the pool that marked the entrance to the flooded portion of the cave. He was standing at the edge. The water was infused with a faint, acid-green radiance — the natural energy of the rocks made visible to his special sight. When he looked down, he could see the opening of the Monster's throat below the surface.

"I've just used the ring to flatline Spalding's aura," he said. "The stone is still hot. The crystal gun went cold just before Spalding died. But it's too late. The energy released by the gun and my ring has ignited the atmosphere. I can feel the growing heat and the instability. The aurora is forming."

"Like the northern lights?"

"Yes. But this is composed of paranormal energy waves. I sense that an explosion will occur very soon. What I don't know yet is if that explosion will be powerful enough to affect the normal wavelengths of the spectrum. But I do know that it might be strong enough to kill me or, at the very least, fry my para-senses. My intuition tells me that my only hope of riding out the blast is to go into the flooded portion of the cave. If I can get enough rock and water between me and the explosion, I might have a chance."

"Where is the entrance to the flooded cave?" Gwen asked.

"I'd be standing on the rim of the pool."

"Describe it to me," Gwen said.

"They call it the Monster for a reason. The locals say it swallows divers whole. Some people say there is an exit to the sea, but no one has ever been able to explore it to the end. Only a handful of people have attempted to get through the cave system. Most were forced to turn back. Those that didn't disappeared."

"But at this point, you are not planning to swim out of here."

"No. I just want to go deep enough to ride out the paranormal explosion I sense is coming. I'm already in my wetsuit because I was preparing to look for the dead analyst. I grab my gear and a flashlight and I go into the pool. I make it into the throat of the Monster. I can feel the explosion and hear it even though I'm underwater. There's a shock wave from the blast, but the water and the rock protect me. When it's over, I surface."

"All right, we are now in that phase of your dream. You are surveying the dry portion of the cave. Tell me what you see."

"Not a whole hell of a lot. Something about the aurora damaged my para-vision. I'm psi-blind."

"Oh, my, I hadn't realized you'd lost your other vision."

"Took me damn near a month to recover. I wasn't sure I would."

"No wonder you retreated to that little town on the coast for a while," she said.

"And no wonder you've had a few bad dreams."

"Speaking of which —"

"Right. Back to this dreamscape."

"I'm psi-blind, but I've still got my normal vision and I've got the flashlight."

"What does it show you?"

"Spalding's body. His flashlight is nearby but it's dead. The explosion destroyed it. I see the crystal weapon, too. It rolled over there by that pile of rocks. But I'm not paying a lot of attention to the body or the weapon because I've just realized that I'm going to have to swim out through the underwater cave system."

He stopped because there did not seem to be much point describing the endless nightmare that was the long swim out of the cave.

"How do you know which direction to swim?" Gwen asked.

"In the water I can feel the current. It's slight but steady. I follow it."

"Not knowing if you're going to come to a narrow place in the cave that you won't be able to get through," Gwen whispered.

Even through the dreamtime atmosphere, he could hear the shiver in her voice.

"I didn't have any choice," he reminded her. "Let's finish this dream therapy thing."

"Sorry. Sometimes I get a little too caught

up in a dreamscape. Okay, I think I've got the lay of the land, so to speak."

"Context."

"Exactly, context. You are about to go back into the water to make the long swim out to the sea but you are still at the surface, looking at the dry portion of the cave. Do you catch another glimpse of the object that you know is important?"

"Yes." Excitement rushed through him. "Yes, now I see it. Something small and white that doesn't look like it should be there."

"Take a closer look at the object."

The dream sequence shifted fluidly around him. He looked away from the frozen curtain of aurora energy and turned to focus on the shadows that shrouded the dreamscape.

"It's over there on the other side of the pool," he said. "It looks like the corner of a piece of paper. I can only see a small edge. The rest is hidden under a rock."

"Hidden?" Gwen pounced on the word. "Are you sure?"

"There's no way it could have landed where it did by accident. It's near the spot where they murdered him."

"Who?"

"The analyst." Judson came out of the

dream on a rush of adrenaline and psi. "He wasn't dead yet, but he knew he was going to die. He tried to leave a message for whoever came looking for him. I have to get back into that cave."

"You're going to swim back through those flooded tunnels?" Gwen asked.

"I don't think that will be necessary. In case you hadn't heard, my father runs one of the biggest mining engineering companies in the world."

"Oh, yeah, right." Gwen wrinkled her nose. "I keep forgetting you're one of those Coppersmiths."

"If there's one thing Dad knows, it's how to dig through hard rock. Opening up the entrance to the cavern will be a walk in the park for him. Probably won't take him more than a few days to get a crew and equipment in place."

"Gee, solve a couple of murders here in Wilby, and then it's off to the Caribbean to solve a few more paranormal crimes involving strange pharmaceuticals and mysterious weapons." Gwen sighed. "You live an interesting life, Judson Coppersmith."

"Yeah, my calendar seems to be filling up lately." The image flashed across his senses. And suddenly it was all there, each piece falling neatly into place. "Damn. Should have seen it earlier."

"What?" Gwen asked.

"The answer is on the calendar."

Thirty-Nine

The town of Wilby rolled up the streets at an early hour. The handful of restaurants were all closed by ten. The last pickup pulled out of the parking lot of the Wilby Tavern shortly before midnight. The staff left twenty minutes later.

Judson waited until the darkest part of the night, and then he went in through the rear door of Hudson Floral Design. He was partially jacked. To his psychic vision, the knives, shears, pruners, snips and thorn strippers arrayed on the workbench gleamed like so much medieval weaponry. The glass vases on the shelves glittered with an acid-green crystalline light.

He moved into the front area of the shop and made his way behind the counter. The door of the small office was closed, but it was unlocked. People who lived in small towns got into some very bad habits when it came to security.

The interior of the office looked much as it had when he and Gwen had talked to Nicole. The torn and mutilated photos were still tacked to the walls.

He crossed the small space and took down the large picture calendar. The first, second and third of August were all marked with the same note. *Feed dogs.*

He took out the list of dates he had brought with him. The *Feed dogs* notes appeared exactly where he expected to find them throughout the year.

The faint, muffled sound of a shoe on the rear steps of the shop sent his senses into full sail. The ring on his hand burned with the heat of a miniature paranormal sun. There was time to get out through the front door of the shop.

He left the office and went around the counter. He was reaching for the doorknob to let himself out into the street when he realized that there were two people on the back steps, not one.

He stopped and waited. The back door opened. The beam of a flashlight speared across the back room and into the front of the shop.

"Hello, Poole," Judson said.

Buddy Poole moved into the room. Gone were the old-fashioned gold-framed reading glasses, the folksy plaid shirt and the red suspenders that he wore when he was behind the counter of the Wilby General Store. Tonight he was dressed head-to-toe in hit-man black.

Poole was not alone. He had Nicole with him. Her wrists were bound behind her back. Her mouth was taped shut. She stared at Judson with wide, terrified eyes. Buddy held a gun to her temple. With his other hand, he aimed the flashlight at Judson.

"Put the gun down, Coppersmith," Buddy said. "Or I'll kill her now."

Judson set the weapon down very carefully on the floor and straightened slowly.

"How did you know I was here?"

"I've been keeping an eye on you," Buddy said. "When you left the inn tonight, I figured you were up to something. I wondered if you were headed for my place. Thought it might be fun to see if you could handle the dogs. But when you didn't drive out on Falls View Road, I realized you were probably on your way here instead. I picked up this bitch just in case I needed some leverage."

Nicole whimpered.

Buddy gave her a violent shove that sent her crashing into the wall. She groaned and slumped to her knees.

Buddy ignored her. He watched Judson with psi-hot eyes. "How did you put it all together, Coppersmith?"

"The old-fashioned way," Judson said. "I started connecting dots. You mentioned that Nicole fed your dogs while you were out of town attending the crafts fairs. When Gwen and I came here to talk to Nicole, I noticed the calendar over her desk. Three days in August were marked, *Feed dogs*. You were gone for those three days, supposedly attending a crafts fair. But one of those dates, the second, was the day you murdered an old lady. I just finished comparing the rest of the dates of the kills. They match up to the dates when you were out of town, the dates when Nicole was scheduled to feed your dogs."

Buddy snorted in disgust. "Unfortunately, that's how Evelyn put it together, too. I got that much out of her before she died."

"You took her computer and cell phone."

"I wanted to see if Evelyn had called or e-mailed anyone else about her suspicions. There was only the one e-mail sent earlier that night to Gwen Frazier. I knew she would probably arrive later and find the body, but I didn't see any harm in that. I was sure that even if Oxley had his suspicions, he would focus on Gwen as a possible killer."

"Then I showed up."

"I knew you might be a problem, especially if you started asking questions. Louise has been a risk for years. Crazy and getting crazier by the day. By then I knew I no longer needed her, so I got rid of her, hoping that would be the end of the matter. I figured all I had to do after that was wait, because sooner or later you and Gwen would leave town and things would return to normal. But tonight I realized you weren't going to give up and go away."

"You're the demon Louise Fuller feared," Judson said. "The father of her only child."

Buddy snorted. "She tried to use my own son to kill me."

"Why not? Zander Taylor was a chip off the old block."

"Except for the crazy gene," Buddy said. "He got that from his mother."

"Nah," Judson said. "Like father, like son. Psychos, both of you."

"Bullshit." Fury flashed in Buddy's eyes. "I'm a professional. I do it for the money. Zander was a gamer. I swear, he was obsessed. Once he got a taste of his kill-the-psychic game, he couldn't control himself. Sooner or later, he would have been caught. I knew I'd have to get rid of him when he started killing right here in Wilby two years ago. But Gwen Frazier took care of the problem for me. Gotta tell you, that was convenient."

"You went to the lab as soon as you heard that Taylor had gone over the falls. You found the camera. That must have been a big relief. You knew your secret was probably safe, but the incident left you with some unanswered questions, didn't it?"

"I knew that Zander didn't jump to his death, at least not intentionally. He lived for the game. All I could assume was that there was some kind of struggle and Gwen got lucky." Buddy narrowed his eyes. "I don't suppose you know how that happened, do you?"

"Sure," Judson said. "I know exactly what happened. You're right — your son was not a suicide. He attacked Gwen and she defended herself. Taylor lost the struggle and went over the falls."

"Zander must have let the rush of the kill get to him at the critical moment."

"Something like that," Judson said.

"Like I said, it was only a matter of time before he screwed up, thanks to his mother. Louise had her uses, but she was not good genetic stock."

"You brought her here to Wilby all those

years ago because you wanted to keep her conveniently available. You needed her to tune the crystal weapon she made for you."

"So you know about my own little gadget?" Buddy raised his brows. "I'll admit I didn't realize you'd gotten that far."

"That gun sure as hell isn't powered by a crystal."

"No, the gun is standard issue," Buddy said. "But it, too, has its uses. It tends to leave the kind of evidence that the police like. When this is finished, the scene will look like a drug deal gone bad. Who knew Nicole was dealing out of her back room and that you were here to buy some merchandise?"

"Why not use the crystal to kill both of us?"

"It's not necessary."

"You mean, you haven't been able to get it retuned since you used it to murder Louise Fuller," Judson said. "You want to preserve whatever energy is left in it because it may take quite a while to find a new crystal tuner. When did it occur to you that you might be able to use Ballinger's records from her days at the Summerlight Academy to locate a replacement for Louise?"

"Son of a bitch." Buddy whistled softly. "You really do know everything, don't you?"

"I had a little help from my friends."

"Sounds like I've got some more cleaning up to do after we're finished here. I blame this mess on Zander. If he hadn't come here to Wilby to find his dear old mom, none of this would have happened. I've been in this business for over a decade and no one has ever suspected me of anything more than selling wilted lettuce."

"Was that when Louise made the first crystal weapon for you? A decade ago?"

"The witch was always fooling around with crystals. Thirty-four years ago, she created the first-generation stones. They weren't nearly as powerful, but they could be used along with some psychoactive drugs to implant hypnotic suggestions."

"You used them to run your profitable little cult in L.A."

"Shit. You know that, too?" Buddy grunted. "What a mess. You're right about the rocks. After I closed down the cult, I used them to make money in a variety of ways — blackmail, investment scams, that kind of thing. But ten years back, Louise came up with a version that could kill without a trace. I realized the possibilities immediately."

"You moved here to Wilby and brought Louise here, as well," Judson said. "You took on a new identity and went into the murder-for-hire business."

"It all went well until Zander arrived looking for his mother. I wasn't aware that he had found her at first. Didn't know she gave him one of the crystals. He was operating on his own, playing his stupid game. Then he heard about the Ballinger Study. He just could not resist."

"That's when you found out that you had a son who had inherited some of your talent," Judson said.

"Obviously, I'll have to deal with Gwen Frazier," Buddy said. "Who else knows what you do?"

"Seriously?" Judson smiled. "You think I'm going to give you a hit list?"

"Yes. Seriously. Because you're wrong about my little gadget. Plenty of energy left in it. Let me show you."

Buddy reached inside his shirt and took out the pendant he wore on the gold chain around his neck. The crystal was a teardrop shape. It was wrapped in a metal frame attached to the chain. The stone glittered darkly in the shadows.

"That answers one question," Judson said. "It doesn't need to be retuned after every kill. I did wonder about that."

"It will work up to three times before it

needs to be refocused. Louise retuned it just before I used it on her. I hate to waste a second firing on you, but you give me no choice. I warn you, you're going to regret your decision. You see, this device can be used to kill very slowly when speed is not necessary. And the pain, I'm told, is excruciating — like being buried alive inside a glacier."

The crystal flashed with dark ultraviolet radiation, but Judson was ready. He sent energy into his ring and got the response he was looking for. The amber stone burned with a searing radiance. The wavelengths collided with those of the dark pendant and sent them rebounding back toward the point of origin.

Buddy gasped when the paranormal radiation from his own weapon slammed into him. He reeled backward, but he did not go down.

He abandoned the crystal weapon, however, and struggled to level the barrel of the weapon.

Judson seized the nearest vase off the counter and sent the heavy glass container and the contents — a couple of quarts of water and a mass of yellow chrysanthemums — hurtling toward Buddy's head.

Buddy ducked instinctively and flung

himself through the doorway into the back room. The vase shattered against the wall.

Judson went through the doorway and kicked Buddy's legs out from under him. The gun landed on the floor.

Buddy fell back against the workbench. He seized a floral knife and came up with it in his hand. He started to lunge toward Judson, but he was not fast enough. Judson used another slashing kick to take him down.

Buddy groaned and fell facedown on the floor.

There was a moment of terrible silence. Buddy started to make gurgling sounds. Judson picked up the gun and set it on the workbench. Then he crouched beside Buddy and turned him slowly onto his back.

The handle of the knife jutted from Buddy's chest. He gazed up at Judson with eyes that were already filming over with shock and impending death. Blood trickled from the corner of his mouth.

"That's the thing about women," he rasped. "You can't trust 'em."

"The problem," Judson said, "was that they couldn't trust you."

Blood and the psychic energy of violent death were already seeping into the floorboards. Judson knew the taint would be detectable as long as the building stood.

Some toxic spills could never be cleaned up.

FORTY

"Don't waste your time trying to convince me that Buddy Poole was going around the country murdering old people with some kind of paranormal weapon," Oxley said. He closed the folder on his desk and cranked back in his chair. "No need to come up with crazy theories to explain this situation. The money trail and the calendar notes work just fine."

"Good to know," Judson said.

"You've convinced me that Poole was running a murder-for-hire operation. But I expect he was using the old-fashioned pillow-over-the-face method or maybe a little poison. Those techniques are very effective, especially when the victims are old and sick."

"You know what, you're right, chief," Judson said. "No need to come up with paranormal explanations. But there will never be any proof, either."

He was very aware of Gwen sitting tensely beside him. Together they faced Oxley across the desk. One of the officers had driven Nicole home after she had given her statement.

"What about Evelyn's and Louise's deaths?" Gwen demanded. "Do you believe that Buddy murdered them, too?"

"Yes," Oxley said. He gave a world-weary sigh. "But I also know I'll never be able to prove it, just like I'll never be able to prove that he killed for money. No way I'm going to try to go after Buddy's clients. Not my job, and I sure as hell haven't got enough to take to the FBI."

"Some folks are going to get away with murder," Judson pointed out. "Namely Buddy's clients."

"Yep, that's a fact." Oxley rubbed the back of his neck. "And I'm real sorry about that, but it happens all the time. You can only do what you can do in situations like this. You know what's important here?"

"What?" Judson asked.

"You saved Nicole Hudson's life, and Buddy Poole is dead in what was a clear case of self-defense that wound up as a tragic accident. That's as much justice as anyone can expect under the circumstances. As far as I'm concerned, this case is closed."

"What about the deaths two years ago?" Gwen asked.

Oxley narrowed his eyes. "No point reopening those investigations because I don't have a damn thing more in the way of evidence. But if it makes you feel any better, I will tell you that I believe Zander Taylor murdered those two people who participated in Evelyn's research project. And I believe that his death out there at the falls was another tragic accident that, by an astonishing coincidence, resulted in rough justice for the victims. I'm okay with that."

Gwen looked at Judson.

"The chief is right," Judson said. "The bad guys are both dead. This is as good as it gets."

"I know," Gwen said.

Oxley cleared his throat. "There is one thing I'd like to know, Miss Frazier."

She turned back to him. "Yes?"

"When, exactly, do you plan on leaving town? Not that I'm marking the days on my calendar, you understand."

"Trust me, I am really looking forward to putting Wilby in my rearview mirror just as soon as I can," Gwen said sweetly.

"Good," Oxley said. "No offense, but I'm real glad to hear that."

FORTY-ONE

"Your mom and I have some good news and some interesting news for you regarding the money that Buddy Poole stashed in that offshore account," Nick Sawyer said.

Judson, phone clamped to his ear, reached the far end of his room. Confronted with a wall, he turned and paced back toward the opposite wall. He did not like the restless, edgy sensation that was feathering the fine hair on the back of his neck. Max watched him from the center of the bed.

"I assume that *interesting* is your way of describing bad news?" Judson said.

"I'll get to that," Nick said. "Before I deliver our report, however, Mrs. Coppersmith and I would like to stress that this follow-the-money thing would have gone much faster if you had remembered to put Poole's name on your list of suspects."

Judson rubbed the back of his neck. The edgy feeling was growing stronger. He knew it meant that he had overlooked something important.

"Poole wasn't connected to the study group," he said.

"Excuses, excuses."

"I'm not in the mood for a critique of my investigative skills. I'm well aware that things have not gone smoothly here in Wilby, but I would like to remind you and Mom that I came into this case cold just a few days ago and it turned out that the situation was a bit more complicated than I had been led to believe."

"No shit," Nick said. "On a personal note, I'd love to know how you got your hands on that offshore account number and Poole's password."

"I used to do some work for a federal agency," Judson said.

"Oh, yeah, right, the Post Office. I keep forgetting."

"Finding that account info wasn't easy, let me tell you. There were dogs. Big dogs."

"Chained?"

"Nope, loose inside the house."

"How'd you get past 'em?" There was professional interest in Nick's voice now. "Dogs can be a real problem."

"I had help," Judson admitted. "I went over to Poole's place with a bag of kibble and Nicole Hudson. She's the one who fed the dogs whenever Poole went out of town on one of his contract jobs. The mutts know her, and they love her. In fact, she's going to adopt them now that Poole is no longer around."

"Did this Nicole know what Poole was doing when he went out of town?"

"No. Tell me about the account."

"We found it right quick after you gave us the number and the password," Nick said.

"But?"

"But it was closed."

Judson stopped in the middle of the room. "Are you sure?"

"When it comes to large sums of anonymous cash, I pay close attention," Nick said. "So does your mother."

"I don't doubt that. Go on."

"Poole's offshore account was emptied quite recently."

"He must have known we were onto him," Judson said. "Maybe he moved the money as a precaution."

"Not unless he did it from beyond the grave."

"Don't tell me —"

"That account was closed about forty minutes after Poole had his unfortunate

423

encounter with a sharp object this morning."

"Shit."

"Whatever. According to the timeline that you gave me, Poole suffered his lethal accident in the floral shop at approximately two a.m. The account was closed shortly thereafter. So, it looks to us like maybe —"

"Like maybe there's someone else involved in this thing." Judson headed for the door. "Someone who not only knew about the offshore account but also knew that it was time to move on."

"Whoever he is, in addition to being very, very good on a computer, he must have his finger on the pulse of what's happening there in Wilby," Nick said.

"He sure as hell does. The bastard has a front-row seat."

Judson yanked open the door and went swiftly out into the hall. Max vaulted from the bed to the floor and dashed after him.

"You're on your own, cat," Judson said.

Max stuck like glue.

Judson opened the stairwell door and started down. Max followed on his heels.

"Are you in a stairwell?" Nick asked. "There's this hollow sound."

"I'm using the emergency stairs. This explains why I didn't find Evelyn's computer or that damn camera at Poole's house this morning." Judson gripped the railing and leaped down the next flight of steps. Max bounded after him. "I'll talk to you later. Call the Wilby 911 number and tell the operator to get someone out to the old lodge immediately. Tell her there's another murder about to take place."

"What's going on?"

"Gwen left a few minutes ago. She's on her way to meet Sundew. And she's alone."

FORTY-TWO

Gwen pulled into the driveway of the old lodge. It was not raining, but the gray skies were growing darker and more ominous by the minute. Wesley Lancaster's rental car was parked under the shelter of the peaked roof at the front entrance. She stopped directly behind him.

His extraordinarily generous offer to buy the lodge to use as a set for his new series had come as a surprise that morning, but the more she thought about it, the more interesting the idea became. The large sum of money would do wonders for her precarious finances while she set up her psychic investigation business.

Wesley was not waiting for her inside his car as she had expected. There was no sign of him lounging impatiently in the entryway, either. It occurred to her that to kill time he had walked around the lodge building to get a closer look at the falls.

She took the code out of her tote and started to key it into the high-tech lock. Belatedly, she realized that the door was unlocked.

She pushed open the heavy steel door.

"Wesley? How in the world did you get the code for the door?"

There was no response from the heavily shadowed interior of the lab. She walked into the energy-infused darkness. The familiar buzz stirred her senses.

The low floor lights came up, illuminating a section around her feet.

She set the tote down on a nearby table and turned to search the shadows. Despite the illumination in the middle of the space, she did not see anyone silhouetted against the glow. She moved forward.

"Wesley? Are you there?"

She saw the body on the floor when she reached the intersection of two aisles. The Viking blond hair was unmistakable.

"Wesley."

She rushed toward the figure, her senses flaring. Relief flashed through her when she saw Wesley's aura. He was not dead, but she could tell that he was not in a normal sleep state. He was unconscious.

She crouched beside him, searching for signs of an injury. The sound of the dead bolt of the front door lock sliding home sent a flood tide of fear through her.

It was only then that she realized the floor lights at the front of the lab were still illuminated.

A familiar voice spoke from the shadows.

"You know," Riley Duncan said, "I gotta thank you and Coppersmith for coming up with a great endgame. I was getting bored with the whole psychic chat room thing. Finding clients for Poole was way too easy."

Her first thought was that Riley didn't look like a killer. He looked like what he was — the front desk clerk at the inn. Then she saw the weak light gleam on the barrel of his gun.

"But you didn't know how to get out of the game, did you?" she said. Instinctively she stayed crouched on the floor next to the unconscious Wesley, trying to make herself as small a target as possible. "After all, Poole was a professional hit man. He killed people for a living, and he did it by paranormal means. He was dangerous."

"Let's just say, I knew that I would have to be real sure of success on the first attempt. Figured I had time. Besides, as long as Poole was working, his offshore account was getting bigger and bigger. Then he told me that Ballinger was onto us. Said he had to get rid of her. Next thing I know, you show up. I knew right away that you thought Ballinger had been murdered."

"Poole knew that as well."

"Yeah, but we didn't worry about it too much until Coppersmith arrived. That's when I did some research online and found out that he might be a problem. That's when Poole decided he'd have to cut his losses and get rid of Louise."

"She was the last one who could connect him to the contract killings."

"There was no way to know how much the old witch really knew or even if anyone would ever believe her if she did talk. But Poole was a real detail guy when it came to his work."

"Besides, by then he knew that he would probably be able to find a replacement for Louise in Evelyn's old Summerlight files," Gwen said.

"You know about those files, huh?" Riley chuckled. "Wow. Didn't see that coming. Nicely played. But I get bonus points because I'm the one who hacked into Evelyn's computer and found those old files. When Poole took the computer that night, he was just trying to cover his tracks. I'm the one who recognized those records for the gold mine that they are. Between you and me, Poole was not exactly a wizard when it came to technology."

"You're the one who ran the psychic chat room, aren't you? You're Sundew."

"Bonus points for you. I'm impressed. You and Coppersmith are much farther along than I realized."

A rush of knowing stirred Gwen's senses. "Zander Taylor was not Buddy Poole's only son, was he?"

"Nope. Zander and I were half brothers. Different mothers, same father. Dad slept with a lot of women when he was running that cult."

"How did he find you and Zander?'

"He didn't even know we existed. I found Poole. Got curious a few years ago and went looking for possible siblings. I located Zander. He was a budding serial killer at the time. I helped him turn his little hobby into a more challenging game. I pointed out that he needed to be more selective when it came to choosing his targets. I convinced him that it would be more fun for both of us if he hunted others like himself, people with genuine talent. Of course, in those days, he didn't have the crystal so he whacked people in a more traditional way. He loved poison because it left no trace and because it always took a while for the downers to croak. That's what he called 'em."

"Downers?"

"Yeah, like those downer cows in the stockyards. The ones sick with that mad cow disease."

"I can tell the two of you really bonded," Gwen said. "How did you both end up here in Wilby?"

"Zander had what you might call a sentimental streak. He knew that I had found him, so he asked me to see if I could track down his mother. Took a while because Poole had pretty well erased her trail after he brought her here to Wilby. But three years ago I found the old witch. Imagine our surprise when Zander and I discovered that good old dad was living here, too."

"That must have been a touching reunion."

"Poole was a little concerned when we first introduced ourselves, but as soon as he found out that we knew all about his murder-for-hire business and that we shared his taste for the game, he immediately saw the possibilities. I'm the one who came up with the Sundew chat room concept. I transitioned him from his old-school business model into a state-of-the-art firm. Crazy Louise, on the other hand, was convinced that her one and only son, Zander, was in great danger from what she called his demon father."

"She gave Zander one of the crystal weapons so that he could protect himself."

"Well, that, too, but mostly I think she hoped that Zander would whack dear old dad. But Zander was a gamer to the core. Naturally, he started using the crystal in his hunt-the-psychic game. Then, about a year later, Ballinger fired up her study, and the first thing you know, she's rounded up a whole flock of real talents. Zander went a little nuts."

"He volunteered for the study. And then he started killing the people in it."

"Couldn't help himself, I guess." Riley grunted. "It was like putting a fox in with a bunch of chickens. Poole and I both got real worried, I can tell you. The whole business was in jeopardy. Oxley may not buy into the paranormal, but he's not stupid."

"Too many mysterious deaths in one small town would get any cop's attention," Gwen said.

"Zander had the sense to make you look good for the first two deaths, but how long could that go on? Poole concluded that Zander was out of control and would have to disappear."

"But Zander went over the falls first,"

Gwen said.

"Problem solved. The timing could not have been better. Poole was very relieved, I can tell you. So was I. But neither of us could figure out what had happened that day out here at the falls. Just couldn't picture Zander a suicide."

"Still, it was convenient for you both that Zander was gone."

"Oh, yeah. We gave it a rest for a few months, and then we went back to business as usual."

"Until Evelyn tumbled onto what was going on when Poole left town to attend the crafts fairs. Now Poole is dead, and you're the one who is trying to clean up."

"Poole was not much of a father, but he taught me a few things during the past three years," Riley said, "the most important of which is to pay attention to the details."

"Why did you hurt Wesley? He wasn't involved in this."

"I needed Lancaster to get you out here this morning so I sent you that e-mail from his address, making you an offer I knew you couldn't turn down. When you took the bait, I got him out here first with a phone call. I told him that you had asked me to pass along a message for you. Something about wanting to meet you out here to talk about his offer. He didn't ask any questions, believe me."

"How do you expect to explain my death?" Gwen asked.

"It will look like you and Wesley quarreled over the future of the lab. Everyone in town knows that he wanted to use this place as a set for his pathetic TV series. They also know that you two had a history. It all adds up to a motive for murder."

"You're going to kill me and frame Wesley?"

"Thought about using Coppersmith, but to tell you the truth, that guy makes me nervous," Riley admitted.

"Want some free psychic counseling advice? That's your intuition pinging you. Pay attention."

"Don't worry, I'm paying attention," Riley said. "After realizing that he somehow managed to whack Poole last night even though the crystal was still fully functional, I knew it would be way too risky to try to use Coppersmith in this game scenario. I'd sure like to know how he survived the crystal, though. Poole had a lot of experience with that gadget."

"I'll bet Judson would be happy to explain to you just how he survived."

Riley snorted, amused. "You've got a

sense of humor, I'll give you that. There's one thing I'd like to know before we end this game."

"You want to know how and why Zander Taylor went over the falls two years ago."

"How'd you guess?"

She moved one hand in a slight motion. "I can see it in your aura."

"Bullshit."

"You're hooked on your game of uncovering other people's secrets and using those secrets against them," Gwen said. "It's a real power trip. That's what drives you. It's right there in your energy field. It has been all along. I knew about your addiction problem, but I didn't put it together until now because I didn't have context."

"It's not an addiction. I'm not like Zander. He was crazy."

"Of course you're addicted. You couldn't quit now if you tried."

Riley smirked. "There's no reason to quit."

"Well, actually there are some very good reasons to quit but none that a wack-job like you would comprehend. So, do you want to know what happened there at the end when your brother went over the falls?"

"Tell me." There was a sudden burst of hungry urgency in Riley's voice.

"I'll do better than that. I'll show you just

435

how he screwed up."

Riley snickered. "You're trying to buy time. This is the fun part. You're hoping Coppersmith will come to the rescue. Who knows? Maybe he will. That's the thing about a really good game. There's always a twist. Okay, we'll play it your way. Show me what happened to Zander."

"He saw a ghost, a couple of them, actually. He went a little crazy. Ran out the rear door and kept going, straight into the river and over the falls."

"Is that the best you can do?" Riley raised the barrel of the gun. "Too bad. I was hoping for a more interesting ending, but if some crappy story about ghosts is all you've got, we might as well end this now."

"I can show you what Zander saw. This place really is haunted, you see. The ghosts manifest in the mirror engine."

"Are you talking about that bunch of old mirrors at the back of the lab?"

"That's right."

"There aren't any ghosts."

"Sure there are," Gwen said. "But it takes talent to raise them in the mirrors."

"Your kind of talent?"

"That's right."

Riley was clearly skeptical, but the energy in his aura throbbed with the need to get answers.

"If you kill me now, you'll never know what really happened at the end of Zander's last game," Gwen said softly.

"Show me."

She held her breath when she turned her back on him and started toward the rear of the old lodge. Everything depended on how accurately she had read his aura.

The bullet in the back did not come. She heard Riley's footsteps echoing on the concrete floor as he stalked her deeper into the maze of workbenches. The strips of automatic lights illuminated and then went dark as they moved through various sections of the lab. She was intensely aware of the hot energy in the atmosphere.

"This place is so weird," Riley said.

"How often have you been inside?"

"Couple of times. Always thought the place was just a big junkyard full of Ballinger's crazy test instruments."

"I'll bet you've never gone into the mirror engine."

"No reason to go inside," Riley said.

"There was a reason. You just didn't know about it. The engine is where Evelyn hid some of her secrets. That's how I found out that your father was still in business."

"You're lying. Why would Ballinger hide

her secrets in this old lab? People keep their secrets on their computers."

"Not always. This may come as a shock to you, Riley, but not everyone trusts computers."

She stopped at the entrance to the mirror engine. In the darkness, the energy locked in the silvered glass seethed and burned. She had no idea how the trapped currents appeared to Riley, but she knew that they were affecting him. He was already aroused by the game he was playing, but under the influence of the engine, his excitement flared higher.

"What's going on?" Riley kept the gun aimed at Gwen, but his attention was on the sparking, flashing mirrors. His growing intoxication blazed in his aura — a junkie sensing a dazzling fix.

"The mirrors are arranged in a specific way to make them work as an engine," Gwen said. "Ever been inside a maze?"

"Sure. Mazes are simple for someone with my talent."

"I doubt if you can get far inside this one. Zander couldn't. He took a few steps in and that's when he started screaming about the ghosts."

"Zander wasn't as strong as I am. With my talent, I know I could go into this thing."

"I doubt it."

"What's at the center?" Riley asked.

"A collection of incredibly valuable paranormal crystals," Gwen lied softly. "They're the fuel source for the engine."

Riley motioned with the gun. "You go first. I'll be right behind you."

She moved through the entrance of the maze. Riley followed. When she looked back over her shoulder, she saw the unholy excitement in his eyes.

"This is powerful," he whispered. "A real rush."

They were deep into the maze now. The dark mirrors reflected their images into infinity. The hot glass also reflected Riley's aura.

It was now or never.

Gwen flashed into the zone and focused on Riley's dreamlight. She found the wavelengths and plunged him into a dreamscape.

Then she followed him down into the nightmare that she had designed for him.

The mirrors still loomed around them, but now they appeared as open doorways suspended over a bottomless sea filled with fog. The peaks of crystal mountains speared the mist. It was a place where no one could survive.

Horror and panic etched Riley's face. He

went to the nearest doorway and looked down into the bottomless well of ice and fog.

"Where are we?" he gasped. "What's happening?"

"We're in a dreamscape," Gwen said. "I created it just for you."

"That's not possible."

"It's true that I usually need physical contact to do this kind of dream work," she said. "But the mirror engine changes everything. It heightens my own talent. That's what Evelyn designed it to do, you see."

The feverish excitement rekindled in Riley's eyes. "Then it must be strengthening my talent, as well."

"No," she said. "It doesn't work like that. It's tuned to my energy patterns, not yours."

The ghosts of Evelyn and Louise appeared in two of the open doorways.

"About time you brought him here," Evelyn said. "We've been waiting."

"Sorry it took me so long," Gwen said. "Things got complicated."

"But you always knew that there was some piece of the puzzle missing, didn't you?" Evelyn asked.

"Yes," she said. "I did."

"I thought no one could kill the demon," Louise said.

"He's gone now," Gwen said.

"I told you that you were a witch like me," Louise said. "But I was wrong. You are stronger, much stronger."

"What's going on?" Riley demanded. "Who are you talking to?"

"The ghosts of Evelyn and Louise," she said. "Don't you see them?"

"No." Riley was sweating now. "But there's something out there. What is it?"

"Hard to say. You're seeing images from your own nightmares. I don't know exactly how they appear to you, but to me your dreamscape is a hall of open doorways floating in midair above an ocean of fog. The jagged peaks of crystal mountains are visible in the mist."

"Yes, yes, that's exactly what I'm seeing now."

"Excellent. That means I've got good control of your hallucinations. This engine really is amazing."

"Make it all go away."

"No," she said. "If I do, you'll murder me."

"No, I won't hurt you, I swear it."

"Zander said that, too. But he was a liar. Like you. Runs in the family, I guess. The only way for you to escape is to run. That's what Zander did."

"Where?"

She waved a hand. "Pick a doorway, any doorway."

"No," Riley screamed.

"Your choice. There's no other way out of here. I'm leaving now. This dreamscape is yours."

She stepped through the nearest doorway — back into the reality of the lab and straight into Judson's arms. Well, into one of his arms, she thought. He had his gun in his other hand.

She felt the brush of fur against her legs. Max bolted past her into the mirror maze. She never knew what the wildly hallucinating Riley saw when he saw Max, but she knew it must have been terrible.

Riley started to scream.

"What did you do to him?" Judson asked. He looked into the mirror engine.

She turned in the circle of his arm and looked into the glittering, sparking maze of mirrors. Riley had disappeared into the labyrinth of energy-infused glass.

"I put him into a dreamscape and I left him there," she whispered. "The same thing I did to Zander Taylor. The only difference this time is that Riley ran into the heart of the engine, not outside into the river."

"He was running from Max."

Riley continued to scream for what seemed like forever. A shot rang out. The screaming stopped.

She heard the first sharp crack a heartbeat later. The hot mirrors started to shiver as though an earthquake had struck.

"Max," Gwen shouted. "Max, come here. Please. You have to get out of there."

To her surprise and overwhelming relief, Max trotted back out of the maze.

"Thank goodness." Gwen scooped him up into her arms.

The tremors grew stronger and increasingly violent. The sound of splintering glass echoed from the heart of the engine.

Judson drew Gwen and Max away from the rainstorm of shattered mirrors. They watched the engine destroy itself.

And then it was over.

The body of Riley Duncan lay in a pool of blood in the middle of the pile of glittering shards.

Only then did Gwen see the blood on Max's paws.

FORTY-THREE

Judson closed the phone, rested one arm along the top of the mantel and looked at Gwen. "Oxley says the hospital told him that Lancaster has a mild concussion. They're keeping him overnight for observation, but he will be released tomorrow. As for Riley Duncan, they're calling it a suicide."

"It was the dreamscape," Gwen said. Absently, she stroked Max. The dozing cat was stretched out alongside her in the chair. He purred steadily. Earlier, much to his annoyance, she had washed the blood from his fur. "Whatever Riley saw drove him mad. Just like it did Zander."

They were back in her cozy parlor room at the inn. It was late. A fire burned on the hearth. Judson had picked up takeout, pizza again. Mostly she was focusing on the glass of brandy that he had poured for her.

The shaky, edgy sensation created by a

combination of bone-deep exhaustion and the aftermath of the heavy adrenaline and psi-burn was still rattling her senses. The recipe guaranteed a sleepless night.

Judson left the mantel and crossed the room. He lowered himself into the other reading chair and contemplated the flames.

"I'm glad that the mirror engine was destroyed today," Gwen said. "I know you said that Sam and his lab techs would want to examine it, but I think it's better that it's gone altogether."

Judson looked at her. "Even though it saved your life on two different occasions?"

"I'm really, really hoping I won't need it a third time."

"You won't," he said grimly. "From now on, I'm never going to let you out of my sight."

She smiled. "Yes, you will, and we'll both be fine."

"No, we won't both be fine. I'm going to have a few new nightmares of my own because of what nearly happened today."

She reached over the arm of her chair and touched him lightly. "Good news, Coppersmith. I fix bad dreams."

He smiled at that, caught her hand and kissed it. "I know you do, Dream Eyes." He threaded his fingers through hers. "Have you decided what you're going to do with the lab?"

"Your brother can have the equipment he thinks might be of interest to him and his techs. I'll let Wesley have whatever is left and the lodge, assuming he still wants it for a set. He may not have any use for the place once some of Evelyn's machines and devices have been removed."

Judson nodded. "Sam will give you a good price for the equipment he takes."

"I'm just glad that a few of Evelyn's machines will be in the hands of people who will truly appreciate them. It means that her work won't be lost."

They drank the brandy in silence for a time. Max rumbled on, eyes closed.

"I wonder what Riley Duncan saw there at the end when he looked at Max," Gwen said after a while.

Judson looked at the dozing cat. "His worst nightmare. Whatever it was, it must have been the final straw — so bad that he turned the gun on himself."

"You know, I really can't wait to leave Wilby."

"I feel the same way about this town," Judson said.

"It's going to be a long night for me." She stirred in the chair. "You might as well go to bed."

"Not without you," Judson said.

"I'm pretty sure I won't be able to sleep much," she warned.

"In that case, I won't sleep, either."

"It's very kind of you to offer to keep me company, but there's no need for both of us to sit here in the dark all night."

He pulled her up out of the chair and down onto his lap. He cradled her close.

"Spending the night here in the dark together is exactly what we need to do," he said. "And after tonight I want to spend tomorrow night with you and the night after that and the one after that and all the nights after that."

Hope and longing whispered through her. "You're talking about giving our partnership a chance to see where it goes?"

"I'm not talking about our partnership," Judson said. "That's a business arrangement. You and I are lovers, remember?"

"Yes," she said. "Lovers. That works."

Maybe not forever, but for a while.

FORTY-FOUR

Three days later, Gwen stood with Judson, Nick and Elias under a large beach umbrella. The shelter had been set up to block the intense sunlight that was grilling the small island. Max was not there. He was currently at Copper Beach where Willow Coppersmith was seeing to it that he got as much fresh salmon as he could eat.

Gwen watched several people use gleaming, high-tech mining equipment to haul the last of the rocks and rubble out of the collapsed cave entrance. All of the tools and machinery bore the Coppersmith logo. The same logo was inscribed on the safety helmets, goggles and uniforms worn by the crew.

Tendrils of energy whispered from the opening of the cave. They raised goose bumps on Gwen's arms. She knew that all four of them felt the faint psi-breeze. At the entrance, the workers hastily moved back.

"Get enough hot energy trapped in a small space and anyone can feel it," Elias said in low tones. "Even folks who aren't sensitive."

One of the men left the group of workers and approached Elias.

"I think there may have been some kind of gas trapped in there, boss," he said. "Not sure what we're dealing with here. Want me to send for some test equipment? I can get whatever we need from the Arizona office within a day."

Elias looked at Judson. "Up to you. Are you okay with going ahead here or do you want to hold off until we see if we can figure out some way to lower the energy levels inside that cave?"

"We both know there's no practical way to lower heavy psi," Judson said. "But I think I can get past that. It's the aurora fire that might be a problem. If that's still burning, no one will be able to get inside. In that case, all we can do is close up the entrance again to make sure no one wanders into the cavern. I'll go take a look."

"I'll go in with you," Nick said. "I like hot spots. They give me a rush."

"Wow, that comes as a shock," Judson said. He started toward the entrance. "Let's go."

Alarm spiked through Gwen. "Hang on,

here, maybe we should think about this a little more before you two go galloping off into that cave."

But Judson and Nick were already heading toward the cave entrance. They pretended not to hear her.

"It's okay," Elias said quietly. "They won't do anything real stupid. At least, I don't think they'll do anything stupid."

"And if they do something stupid?" she asked.

Elias shrugged. "In that case, you and I will have to go in and drag their asses out of that damn cave."

"Oh," Gwen said. "Yes. That's exactly what we'll have to do."

They watched Judson and Nick don some safety gear and disappear into the cavern.

"Well, they're not rushing back out, so it looks like they didn't run into anything they couldn't handle," Elias said.

Gwen surveyed the array of equipment and the crew of workers. She was no expert, but it seemed to her that there were a lot more people standing around than were required to do the job.

"You sure got this project set up in a hurry," she said. "I'm impressed. This is one of those small islands with a huge government bureaucracy. Doesn't it usually take days, weeks or even months to get the proper permits before you start doing major earth-moving work in a location like this?"

Elias snorted. "Not when you hire a lot of the locals, spend a lot of money in the local business establishments and pay off the right people all the way down the line. You'd be amazed how fast you can get a project like this going."

"You're good, Mr. Coppersmith. Very good."

"I like to think so." He paused. "But this project was downright easy."

"And if it hadn't gone smoothly, you'd have flown in with a small personal army of private security guards, heavy equipment and all the manpower required to open up that cave for Judson."

"Well, sure," Elias said.

"Whatever it took, because he's your son and you knew he needed to get back inside."

"Yeah, that pretty much sums it up." Elias studied the cave entrance through his dark glasses. "I could tell from the way he talked on the phone that it was damn important for him to get back in there."

"Yes," she said. "It is."

Elias rocked on his booted heels. "He's looking a hell of a lot better now than he did when he first came back from this island."

She remembered the hot energy that had burned in Judson's aura the night she had met him for dinner in Seattle.

"Yes," she said. "He's fine now."

"Thanks to you."

"No, Judson just needed some time to heal after the psi-burn he took here."

"You helped the process along. Willow and me, we won't forget what you did for Judson. The family owes you. If you ever need anything, all you've got to do is ask."

She smiled, touched. "Thank you, Mr. Coppersmith. But that favor has already been paid off. Judson helped me close out that unfinished business in Wilby. We're more than even, believe me."

"Good." Satisfaction etched Elias's craggy face. "Willow says it's better that way."

"She's right," Gwen said. "This way everyone is free to move on."

"Yep. Willow says it's not good for a woman to worry that a man might think he's in love with her just because she saved him from some bad dreams. She says when it comes to a relationship, a woman needs to know that there's something deeper and more lasting involved."

Gwen caught her breath. "Your wife is a

very wise woman."

"She is." Elias looked at her, sunglasses glinting in the hot light. "I'm not so dumb, either."

Gwen laughed. "No one would ever call you dumb, Mr. Coppersmith."

"Judson is in love with you."

She turned away to look at the cave entrance. "It's too soon to know."

"Not for a Coppersmith. The question here is, are you going to break his heart?"

She flushed. "I really don't think this is the time or place to talk about that sort of thing."

"Can't think of a better time or place. It's a simple question. Are you going to break my son's heart?"

"Mr. Coppersmith, for heaven's sake —"

"Willow says that if you do intend to break his heart, it ought to at least be for the right reason — not the wrong one."

Gwen realized she was starting to get mad. "Assuming I do have that power — which I very much doubt — what would constitute the wrong reason for breaking Judson's heart?"

"Doing it because you think it's for his own good," Elias said. "Worst damn reason in the world."

She froze. "But, if he doesn't know his

453

own mind —"

"No such thing as a Coppersmith who doesn't know his own mind." Elias broke off and focused his attention on the cave entrance. "Here they come. Doesn't look like they got fried while they were inside."

Gwen followed his gaze. Judson and Nick emerged from the cave. Automatically she raised her senses and studied the auras of the two men. They both looked normal — at least as normal as the auras of two powerful talents could look, she thought.

"They're fine," she agreed.

Judson stripped off his helmet and put on his sunglasses. He walked to where she and Elias stood. Nick accompanied him, grinning with excitement.

"Still damn intense in there," he said. "Makes for a great ride."

Elias looked at Judson. "Find anything?"

"Maybe." Judson held up an object that looked like a flashlight. "This is the weapon that Spalding used on me. I'll have Sam and his techs take a look at it."

Gwen frowned. "But that's not what you were looking for in your dreamscape."

"No," Judson said. He reached into his pocket and removed a slip of paper. "This is what I went down there to find."

"What's that written on it?" Elias asked.

"I think the name of a business firm and the town where it's located," Judson said. "Anyone ever heard of Jones and Jones in Scargill Cove, California?"

FORTY-FIVE

The voice on the other end of the connection sounded like the low, ominous growl of a bear.

"This is Fallon Jones," the bear said. "Who are you, and how did you get this number?"

"The name is Judson Coppersmith," Judson said. "Got the number from a guy who's really good at tracking down information online."

Nick smiled and drank some of his beer.

There was a brief silence on the other end of the phone.

"Coppersmith as in the Coppersmith mining company?" Fallon Jones said. He sounded interested now.

"Yes. And also as in Coppersmith Consulting," Judson said.

"Never heard of Coppersmith Consulting."

"We're a small security outfit," Judson

said. "Specializing in psychic investigations. Sort of like Jones and Jones."

"Yeah? Lot of psychic investigation agencies out there. Most of them are frauds."

"We're a little different," Judson said. "Like you. And by the way, we've never heard of you, either. But we need to talk."

"Why is that?"

"I'm calling from a small island in the Caribbean. We pulled what's left of a man named Daniel Parker out of an underwater cave today. He was murdered a little over a month ago. He left a message for whoever found him, a scrap of paper with the name of your firm on it."

"You're right," Fallon Jones said. "We need to talk."

FORTY-SIX

"This Jones and Jones agency had Daniel Parker working undercover in yet another low-profile agency affiliated with the government's intelligence community," Judson said. "He vanished without a trace over a month ago. Jones said they tracked him to an island in the Caribbean but not to this island. That was the end of the trail."

Nick studied the screen of his computer. "From that point on, Parker paid cash. Chartered a boat to bring him to this island where he evidently intended to meet up with Spalding."

"Jones says he thinks Parker stumbled into Spalding's operation while he was working another case," Judson said. "Instead of reporting back to Jones and Jones, it looks like Parker went rogue. Saw a chance to make some easy money. Jones thinks he probably tried to blackmail Spalding. But if that's the case, Parker was way out of his league."

They were gathered on the veranda of the hotel's open-air bar. Gwen lounged in her chair and toyed with the little umbrella in her colorful rum-based drink. She contemplated the glorious island sunset. It was the same color as her drink.

"Spalding planned to go to work for this Nightshade bunch that Jones told you about?" she said.

"Jones says Nightshade is a group of talents who have developed some kind of formula that enhances a person's natural paranormal abilities," Judson said.

Nick's platinum brows shot up. "Cool."

"Not so cool, according to Jones," Judson said. "Apparently, there are some major side effects, the kind that make 'roid rage look like a common cold. Also some serious withdrawal issues. Skip even a few doses and a user will sink rapidly into insanity. Suicide is the usual result. Jones and Jones has an antidote, but no one ever calls for it. Nightshade would prefer not to leave any trail."

"Damn," Nick said. "Why does there always have to be a downside? Guess we now know what happened to the two guys you took down here on the island before you went on that last dive."

"Yes, I think so," Judson said.

"They ended up in the local hospital," Gwen said. "Their boss was dead. You were swimming for your life, and there was no one around to give them a dose of the drug or call this J-and-J outfit." She sighed. "How sad."

"Except for the part where they murdered one guy and tried to kill me," Judson said.

"Except for that part," she agreed.

"I got the strong impression from Fallon Jones that Nightshade has a company-wide policy of abandoning its agents who are unlucky enough to get caught," Judson said.

Elias whistled softly. "Tough outfit."

They watched the sunset in silence for a while. The men drank their beers. Gwen sipped her umbrella drink. After a while, she looked at Judson.

"Sounds like your former client, Spalding, and his two men sold their souls to this devil called Nightshade," she said.

"According to Fallon Jones, his chief client, an organization called Arcane, has been trying to control rogue talents, including Nightshade, since the Victorian era," Judson said. "We stumbled into the middle of a turf war that has been going on in the shadows for more than a century."

Elias snorted. "More like they stumbled

460

into us."

"Regardless of your point of view, contact has been made," Judson said. "And early indications are that the Coppersmiths and this J-and-J agency are on the same side."

"Or maybe just temporary allies," Elias said. "There's a hell of a lot we still don't know about this Arcane bunch."

Judson's smile was cold. "And a hell of a lot they don't know about us."

"And it's going to stay that way," Elias said. His voice was flat and hard.

"Right," Judson agreed.

"Hey, everyone's got secrets," Nick observed. "Doesn't mean you can't do business together."

"No," Judson said. He drank a little more beer and lowered the bottle. "It doesn't mean that at all."

Gwen sensed the energy in the atmosphere and smiled. She was feeling it, too, she thought.

"I get the impression that this Fallon Jones person may have suggested a business arrangement of some sort?" she said.

Judson watched the hot sunset streak the sky. "Jones mentioned that his agents work on a contract basis. He brought up the fact that he could use the expertise and the vast resources of an experienced security consulting firm that had global connections and a very solid cover."

Elias paused his beer in midair. "Vast resources?"

"He recognized the Coppersmith name," Judson said.

"Huh." Elias thought about that. "Well, he's right about one thing. Coppersmith, Inc., would make a hell of a cover. Our business interests give us an excuse to go just about anywhere in the world at any time. Hell, we've got our own jets, our own helicopters, our own ships."

"It occurs to me," Gwen continued, "that Coppersmith Consulting is in need of a new client to replace the one that recently went out of business."

"That occurred to me, as well," Judson said.

"If you're taking on a new client, you're going to need to hire some new talent," Gwen said. "Someone who can talk to ghosts at crime scenes, for example."

"And maybe a guy who can get through locked doors," Nick said. "One who can hack into just about any computer. Someone with connections in places where those ritzy Coppersmiths generally don't hang out."

His tone was as cool and cynical as ever,

but Gwen recognized the hope and longing just beneath the surface. Like her, Nick was looking for a place he could call home, a place where he belonged. He was searching for a family of his own.

Judson smiled at Gwen and Nick. "Coppersmith Consulting is hiring, and the firm could use your talents."

Nick nodded once, satisfied. "Just so you know, since I've been assisting your father, I've developed a taste for first class when it comes to travel and accommodations. That corporate-jet thing sure is convenient."

"I've created a monster," Elias said. "But his B-and-E skills make him worth it."

FORTY-SEVEN

That night, Judson made love to her beneath a brilliant Caribbean moon that splashed the sea with silver light. Gwen abandoned herself to his touch, savoring the tenderness and the power that he brought to the bed they shared. But it was the sense of intimacy that flared between them that she would treasure all the days of her life.

When it was over, Judson rolled onto his back and pulled her down across his damp, heated body.

"I love you, Dream Eyes," he said. "I have since that night in Seattle."

She laughed. "You were looking for some hot sex that night because you thought it would take your mind off the dreams."

"That's what I told myself at the time, but when I didn't get the hot sex, I realized I was wrong."

"And just how did you figure that out?"

He smiled and twined a strand of her hair

around his finger. "Because it dawned on me that if I couldn't have hot sex with you, I didn't want to have it with anyone else, even if it meant that I wouldn't get a break from the dreams. How long is it going to take for you to figure out that you love me?"

"Oh, I fell in love with you that night, too," she said.

"Is that right?" He looked pleased.

"I knew from the start that you were the one I'd been waiting for. But I screwed up our first date when I offered to fix your dreams, didn't I? You got pissed off and disappeared to Eclipse Bay."

"You felt sorry for me because of the dreams. Pity was the last thing I wanted from you."

"I knew you were having a few dream issues and I was sympathetic, sure. I also knew I could probably fix your dreams. But that had nothing to do with falling in love with you."

"You're positive?"

"I told you," she said. "I never sleep with clients. I certainly don't fall in love with them, either. I love you, Judson. I have from the start and I always will."

"Glad we got that settled." He smiled and framed her face between his hands. "I could only think about two things that month in

Eclipse Bay — you and that damn recurring dream. It was only a matter of time before I went looking for you. But I told myself I needed to clear up the dream issues first. Then Sam called and told me that you had a problem."

"What a coincidence. I spent that month telling myself that I would see you at the wedding," Gwen said. She touched one fingertip to the corner of his mouth. "I had a cunning plan."

Judson's eyes gleamed with laughter. "What was your cunning plan?"

"I wasn't going to say a word about your dream issues at the wedding. I was going to pretend that I couldn't see a thing wrong in your aura. Instead of talking about my terrific skills as a psychic counselor, I was going to try to seduce you instead."

"A very cunning plan, all right. I can guarantee you that it would have been successful, too."

"Do you really think so?"

"Without a doubt," he assured her. "I can prove it."

"How?"

"You can try your cunning plan on me right now and we'll see if it works."

"What a brilliant idea."

She kissed him there in the moonlight and

put her cunning plan into action.
The results were extraordinary.

FORTY-EIGHT

The day of the wedding had been made-to-order for an outdoor ceremony. Legacy Island was bathed in the warm glow of a summer light that was unique to the San Juans. But it seemed to Gwen that the Coppersmith family compound at Copper Beach was illuminated with a little extra energy.

The sun flashed on the surface of the sea. The air was so crystalline that the small, neighboring islands appeared to be within touching distance. And as if hired by the wedding planner to make the picture-postcard scene perfect, a pod of majestic orcas cavorted offshore. They danced in and out of the water as though their sleek, black-and-white, multi-ton bodies were weightless.

"You look beautiful," Gwen whispered to Abby.

They were in a small alcove of the old mansion that Abby and Sam now called home. Gwen was making final adjustments to the elegant folds of Abby's satin and lace gown. Through the open French doors they could see that the rows of linen-draped folding chairs on the groom's side of the aisle were filled.

In addition to the Coppersmith family and friends, all of the local residents of the island had been invited to the ceremony and the reception. Judging by the throng, Gwen was sure that everyone on Legacy had accepted the invitation.

But the bride's side was not empty. True, Girard, the wedding planner, had discreetly packed that side by ensuring that many of the locals were seated there. But Abby's stepbrother and her half sisters had shown up. Her father and stepmother had sent regrets, but given that they were currently locked in the midst of a nasty divorce, that had not come as a surprise to anyone, least of all Abby.

Gwen knew that Abby had been genuinely touched when a handful of her reclusive rare book clients arrived. Grady Hastings, a young man who had been involved in the case that had brought Abby and Sam together, was also present.

"Why am I nervous?" Abby asked. "I shouldn't be nervous."

"Brides are always nervous," Gwen said.

"How would you know that? You've never been a bride. Wait until it's your turn. We'll see who's nervous."

Nick appeared at the entrance to the alcove where Abby and Gwen waited. He always looked good, Gwen thought. But he was especially dashing and sophisticated in his new, elegantly cut tux.

He smiled at Abby and Gwen. In a rare show of emotion, moisture glinted in his eyes.

"I have the most beautiful sisters in the world," he said, his voice uncharacteristically husky.

"And we have the most handsome brother on the planet," Gwen said.

"I'm happy for you, Abby," Nick said. "You're getting a real family."

"I've already got a real family — you and Gwen are as real as it gets," Abby said. "I couldn't ask for a better family. I'm just adding on a husband and a few new relatives today."

"Things will be different now, though," Nick said.

"No, they won't." Abby stepped forward and stood on tiptoe to kiss his cheek. "Nothing will ever change what the three of us have."

"We will always be family," Gwen said. She kissed Nick's other cheek and stood back.

"Okay, then." Nick looked satisfied. He blinked away the sheen of tears and offered his arm to Abby. "Let's do this. I think Sam is getting nervous."

"Nothing makes Sam nervous," Abby said.

"Trust me, the possibility that you might run off and leave him standing at the altar is more than enough to scare the living daylights out of him," Nick said. "Speaking personally, I sort of enjoy that look of incipient panic in his eyes."

Gwen smiled. "But it's not going to last long because Abby is not going to leave him at the altar."

"No." Abby wrapped one white-gloved hand around Nick's arm. "Never."

The musical cue sounded.

"Here we go," Gwen said. She gave Abby one last sisterly kiss, careful not to spoil the bride's makeup, and picked up the basket of flowers.

Sam was waiting at the altar but he was not alone. His best man, Judson, was there, as well.

Judson never took his eyes off her as she walked slowly and serenely down the aisle to take up her place as maid of honor. She smiled at him from beneath the brim of her flower-and-bow-trimmed hat. The heat of love burned in his eyes.

Sometime later, Gwen stood just inside one of the large, white tents that had been set up for the reception and watched the bridal couple finish the first waltz.

"Got to hand it to Girard." Nick swirled champagne in his glass. "He pulled the whole thing off without a hitch."

"If you ask me, that man should be commanding troops," Judson said. "The military missed out when Girard decided to go into the wedding planner business."

"He did command troops for a while," Nick said. "Girard was in the Marines for ten years."

Judson smiled appreciatively. "I believe it. Not everyone can get away with telling a bunch of Coppersmiths and the entire population of Legacy Island what to do and how to do it. Between you and me, is Girard his real name?"

"Can't tell you that," Nick said. He sipped his champagne and lowered the glass. "I was sworn to secrecy on the subject. Now, if you want to discuss his tats —"

"No," Judson said. "I don't."

"Pity," Nick said. "Real works of art."

"I think it's time to change the focus of this conversation," Gwen said firmly. "Tats and names aside, Girard produced an absolutely gorgeous wedding. Of course, it helps that Abby and Sam are so perfect for each other. Look at the way they're gazing into each other's eyes. You can feel the good energy from here."

The waltz came to a slow, elegant stop. The crowd cheered when Sam kissed Abby. Then, abruptly, the musicians changed tempo, the signal that everyone was invited to dance.

Nick put down his wineglass with grave deliberation. "If you'll excuse me, I'm going to ask Girard to dance. He'll probably give me some static because he's very conscious of his responsibilities and position as the planner."

"Tell him I said that at a Coppersmith wedding, everyone dances," Judson said, "including the wedding planner."

Nick flashed a brilliant smile. "Thanks. I'll do that."

He glided away through the crowd.

Judson took Gwen's hand.

"Dance with me, Dream Eyes?" he asked.

"Certainly." She let him lead her out onto the crowded floor. "I'll even promise not to crash your dreams while we dance."

He pulled her into his arms. "You're welcome in my dreams anytime." He tightened his arms around her. "I love you, Dream Eyes."

"I love you, Judson."

The Phoenix stone on Judson's hand burned with the heat of summer light and the fire of love.

ABOUT THE AUTHOR

Jayne Ann Krentz is the author of more than fifty *New York Times* bestsellers. She has written contemporary romantic suspense novels under that name, as well as futuristic and historical romance novels under the pseudonyms Jayne Castle and Amanda Quick, respectively. She earned a B.A. in History from the University of California at Santa Cruz and went on to obtain a Masters degree in Library Science from San Jose State University in California. Before she began writing full time she worked as a librarian in both academic and corporate libraries. Jayne Ann Krentz lives in Seattle.

LTP F   NCKL

Krentz, Jayne Ann

Dream eyes

$15.99   02/27/2014

CPSIA information can be obtained
at www.ICGtesting.com
Printed in the USA
FFOW05n0736211213

9 781594 136719